From Chicken Little to "chicken-hearted," our clucking, two-legged, feathery friends have been routinely slandered and derided. The most notable exception, the Little Red Hen, was a paragon of chick-lit domesticity. But what if she'd also been a natural-born genius, an Einstein among chickens? Sunshine Bell is the largely true story of just such a chicken. You may have eaten one of her siblings.

SHOCKING, EXCITING, AND IN THE END SIMPLY INSPIRING. . . THE STORY OF A CHICKEN WHO REFUSED TO BE JUST ANOTHER GALLUS GALLUS DOMESTICUS!

Some Reader Reactions:

"Better than Harry Potter!"
　　　—Alexander Boykin Bell, *The Ephesus School News*

"Long overdue. . . At last, a story that tells the truth about a much maligned species, one that has done more to help humankind than any other except the duck."
　　　—Luther Burbank Merganser, *Quackery for All*

"Egg-zactly what the doctor ordered! Sometimes scrambled, sometimes hard-boiled, but always appetizing—though I'd take some portions with a grain of salt."
　　　—Nathan Bjornstrom, *Egg Fanciers' Monthly*

"Dangerous and utter nonsense. . . if chickens were truly this smart, you could kiss your drumsticks good-bye.
　　　—Cynthia Snivveler, *Batter Up! / An Essential Guide for Fryers*

"Like a feminist *Animal Farm* without the pigs! Everyone else but not the pigs— it's a good example of what to expect when hens are put in charge."
　　　—Marcus A. Trotter, *Boaring In: The Natural Order of Things*

With easy to follow suggestions for becoming a genius too!

SUNSHINE BELL

The Autobiography of a Genius

an annotated edition by

Ben Dunlap

Grateful acknowledgement is made to RiskPress Foundation for making The Divers Collection possible.

Cover art by Helen Berggruen

Cover design by William Salit

Author photo retrieved from alchetron.com

Editor photo by Mark Olencki

San Francisco, California

FOR ALL MY PRETTY CHICKENS
and their Dam

(editor's dedication)

ABOUT THIS BOOK

It may well be that wisdom is often just a matter of grasping familiar platitudes at a much deeper level of understanding, but how is that to be done except by seeing things anew? Along with her vibrant wit and sense of adventure, that's the gift to be found in Sunshine Bell's remarkable story of her life.

Her achievement clearly merits the fame she's won, but in completing my own much humbler task of helping edit her text, it became clear to me that her very compelling thoughts on language and reputation could be further enhanced by additional background and context. That led first to a glossary of words selected by Ms. Bell and *italicized* in the text with definitions, comments, and guides to pronunciation. At her suggestion, we also compiled notes keyed to asterisks (*) in her story to provide even more intriguing information. Finally, she agreed to include a very revealing interview conducted by Alexander Bell in 2009 as well as a list of the major characters, species and breeds appearing in her account—and at that point we realized that we'd unconsciously constructed what is known as a metafiction.

As to how you choose to consume this autobiographical smorgasbord, I can do no better than quote Ms. Bell herself: "Readers should feel entirely free to nibble on our side dishes during their literary meal or to bolt them all down afterwards as dessert—or even, if they prefer, to leave them completely untouched as if they're slugs on toast." If you feel you're confronted by slugs, however, the fault is mine alone.

Ben Dunlap
March 10, 2021

CONTENTS

INTRODUCTION

Wondrous the gods, more wondrous are the men,
More wondrous, wondrous still, the cock and the hen.

—William Blake*

F irst of all, I can fully understand why you might want to get on with my wild and funny, often quite dangerous adventures while skipping over my offer to help you become a genius—especially when I'm confirming here at the start that I really am a chicken and only a hen at that. I say "only" because, as you probably know, there are lots of stories going around about handsome, boastful and foolish roosters, but the odds are probably very high that if you've ever read even one that's mainly about a female chicken, it must have been a little red hen. . . whereas I myself, as you can tell from any of my publicity shots,[1] am plump, and squat, and speckled all over in dingy shades of black and white. Even more to the point and regardless of how I look, you're probably already asking yourself what I could possibly have to share that you'd be eager to learn.

Well, depending on your age and openness of mind, I think you might be surprised to find how much we have in common. To support that claim, I could quote a scientist like Frans de Waal*, a distinguished primatologist—which is just a word for those who choose to study their closest animal cousins. He's admitted for example, on behalf of your fellow humans that "we have the long tradition of downplaying what animals do and considering animals

---

[1] There's one such photograph at the end of this book.

dumb and below our level, and we consider ourselves as absolutely unique." Or I could cite the evolutionary biologist Andy Sih,* who's acknowledged that, despite such *condescension* by his species, "In other animals, there is a history of realizing that a few individuals—a very few—might do things that no one else in their species has done before. . ." like thinking, achieving, and feeling in ways that seem extraordinary.

"So what?" you might object. "You expect me to read *The Adventures of a Brighter than Usual Earthworm?*"

Actually, that could be very informative if you happen to agree that earthworms are delicious. But no matter how clever you or the earthworm might be, the real problem would lie in how you'd expect to communicate. For instance, if you and I were to meet face to face, I'd begin my story by saying, "*Kraak krak brrrlkk ☼ krūwwwk!*" Or, in other words, "I was born on a beautiful bug-filled day!"*

But unless you happen to speak Chicken, you'd have no idea what I'd said. The fact that I've learned to read and write in English would enable me to scratch out letters in the dirt, but, even if you understood what I was doing, it would be only slightly more efficient than sending out smoke signals—which I gather was once your latest technology.

So what would work better? A computer or smart phone, of course, assuming I'd learned a few basic things and knew how to hunt and peck—which, fortunately, is a skill every chicken is born with. Then, if I was fairly smart and ready to go to work, all I'd need is a teacher who believed I could learn whatever I wanted. That was important for me, you see, and, unlike millions of other young chicks, I had not one but two such teachers who, because I was reading or writing within a couple of weeks, declared I was truly *prodigious*, meaning brighter than most at that young age—just like that earthworm of yours.

But the truth of the matter is that, because I'm a chicken, I've got a somewhat special point of view based on the unavoidable fact that, unlike you, I'm never going to vote or drive a car or eat a meal at KFC—the very thought of which makes me shudder! At the same time though, I'm also aware that I grew up a great deal faster than you and have happily gobbled down snacks you wouldn't go near. In fact, you might even say I've had a *prodigious* appetite for all sorts of things you're very unlikely to take a fancy to.

In that respect, I hope we'll agree that it takes all sorts, and I might as well confide that many would claim I'm simply undocumented. It's true that I don't have a birth certificate, and though there might be a bill of sale somewhere in Chapel Hill, that's no real proof of citizenship. But I know for a fact that I was raised right here in North Carolina, and, when we get right down to what's really basic, I'm an upright *biped** like you and resemble you far more than you might think—except for how I look and talk. . . and, as I've already mentioned, my wildly adventurous life so far.

Which takes me back to why, in addition to all the many close calls I've had, I think you should want to read this book. It's called an *autobiography* which, as you probably know, means the story of my own life, but I hope you'll also find some simple but useful ways of showing your own potential in the very best possible light—and not just by playing clever tricks. In my particular case, the "genius" label* was only tacked on when people who'd thought I knew nothing at all discovered I knew a little bit more than they in their snootiness had assumed. But all of a sudden in one fell swoop,[2] I went from being dismissed as merely a dull-witted bird to being considered a wondrous hen—which changed my life so totally that I'm willing to bet what worked for me will also work for you and that you quickly find you're considered a genius too.

All creatures are wondrous in their way, though some can get so stuck on themselves that all they care about is for others to be exactly like them, which is what Frans de Waal was saying. And we can get down on ourselves as well, for, as a very real genius named Albert Einstein* pointed out, "If you judge a fish by its ability to climb a tree, it will live its whole life believing that it is stupid."

That's why what you're about to read is more than an autobiography. It's also a sort of self-help guide[3] that, if it works as I hope it will, will not only keep you out of the fire but out of a frying pan as well. In the long run, that should matter to you as much as it has to me. . . if you happen to know what I mean!

---

[2] The phrase "in one fell swoop" was probably first used by Shakespeare in his play *Macbeth* to describe a hawk swooping down on a hen and her chicks, but now it simply means "all of a sudden."

[3] For further details, see Appendix II: "An Interview from *The Ephesus School News.*"

MY LIFE SO FAR

An Autobiography

Chapter 1

I was born on a beautiful bug-filled day!

That's what I was told, at least. I can't be entirely sure because I was in an incubator at the time somewhere or other in Chapel Hill—on a farm, in a shop, or maybe at a fair. Don't ask directions from an egg.

But I was hatched—that much is clear because, once you're out of one, there's no getting back inside—and the first thing I probably did after that, though this is a little vague as well, was to continue pecking about in an aimless sort of way, the way new hatchlings tend to do without much sense of why they should bother. What I did next in all likelihood would have been to topple over like lots of biddies I've observed who're giddy at first to find themselves alive but so worn to an absolute frazzle by getting out of their eggs that they tend to yawn a couple of times, blink once or twice while looking around, and utter a sleepy "pee-peeep-peeeep"—which in Chicken means simply "me. . .me. . .meeee!" Then they yawn, lie down, and take a snooze, which I'm guessing I must have also done.

The next thing that I remember now is waking up in some sort of box with a whopping big human face bobbing about overhead like one of those smiley-faced suns in books that are beaming down at everything because they're just so enormously pleased with whatever's going on—which, in my case, of course, was actually nothing much. Later, when I was still learning how to write in English, I said I thought that face had looked "guy-jan-tic." But, except for mispronouncing that rather simple word, my reaction was mainly because, to a newly hatched chick, nearly everything looks gigantic and partly because the smiling face was leaning so close to mine, staring and saying excitedly, "Get this one, Mama! This is the one we want!"

Or something like that. I couldn't really understand, though I think some words are probably universal, one of them being "Mama." So what I actually heard was more like "blah blah Mama, blah blah blah," and I thought to myself in a wordless way, "Well, that makes sense, I guess!"—somehow I'd simply assumed there'd be one of those about. So I yawned and answered "Peeeep peep, Mama. Peep, peep!" which made the face break into a smile as if to say it was happy to share its mama with me.

It was dizzying to learn so many new things at once. They put me into a smaller box that wasn't much bigger than my egg except it was square with little holes, and, though I couldn't see what was happening after that, I realize now that they took me outside and into an automobile—which, in any case, I couldn't have identified. Then we started to move again in a smooth but slightly shaky way that wasn't so bouncy up and down, headed towards what I'd later learn was a house at a place called Birch Circle—"*our* house," I should have said—with a truly enormous brother and a mother I hadn't seen clearly yet while assuming she too must be quite big plus somebody else whose voice I could hear laughing and talking now and again.

It would take me a while to figure out that my brother the giant was known as Jones. Our mother was Boykin—Boykin Bell—and there was another giant brother, smaller than either of them, whose name I learned was Zan, which was short for Alexander. . . and all of us, I gathered, were Bells, whatever that was supposed to mean, though an idea began to stir in my brain that I was a future giant too who someday soon would be thudding about weighing as much as an incubator while looking around for things to eat at least as big as my newly hatched self.

Jones opened the box so I could see as he carried me into the two-story house where my life as a genius would shortly begin. At least, that's what was later *alleged*—meaning it's what some people would say in newspaper stories or on TV or even at a big state fair. But that wasn't a glimmer yet in my mind as Zan peered down examining me and saying I must have lost a toe that was probably somewhere loose in the box. It wasn't, of course, as Jones explained, lifting me gently in his hands once we all were safely inside while I, not knowing exactly why because I'd never tasted one, was checking about for bite-sized bugs. . . of which, I thought, there were pitifully few.

At the same time, for no apparent reason, it began to cross my mind from what I'd seen of Jones that, even if I was his sister except with fewer toes, it wasn't just size that made me feel so different. If I was going to look like him, I'd also need to get rid of the fuzz that was covering me from beak to claws and grow some fingers on my wings. . . and, even more improbably, my knees would have to bend in the opposite direction. But we've got to play with the cards we're dealt, and I'd quickly learn how useful mine are if you're looking to peck about in the dirt—so much so that I've often thought that, if human legs were more like mine, they'd be wanting to eat more things that crawl and probably fewer that fly.

But thoughts of that sort were quickly *dispelled*—which means they were made to disappear—when Jones explained we were now in his room as he set about making a nest for me in the pillows on what he said was his bed. Zan crumbled some breadcrumbs next to me, and I did what I guessed they wanted from me which was eating some crumbs and looking around at the treasures piled up throughout the room as if it was Ali Baba's cave*. . . though I hadn't yet read about that, of course.

To begin with, I could see a second big padded platform like the one I was standing on, and because it had a pillow too, I thought it must be Zan's. He also called it a bed, and it occurred to me that they must be very fond of boxes so long as the lids were removed—but then I realized that even the room we were in was just an even larger box with its lid still on it overhead that Jones and Zan said was a ceiling, and in between one end of the beds was a different sort of box atop some scrawny long legs that looked a bit like their own. It was called a desk, they said, while on the walls hung some flat colored things that I couldn't make much sense of at first, though, once I'd figured them out, I found them very informative. They were "pictures" according to Zan, who was pointing to one I'd eventually recognize as a really colossal dragon* armored with gumdrop scales in the company of a tiny man dressed in a metal suit and, despite some sort of stick in his hand, wearing the uneasy look of something about to be eaten. There were happier pictures too of a strolling teddy bear smiling serenely to himself and toadstool houses in the woods for tiny bug-like villagers. For all I knew, which was practically nothing at all, they showed the world as it actually was.

I gazed and pecked and, knowing no better, did what chickens naturally do, though nobody seemed to notice at first because they listened instead to what I was trying to say.

"Did you hear that?" Jones said to Zan. "Sunshine just told us 'peepity peep peep peep!'"

"Peepity peep. . . peep peep!" repeated Zan, though he didn't know any Chicken yet and what he'd said just sounded to me like "Whattaya what what what!"

So I said it again as loud as I could. "PEEPITY PEEP PEEP PEEP!"

"You see! I told you!" Jones hooted, starting to crow and flapping his arms.

I cheeped as winningly as I could, flapping back at him.

"SUNSHINE!" he said delightedly, using that name a second time.

That puzzled Zan and me as well.

"You called it Sunshine," Zan observed.

"What?" Jones said distractedly.

"How do you know that's his real name?"

"Because," said Jones, "she's very bright. . . and she hops and shines and feels so warm."

"You mean it's a *girl*?" That puzzled Zan too. He seemed a little disappointed, not pointing out that the sun doesn't hop.

"A hen," said Jones *emphatically*, acting like an older brother. "She's way too pretty to be a boy. If she were a boy, she'd be something else. . . like Gorp or Thor or, I don't know, like Uncle Freddie Crookedbeak."

"Uh-oh," said Zan.

That's when they noticed what I'd done, some dainty deposits I'd just dropped.

Zan saw them first, exclaiming "Yuckkk!" while sounding intrigued and a little *appalled*. "Look at your pillow! That's a mess!"

Jones bent down for a closer look, and I repeated my "Peepity peep!"

This time it caused a different reaction. "Doo doo," said Jones in a clinical tone. "So that's what she was trying to say. 'Peepity peep' means. . . where's that pad I took to school? I need to write down what she says."

Zan started to giggle. "Peepity poop! Peepity poop!"

"Hand me a Kleenex!" ordered Jones.

But Zan was halfway to the door as Jones was plunking me back in the box, the little one where I'd been before.

"MAAAA!" Zan shouted down the hall.

"Shut up, Zan!" demanded Jones as I peeked over my cubicle's edge. He'd yanked thin sheets of paper up and was rubbing away at my mistake as footsteps hurried down the hall with a clatter and clicking new to me.

Chapter 2

The first to arrive was Boykin, whom I'd heard but hadn't seen before, trailed by two wild-eyed creatures who loped in horizontally instead of in an upright way and might have reminded me later on of the dragon in that picture.

Odd, I thought, so many legs! Humans and chickens have only two matched by a pair of arms or wings. But the eager and noisily snuffling beasts that seemed to be boarders of some sort came scurrying in on four legs apiece, not very useful for trying to fly or even for eating with a spoon but probably very well designed for chasing whatever they want to catch. . . which, in the case of the smaller one, clearly seemed to be me.

As soon as she'd caught a whiff of me or maybe even the driblets I'd dropped, that creature, whose name was Nellie, started dancing about excitedly, bawling in a language I didn't know—though it sounded a lot like Russian to me. I didn't know Russian either, of course, so it would have been equally true to say I thought a Russian was barking at me. But, either way, it didn't let up.

"RURRR-RURRR-RUFF!" she jabbered and growled, poking her snout in my direction, then followed that up with, "RUFF-RUFF-RURRR!" as if she didn't have good sense.

I sensed she probably meant no harm, but it was alarming just the same, and I made a little note to myself to listen and learn every language I could as soon as that seemed *feasible*. The other creature was named Maud Gonne and appeared to be older and more *sedate*— calm and mildly curious—looking from Jones to Boykin and back as if to *fathom* what was up. She had a somewhat graying coat of what must have once been curly black hair and, being less excitable, wasn't eager to squabble so that after a while, because of her, the three of us would become good friends. I soon gathered that they were adopted like me and was reassured by how quickly they seemed to understand that I'd be part of their household too. They're dogs, as I'd eventually learn—good-hearted creatures on the whole, though woefully *inarticulate*, which means they're not so good with words. . . though, in all fairness I have to say, they're better at listening than speaking.

I wouldn't hold that against them though, because, after years of studying Dog, I still find it a hopelessly limited way of expressing what you think or feel. To give a single example, there's simply no translation for what Nellie was yawping about when she first laid eyes on me. If you asked me even now to translate what she meant, all I could possibly do is repeat, "Rurrr-rurrr-ruff, ruff-ruff-rurrr!"—which means about as much as a squeaking shoe. But, if you happen to have an ear for music, I'm sure you'll hear the difference in tuneful lines like these from a well-known Chicken lullaby:

> Brr-brrrr-brrawk, brrawk brr-brr-brrawk,
> Brrawk-brrr brrawk-brrr awwwkk. . .

which is easy to turn into human talk: "Sleep, little chick, under Mama's wing / Sleep, now, sleep, now snugly, sleep!"

How simple but lovely can you get? As one of your human authors once said, "the poetry of earth is ceasing never."* That's true in the broadest sense, of course, but I think it's also true that, while some creatures are admired for strength or speed, others, especially birds, appear to be more expressive. I'll never dance like a butterfly, and, though they're good at many things, dogs won't ever sound *mellifluous*—which means they'll never bark or whine with voices flowing like honey. So Nellie was not mellifluous, and the look that I saw on Boykin's face as she rushed into the room wasn't as sweet as I'd hoped a mama's was going to be.

"What's the matter?" she asked with a bit of a frown.

"See?" pointed Zan as if proud of having seen it first. "What Sunshine did. . . like teeny doo-doo M&M's!"

Boykin called back down the hall. "Greg! You'd better come look at this."

I heard heavier footsteps clomping our way and supposed they must belong my new father, Greg, whose voice I'd heard inside the car and who, being the oldest and biggest Bell, made our family add up to seven in all. I didn't really know how to count, but that included a mother and father, two brothers, two four-legged hangers-on—somewhat distant but friendly relations was how I thought of them now—and the newest addition, me. Later I'd learn there was someone else, an older sister named Bevin who was off at a college that Boykin's father runs, and that would raise our number to eight. But for the time being, at least, it was seven including me, and, while waiting for Greg to consider the thing that I'd just done, I tried my best at sizing each of us up.

My brother Jones was *imposing*, I thought—approximately four feet tall with a feathery-looking mop of hair and a modest but well-shaped sort of beak. His eyes were dark and very quick, and he laughed whenever I spoke to him in a way that almost made me think he'd understood what I'd just said. I'd soon discover what pleasure he took in learning about new things—including how to speak Chicken*—and teaching them to others as well. . . and, in some ways, as my first human friend, he'll always be my best.

But Zan was very special too. He had a way of adding what seemed like footnotes of his own to every pronouncement Jones would make—the way the comments of birds or squirrels can warn of trouble brewing ahead or offer up carefree melodies to help embroider good weather. His expression always seemed amused as if he could guess how others might react if what he was imagining took place, though it didn't seem to matter a lot whether it actually happened. Also, he could throw and catch better than anyone.

Boykin and Greg were grown-ups, of course and, no matter how easy-going they are, most grown-ups think a lot about rules—as I do too more often than not. But Boykin spoke in a husky sweet voice that danced and bobbed in a rhythmical way like lizard's feet on a tabletop. She laughed like an engine starting up, and she was fun to be around—though she worried sometimes because she had to make sure everyone else was having fun too.

What was lucky for her was marrying Greg, who knew that the secret to having fun lies often in catching it on the wing. His curly hair was Buff Orpington blond, and spectacles made his eyes look big, and he had such an easygoing way that he never was mean to anybody, even to bats he'd find in the attic—though he'd make it totally clear when he did that they'd absolutely have to leave, and you've never heard such twitters and squeaks. I'd been listening to their back and forth when I was in the house at night but couldn't make out a word they said, and then I learned it was meaningless. . . like the sound of a bouncing tennis ball, just beep and ping and weeek-weeek-weeek as if they'd all gone batty!

By comparison with such goings on, even Nellie actually had some sense. She was skinny and peppy with short black hair but wasn't reflective in the least. Maud Gonne, with her tangled out-of-date coat, had been named for a famous raven-haired beauty who'd *spurned* an even more famous poet*—and, because she'd seen a bit of the world before arriving in Chapel Hill, Maud Gonne was always gentle with me. Her nose was wet and Nellie's was not, though I never knew what to make of that. They both ate meat which, like their extra pairs of legs, was different from the rest of us—though Boykin would make an exception for shrimp because, she said, she loved them so, and I'm well aware, regarding my diet, some bugs might argue they too are meat. . . which, technically speaking, they might be, but only in a McNuggets way, which I advise you to avoid.

In any case, the point I was trying to make to myself as Greg came thudding down the hall, was that no matter what awful thing I'd done, I was suited by nature to be a Bell because we were such a *diverse* lot.

"What?" said Greg. He loomed very large.

Zan pointed to what he said was poop while Jones had a worried look on his face.

"Psittacosis!" said Boykin, looking concerned. "I knew this was a bad idea. They'll both come down with psittacosis."

"What's psittacosis?" Jones inquired.

"Yeah, what's. . . whatever he said?" asked Zan.

"It's Parrot Fever," answered Greg while cocking his head to the side. "From the word for 'parrot' in Greek, I think. It's like the flu."

"It's more like typhoid," Boykin declared. "And it's no laughing matter," she tacked on. "I want that chicken out of here."

"Aw, Mama!" cried Jones. "She's just a biddy! Really, she didn't know any better."

Zan leaned to get a closer look. "Sunshine's a *parrot*? I told you so!"

"No, you didn't," Jones replied.

"Greg," Boykin said as if she meant it, "you'll have to build a coop outside. This is unacceptably unhygienic."

"And a *Greek* parrot too!" Zan nodded to Jones while Nellie added "Ruff-ruff-rrrrr-ruff!"

"Well. . ." Greg pondered, cocking his head on the other side and rolling his eyes as if deep in thought.

At that point I saw it was up to me. One thing you should know is that chicks, as a rule, are pretty much good to go from the start while humans at a similar age are barely able to find their toes —as if, having more toes to worry about, it takes them more time to figure it out. It's true that, at that particular point, I was technically only one day old, but the chips were clearly down, as it were, and I needed to think as fast as I could.

So, calling to mind what Jones had done and putting two and two together—or, as I'd later chant to myself, "two bugs, four bugs, six bugs. . . a *dollop*!"—I made a truly *prodigious* jump, flapping my puny little wings and landing just barely on the desk. Then I hopped to the box that Jones had used when yanking thin sheets of paper out in order to clean things up a bit, and, imitating what he'd done, I used my beak to tug one free. As it floated down onto the desk, I hopped and stood on top of it. Then I focused as hard as I possibly could on making a few more driblets appear on the tissue that I was standing on.

"Just get a load of *this*!" I cheeped

The effect was instantaneous, like pulling a rabbit out of a hat or making an elephant disappear.

"DID YOU SEE THAT?" Jones crowed aloud.

"More doo doo!" noted a sharp-eyed Zan.

"*Greg*?" asked Boykin, sounding awed.

"I swear I don't believe it," said Greg, shaking his head and waving his hands.

"Is what we just saw *possible*?" She looked as if I'd whistled "Dixie"—or, given our family's musical tastes, something more like the Grateful Dead*.

Maud Gonne and Nellie had nothing to say.

"She *knows* what she's doing," Jones exclaimed. "A genius chicken! She's got to stay."

"She's not a parrot?" Zan complained.

"Let her stay there on the desk," begged Jones. "I'll make a sanitary nest, and she can live in here with us."

"With plenty of Kleenex," Zan chimed in.

"Well. . ." Boykin seemed to hesitate.

Greg clearly had a project in mind. "I'll start building a coop outside in the yard. And maybe we ought to get her some friends."

"More chickens?" asked Zan. "Including a boy one just for me. Maybe I'll call him Dynamite!"

Boykin and Greg were exchanging a look.

"It'll have to be a girl," Greg said. "No roosters permitted here in town. . . and, to tell you the truth," he added to Boykin, "that might be true for hens as well."

I judged from the look on Boykin's face that she saw me now as a *refugee*. "Well, okay," she began to *relent*. "At least until we work things out."

And that's how two decisions were made that would deeply affect the rest of my life. I belonged to a family whose name was Bell, and, whether I was a genius or not, I'd learned that I was smart enough.

Chapter 3

In many respects, this is the most exciting part of my story because it's when I truly began to learn what wasn't already inside my head—for, though I might have been smart enough, I certainly didn't *know* enough. In fact, I really knew almost nothing at all. But Jones, who'd just reached the age of ten, was a student at nearby Ephesus School and was studying nearly everything, including subtracting and long division as well as all sorts of literature and other stuff like history and French and even a little music. At the same time, Zan, who was only six, was eager to learn what Jones would share. . . which, as things turned out, was quite a lot. And I got to eavesdrop on it all—which simply means I listened in, tucking away whatever I heard.

That desk became a roost for me. Whenever Jones read aloud from his books, I'd move up closer so I could see and cock my head the way Greg did, trying to figure the pictures out. But all I could make of them at the start were colorful splotches and squiggly lines that seemed to wander in all directions. Then, by watching their eyes as Jones and Zan paused to talk about one, I saw they weren't scanning it line by line but moving here and there on the page as if they both were hunting for bugs, and I listened to what they were saying for clues until, finally, one day it dawned on me.

That happened when Jones, who was playing the teacher by reading out loud, asked Zan to point to Chicken Little*. I thought at first Jones must mean me since, compared to them, I was still *Lilliputian*. But imagine how perplexing it was when Zan's finger went to a splotch on the page and, "There," he said, "that's Chicken Little!"

I looked and listened more closely then and all at once understood that, while Jones *deciphered* loops and scratches arranged in lines as code for words, what Zan was peering at instead was a smaller and flatter feathery thing fully equipped with a beak and wings—a depiction of a chicken, in fact, which, except for its mostly yellowish hue resembling the color of Greg Bell's hair, could easily have been a brother of mine.

So that was the secret—now I could see it! Not only the pictures on a page but the others around me on the wall and even on a computer screen. That might not seem so *momentous* to you because it's probably something you assume you just naturally knew right off the bat—though you didn't, of course, any more than you could read from the start without ever needing to be taught. . . which, of all the things I didn't know yet, was what I most wanted to learn.

But now that it all made sense to me, I felt completely *mesmerized*—as if I was hypnotized, that is—by the story that Jones continued to read in his grown-up teacher's voice while Zan and I both peered at the book.

"'Turkey Lurkey looked skeptical,'" Jones read on. "'But how do you know the sky is falling?' he quite reasonably wanted to know.'"

"Who's talking?" asked Zan.

"Turkey Lurkey," said Jones.

"Not in the picture," objected Zan, pointing at the book. "You can see that his mouth's completely closed."

"Right," Jones sighed. "He's just waiting to hear the answer."

So we waited to hear the answer too.

"'Because I saw it with my own eyes,' Chicken Little replied, 'and heard it with my own ears. . . and part of it fell on my head.'"

Well, I thought to myself, that makes him sound very silly. In fact, it made me think of a notion of mine when I'd first seen the sky that it was just the dome of another, gigantic, egg—the sort of idea that seems okay if you use it as a *metaphor*, a comparison which, though not really true, can be very provocative. But the more I heard of Jones' story, the more it seemed to me unfair, like calling somebody "chicken-hearted" as if all chickens were namby-pambies or saying that bats are generally "batty". . . which I just did, I realize, and for which I now apologize.

The truth of the matter is that, among every sort of animal, some are merely dumb and scared while others are admirably smart and brave—which is also the case with humans as I'm sure you've discovered by now yourself. And, as far as I'm concerned, whoever's amused by putting others down is like an ignorant little chick who struts about and preens after dumping some pellets of *guano*.

Yes, guano's what you think it is, and, regarding that story of Chicken Little, if someone who runs about screaming at night that "The British are coming! The British are coming!" is considered to be heroic*, why should we call somebody a dope for warning us that the sky is falling. . . or, when it comes to that, that our planet's getting much hotter? And what if the British hadn't come—would we ridicule Paul Revere for having been a coward?

I don't mean to get up on a soapbox, but I've just recently learned about an old woman in Italy who, after living most her life a few miles from the sea without ever having seen it, was taken one day to a beach where she clapped her hands and cried, "Jesu! Jesu! What a sight! It looked as if the sky had fallen all over the earth!"* To me that's a wonderful sort of footnote for the story of Chicken Little—who, by the way, is also known as Henny Penny, just to make it more insulting to us girls. But then, of course, it's the roosters who get to crow.

Anyhow, as I watched and listened while Jones was reading aloud, I began to learn how books are supposed to work, and, once I'd started to figure that out, I found a way to open them up as long as they'd been left on the desk, turning the pages with my beak and studying all the loops and squiggles along with the colorful pictures.

Usually, in the beginning, I did it while Jones and Zan were at school, but then one day, when Jones came quietly home, I was so *engrossed* in a book that I didn't have time to close it before he saw what was up—and being the sort of person he was, he decided that he would help me. He's a natural teacher, as I've said, and, in no time, I was utterly hooked, beginning to read the simplest books in just a couple of days. . . and the more I learned, the more exciting it seemed to read and learn some more.

As I've already mentioned in passing, what I needed to help me communicate would be some sort of computer, and, by a stroke of good fortune, Jones had gotten one for his birthday and was leaving it in sleep mode on his desk when he went off in the morning. That was marvelous for me, and, as soon as I'd learned to wake it up and gotten the hang of pecking its keys, I discovered new things in endless chains as every new fact would lead me on—from pearls to *pinochle*, *pomegranates* to *pugs*, penguins to *pimentos*, on and on. Arithmetic seemed to come naturally, especially after hearing Jones explain the basics to Zan.

"One and one make two," he'd said, laying two pennies on the desk. "And two and one make three. . . one, two, three."

"Let me!" cried Zan excitedly, grabbing the pennies in his hand and trying to lay them out himself.

I watched, imagining bugs instead—one plus one and you've got lunch!

Jones put two pencil marks on a pad. "One plus one. . ."

"Equals TWO!" Zan said triumphantly.

"And two and one. . ."

"Make THREE!" cried Zan, taking the pencil and adding a mark just like the two that Jones had made.

"Good," beamed Jones approvingly. "Those are called Roman numerals, okay? But, see, if we keep on adding marks, they're going to *proliferate*." He stumbled as he pronounced that word, which he said his teacher had used at school. "That means they'll multiply really fast. So, here's a simpler way to count." What he drew was like the neck of a swan. "That's how you write a number two. . . and here's the way you make a three."

The figures he sketched I'd seen before on the keyboard of his computer without being able to figure them out—though, because I'd watched what they called tee-vee at night sometimes with Jones and Zan, I noticed that what he drew as a three resembled Mickey Mouse's hands which have that same number of fingers. They're really just toes, I should probably say, but he's always got them stuffed in gloves as if he's embarrassed that real-life mice are running around with five instead. And in case you'd like to know about mine, the breed I belong to all have four—though, for reasons that must be obvious, I've never considered wearing gloves since they'd get in the way while scratching for bugs.

But, anyhow, it happened one day while Jones was teaching numbers to Zan that Greg came striding into the room and said the time for a change had arrived, which sounded a wee bit ominous. Jones picked me up protectively while Zan, who looked quite worried I thought, began to wrinkle up his brow, and though Greg, like all the other Bells, wasn't himself a *carnivore*—which simply means he didn't eat meat—people can sometimes change their minds depending on how hungry they get or how edible "lesser breeds" might appear.

Most animals have a certain expression when appraising you as a possible snack, and, if you should ever encounter it, you need to be ready to scamper off—for, at least as long as we stay on our feet, there'll still be a chance of getting away. That's why small creatures seem so upset whenever you try to pick them up.

That's generally true of chickens too, though there're many exceptions of which I'm one—maybe because, when I was young, I wrongly thought I was human too. And yet, I can't help asking myself how any smaller human might feel tucked under a giant rooster's wing or poked and prodded by its beak. But thanks to Jones' care and concern, I'd always felt safe when he was around. So I was glad to be in his hands when Greg led the three of us down the hall, across the kitchen, and out the door followed by Nellie and Maud Gonne who seemed to sense that something was up.

Chapter 4

I should have guessed what was going on with all the banging and buzzing outside, but I'd been so immersed in learning math that I'd simply tuned such distractions out. It was only when we saw the results that I learned what the racket had been about—a *palatial* hen coop Greg had built that was nearly as tall as he could reach with a floor just high enough off the ground for chickens to scratch or nap in its shade. It also had a ladder-like ramp that led to a door some ten inches square and a human-sized entry off to one side that was fastened shut with a metal latch.

When Greg opened that larger entrance way to let us peer at the roosts inside, we saw there were feeders and water-trays sitting atop some freshly laid straw, and surrounding the coop was a sizable run protected by a chicken-wire fence that Nellie and Maud Gonne went to inspect by sticking their noses through the holes. That was easy enough if they wanted to sniff, but opening their jaws just couldn't be done—an extra sort of safety device revealing how shrewdly all had been planned. No wonder Greg was looking so proud of his lavish backyard Taj Mahal*.

Zan, as usual, spoke up first. "Can I live out here?" he wanted to know.

"It's just for chickens," Jones declared, ignoring the open human-sized door. He'd never seen a coop before but, remembering what his parents had said, he held me so I could see it too. "And it's really a palace!" he exclaimed.

Zan reached out to pat my head. "For Princess Sunshine to enjoy."

"And for all the other chickens too!" said Boykin whose voice I recognized as she slowly descended the stepping-stones that led away from the front of the house.

She was holding a box in both her hands and, turning my head for a better view, I saw that it resembled the one I'd traveled in the week before except it appeared much bigger.

Nellie, who needed only a whiff, quickly entreated, "RUFF-RUFF-RURRR" which, as you may remember, is one of the much-used phrases in Dog that almost everyone understands. "Just gimme a little taste!" she begged, then added with a plaintive whine, "Or even a lick would probably do!"

Maud Gonne snuffled and poked her nose a little bit farther through the wire as Boykin, paying them no attention, opened the gate into the pen for Zan and Jones to enter with me. Then, closing it after we were in, she carefully put the box on the ground and lifted its lid dramatically so we all could see what it contained.

The sight was simply wonderful—five lovely little featherlings just slightly smaller than I was then but blinking and peeping and gazing around at all the Bells surrounding them. Then one of them boldly lifted its head and, turning it sideways, stared at Zan.

"Thor!" Zan exclaimed ecstatically, and, leaping about outside the pen, Nellie chimed in with a joyous bark as if he'd shouted "hambone!' instead.

"Can we name them, really?" Jones asked Greg.

"If you want to change their names, you can, but these have labels on the box—all but one," Boykin reported. "And all of them are girls," she said.

"Even Thor?" Zan's glum expression said it all.

"Well, let's see then," Boykin declared. "She'd be the one without a name. . . and Thor must be short for Thorazine. She's different in other ways as well—the others are all Rhode Island Reds."

"So what is she? Thor. . . Thorra. . .?"

"Thorazine," Jones nodded and said, repeating what he'd heard Boykin say.

"Yeah, but. . ." said Zan, "if she's not from Rhode Island, where's she from?"

Nobody seemed able to answer that, so they studied the chick while trying to think. Unlike the others' russet and gold, her feathers were speckled black and white—like mine, but with long slender legs, a rosy beak, and yellow feet.

"She's a Dominicker," Greg observed.

"Thaaat sounds good!" Zan happily said. "And the ones from Rhode Island, what are their names?"

"Well, this one's. . . Jo," Boykin replied, lifting her carefully from the box and setting her gently on the ground.

Leaning towards her, I peeped, "Hi, Jo," in what was nearly a grown-up cluck. "And welcome to our swish new home."

"Hi," she shyly peeped at me.

I wriggled until Jones put me down, then Jo and I made friendly sounds.

"And this one's Meg."

"Hi, Meg," I said. "My name is Sunshine . . . Sunshine Bell."

"And Beth."

"Hi, Beth."

"And little Amy* last of all."

"We're going to be so happy," I said, wishing the Bells spoke Chicken too so they could say that for themselves. "There's so much here to learn," I peeped, again in a sort of semi-cluck.

"And eat?" asked Beth.

"Oh, lots to eat. But so much more that we can learn."

"Like, really!" Meg let out a yawn. "You mind if we do the eating first?"

"Sunshine's so different," Jones observed while sizing the new arrivals up. "Why haven't you said what breed she is?"

"No reason, really," Boykin replied. "She comes from Scotland like all us Bells—at some point in the past, at least. . . and they'd call her a Dumpy over there."

That was news to me too at the time, and the name seemed less than flattering as well. "But Sunshine's better!" I tried to cheep, though none of my family understood, and, in any case, they seemed to agree.

"She's very special," Boykin said, smiling and nodding down at me.

"Thorrr-a-zine!" Zan crooned her name, stressing how close it was to Thor. "Can I pick her up and show her around?"

"As long as she doesn't object," said Greg.

I could see the distress on Thorazine's face. She was frantic for Zan to put her down, and, though I urged her not to fret, she was much too frightened to comprehend. It's hard, you know, when a place is new—like your very first day attending school. . . according to Zan, whom I believe. But, for all the newbies but Thorazine, school wasn't at all what they had in mind. They wanted an endless recess instead, which I was very sorry to find.

I wanted to be a teacher like Jones, but, looking back on my efforts at first, it's almost comical to recall how little interest anyone showed, and maybe that was partly because it was fairly well established by then that I'd spend mornings and nights in the house with only a few hours in the coop hobnobbing with the other hens. That seemed to upset their notions of order, and, after only a couple of days, I found when I joined them in the run that I was more or less *ostracized* except for my friendship with Thorazine—who'd also, from the very start been treated by the Rhodes Island Reds as if she somehow didn't belong. As soon as I tried to share what I knew—like how to drop pellets while in the house—all four would point their beaks at the sky, saying I'd just been showing off in a crude and very un-hen-like way.

"I wouldn't behave as coarsely as that," Jo cackled to the other Reds, "no matter where they let me sleep!"

When they saw Jones open the gate to let me enter in the run, they'd toss their beaks in the air again in order to sneer at Thorazine for being so glad to see me back that she'd ruffle her wings and nod with a cluck as I sped over to say hello. I was still enough bigger than all of them that they were mostly *wary* of me, but they constantly tried to pick on her when I was away inside the house, and sometimes, though she never complained, it looked as if she'd been mugged in the dark. I was indignant on her behalf, though I knew attempting to intervene would only make things worse for her, so I was delighted that, after a while, Thorazine grew to be largest of all. Soon they'd have to leave her alone, if only for fear she'd *retaliate*—which means to get even, tit for tat. She didn't, but she knew she could.

Chapter 5

I've admitted how badly I failed at first in my efforts to be a teacher, though I'm sure you realize by now that I haven't entirely quit trying. And despite that disappointment, I made considerable progress as a student, especially in math to such an extent that I really can't understand why humans suppose that girls don't like it much. In little more than a month, I'd advanced to algebra and was working away at equations known as *quadratic* because some of the numbers get "squared" and "quad" means four in Latin—so that four-footed creatures like dogs and cats are also known as *quadrupeds* while you and I are *bipeds* as, of course, you know by now.

Also, I can't help adding that all that mixing of words and math is a lot like sounds and numbers in music, especially in the way that everything fits so neatly together that, when you get to the end and whatever the problem was has been completely resolved, what you really most want to do is throw back your head and crow. . . which, distressingly, most hens can't do—or can't do very well*—though we can cluck and cackle along like sopranos instead of baritones.

As it happens, the Bells are a very musical family, and, when Jones and Zan were home, there was always music somewhere in the house if only on the radio, though Greg could play any instrument and Boykin sang and Jones on his own had learned piano while Zan kept time on homemade drums. . . so that soon I found I could cackle along and recognize some of my favorite bands—like the Rolling Stones* and the Grateful Dead as well as the Beatles and The Doors and started to learn the words of songs like one called "Satisfaction" and another that was truer than I knew, "You Can't Always Get What You Want." Hearing them always set me off clucking and hopping about.

But no matter how eager I was to share whatever I'd managed to learn, it was more than I could convey even to Thorazine who was endlessly willing to listen. So I had to content myself with trying again and again to explain how adding two bugs to one will give you three bugs for lunch, scratching two lines in the dirt and after that another, then explaining what I'd just done. On one of those occasions when Thorazine ducked and brawked with utter confusion, I felt so sorry for mixing her up that I got some seed-bits in my beak and carefully laid them out next to the marks I'd made.

"Okay," I said. "Now, look. . ."

I was dimly aware of Amy and Beth who were watching us from a distance.

"Like who gives a creepy-crawly slug, Miss Stumpy Legs from wherever?"

"Not Dum-Dum Dominick, that's for sure!"

They laughed and cackled up such a storm that Jo and Meg came running over, and all four stood there jeering at us.

"Ignore their silliness, Thorazine. Eventually, they'll understand." I was trying to reassure my friend, though I'd started to doubt they ever would.

All they cared about, it seemed, was stretching their necks and grooming their feathers and talking about their favorite bugs or whatever it was they were planning to do as soon as a rooster showed up in the yard. How they knew about roosters I never found out, but what none of us could have guessed back then—including me as well for all my reading in books and learning to scan the internet—is what it's really like in a world where you yourself are somebody's bug and those who'd wash you down with champagne will take it for granted when hearing you squawk that you're mindless and *expendable*.

That's another big word, but, when something's considered "*expendable*," nobody really cares if it's being made into buttons or getting served up for lunch. I'm sure you must have heard of Chick-Fil-A, which sounds about as awful to me as what happened to humans called Hottentots*—who're now very nearly extinct, at least as a separate people, though for the longest time nobody seemed to care because they didn't look or behave like those who were then in charge. It somehow seems worse in a way when you're not even thought of as food.

That bothers me a lot, though all I can suggest is that, if such thinking is ever to change, we've got to let others know what it's like to be in our shoes—or without any shoes at all—and that means learning and teaching everything we can. For we can't just *mosey* along as if there's nothing to be done. . . which is why, despite my dear friend's puzzlement and mockery from the others, I kept scratching out numbers in the dust and, on one particular afternoon, was so focused on trying to explain that I never saw Jones as he walked up and left and then came back again with Greg and Boykin and Zan.

It was only when I heard an inquisitive snuffle and turned to see Maud Gonne jabbing her snout through the fence that I realized they were standing there, silently staring down at me. They didn't move, and nobody said a thing—except Maud Gonne who went on snuffling, her way of saying "What? What? What?"

It occurs to me now as I look back that, if I'd arrived from outer space assuming the form of a chicken and then, when I thought nobody could see, had changed back to my alien self, my family couldn't have been more shocked. All during the months before, I'd taken my progress for granted, knowing that through no fault of their own they'd had no way of assessing what I'd been taking in. I'd never expected praise or applause. but now I got both in spades.

They seemed so proud, in fact, that they looked almost alarmed, whispering to each other until Jones declared out loud with a sort of proud finality, "Sunshine is a *genius!*"

"Another typical Bell," added Zan, and everyone laughed.

They picked me up and took me inside, and, once they knew for sure that I truly understood whatever they wanted to say, they asked me to demonstrate how I'd opened Jones' books and managed to turn the pages and learned to operate the computer on his desk. They kept it all secret for a while except for telling some relatives like both of Boykin's parents, neither of whom I'd met.

Our sister Bevin visited for the weekend and talked about the college that she attended. It was called Wofford, she said—the name of which sounded to me like something Nellie might say—and contained a lot of smart people but no chickens anywhere except. . . she paused, and, changing her mind about what she'd been going to say, she mentioned a dog named Chaser*, a brilliant border collie who, as everyone would soon be aware, was the smartest dog in the world.

Our cousin Boyd, who was only a baby then, also came to call. His father was Boykin's brother, Ben, and he talked about Sequoyah*, not a chicken but what he called a Cherokee who'd invented an alphabet because his people long ago had had no way of writing their language down. And Ben said maybe, if I decided to try, I might just do the same sort of thing for animals everywhere. . . or for chickens anyhow. That was very flattering, and his opinion was shared by Susannah their sister in San Francisco—whose name reminds me of mine, with six of the same eight letters, and when I cackled that briefly to her over the phone, she did an excellent job of cackling back in a way that was quite amusing.

Boykin's parents came too, and I learned from her that Pa Ben, the head of Bevin's college, had been a beatnik* when he was young. I had no idea what a beatnik was, though to many that would have been a very odd combination, at least according to Boykin. Annie Rooney*, his wife and her mother, had been a reluctant debutante who was currently spending much of her time reading Marcel Proust* which would sound even weirder to some, Boykin said with a shrug— though now that I've read Proust too, I think it showed good sense. The two of them lived a long way off at the far end of the state, and, when not in their campus house, hung out at what Pa Ben described as a horse farm minus the horses—the best sort, he explained, for doing some thinking and writing. He'd been both a teacher and writer and said he strongly agreed with Ben that, if I should someday find a way to share my personal views, it would strike most humans as being akin to news from another planet.

He didn't elaborate, but, since I've just described myself as an alien from outer space, I guess I can add that he planted a seed that's come to *fruition* in this book—which simply means it's bearing fruit, a process that started that very day and soon was changing everything.

Jones was so proud of the part he'd played that he told his teacher how quickly I'd learned whatever it was he was trying to teach and then, with Boykin and Greg along, took them and me to visit his school, where I showed the teacher and her class how I'd figured out arithmetic.

—

I'd have liked to discuss it a great deal more but, since no computer was ready at hand, I couldn't converse with them in words and decided to stick with numbers and signs as the language we all knew. So I added and subtracted, divided and multiplied—which all went well enough. But, once I'd started in on some easy quadratic equations, it seemed some dignitaries who'd been invited to watch began to grow uneasy, and the principal, who was head of the school, told Boykin and Greg they'd better take me home before suspicions arose of "demonic possession" or something even worse.

They did as he suggested, but the local paper next day had a photograph of me with a headline that announced, "Miracle Chicken or Hoax?" And, after that, there were jokes and far-fetched explanations, including one that implied I really had come from outer space and another that declared that "this so-called Scots Dumpy chick" was just another illegal from a socialist foreign country who hadn't yet "met the Colonel*." For a while, I had to stay inside the house completely out of sight. Then, gradually, the furor died down, and I went from being an Einstein Chicken to being just another bright Bell—but one that had, in a manner of speaking, rung loudly and fallen silent.

It wasn't long after that that I laid my very first egg.

Chapter 6

From chick to *pullet* my life had changed, but when I was nearly six months old that egg appeared and life in the coop took a turn for the worse. Mine wasn't the only egg, you see. All us hens were laying them, but without a rooster stalking about, there wouldn't be any baby chicks—so there was bickering instead, more and worse than ever before. Despite my friendship with Thorazine, I stayed in the house as much as I could, immersing myself in learning new things and hatching all sorts of *grandiose* schemes for saving the rest of Chickendom. My family took the eggs away, but that too added to the stress since none of the other hens had a clue about what had become of them, and I kept what I knew to myself.

Thorazine, meanwhile, grew and grew. So her former tormentors left her alone, attacking each other for a change over such foolishly trivial things as who'd first spotted a ladybug* or got to perch on the highest rung while dozing off in the coop. Thorazine could have ruled the roost if she'd thought it was worth the fuss.

But then one day, when Jones had decided I needed a little exercise and put me outside in the run, she took part in an awful ruckus. For nearly a week before, I'd been eyeing a chickweed clump growing outside the fence, close but not quite close enough for anyone to snag. All the hens had had a try by stretching their beaks through a hole in the wire, but it had remained just out of reach.

Still, rain and sun make everything grow, and the clump looked truly *delectable*—"extremely delicious" in other words—and we'd all been successful in the past with things that grew or imprudently crawled a hair's breadth closer than before. We'd learned to choose the exact right hole while, if it was some greenery, hoping its roots hadn't grown very deep and a favorable breeze might bend it enough that, by stretching and nabbing the tip of a sprig, we could yank the whole *bonanza* loose and, with that trophy gripped in our beaks, gleefully race about the yard as every hen would stop and stare before launching themselves in a greedy pursuit, ducking and squawking and doing their best to snatch whatever they could for themselves. It would be an unseemly free-for-all, but it was always the same.

On the afternoon I'm talking about, Meg, who'd gotten off on her own to study the chickweed one more time to see if it might be reachable, was turning her head this way and that. Deciding there might just be a chance, she darted her head through the honeycomb wire, and, probably to her great surprise, managed to grab a stalk of the clump. Then, bracing her feet, she shook it a bit before tugging on it with all her might. . . and the whole plant suddenly tore loose as she fell backwards onto her back clutching it like a leafy cloak that covered her from beak to feet.

As she scrambled to get upright again, we heard her exclaim with her mouth still full, "Oh, m'gosh! M'gosh! M'gosh! M'gosh!"

Amy saw what had happened at once. "Whooeee!" she shrieked, scratching up dirt and making a bee line straight for Meg.

Jo saw Amy, and Beth saw Jo, and in seconds there followed a wild *melee*, a furious flailing of claws and beaks with shrieks and feathers in the air.

"I'd stay out of that if I were you," I tried to caution Thorazine.

But her urge to dive in was too great, and she went thudding towards the brawl, jostling the smaller hens about while pecking and getting pecked in return before vanishing into a cloud of dust amid furious screeches and flapping wings.

In seconds the weed had been torn to bits. Heads were bleeding, and one of Meg's eyes appeared no more than an empty socket. Thorazine finally stalked away with tattered bits of a chickweed stem while the others looked on resentfully and Meg began to stumble about, brrrkkking incoherently.

I was truly horrified.

It had been no more than a couple of days since, fully aware of my ancestry now, I'd memorized some stern advice written by a fellow Scot* whose name was Lord Macaulay. "Live strictly and think freely," he'd urged, while you "practice what is moral and believe in what is rational." He'd called those admirable words a "counsel of perfection," but after watching that *donnybrook*, I felt how hopeless it would be to expect such excitable creatures as us—and maybe most of you humans too—to rise above our appetites.

I was still brooding on such pessimistic thoughts late on the following day when I found myself once again in the coop, this time to stay there overnight because Greg, who played with a bluegrass band he'd decided to call The Chicken Wire Gang, was also the *impresario*—or person who manages some big show—for a festival* outside Chapel Hill. He'd be especially busy that night, and Jones and Zan were performing too in something they'd practiced for a week, and they'd all be camping out in tents along the riverbank.

I'd heard Nellie and Maud Gonne making big plans and naturally had high hopes myself of being invited to tag along. But just as naturally, I suppose, I was told it wasn't the sort of event at which an unattached hen like me was likely to feel very comfortable—so I'd have to sleep in the coop.

After Jones took me to the run, I heard the car as they drove away and did my best to settle down in a "thinking freely" state of mind as the evening and darkness slowly came on. It was quiet, almost somber, in the yard. Thorazine seemed to be dozing off in a cool spot under the coop while Meg was perching alone inside, recuperating as best she could, and Amy, Jo, and Beth were strolling about in seemingly aimless directions, clucking distractedly to themselves and pausing to scratch a bit here and there as if they couldn't remember why. Finally, it was totally dark, and one by one they wandered inside as, trailing behind them, I entered too and, finding a place on the middle rung that was fairly close to Thorazine, I closed my eyes and fell asleep.

I'm not sure when I became aware that something had invaded the coop. I'd heard a thump and the clank of a hasp and the creak of one of the big door's hinges. I'd roosted nearest to that door and was startled at once by a blinding light as a voice began to coax and growl in a low and very menacing way, "EYE-in-stein! Oh, EYE-in-steinnn!"

Beth and Amy ruffled up. The light left me and focused on them.

"Let's see now," muttered the growly voice. "Which one of you is the brainy one?"

I remembered that caption and photo of me that had run in the local paper, but some humans, I think, are inclined to suppose all chickens look more or less alike. Also, of course, except for our size, Thorazine looked a lot like me, and the giveaway of my dumpy short legs was hidden as long as I stayed on the roost.

"It's her! It's her!" I heard Beth scream, waggling her wings in my direction and provoking a general panic.

As Meg flew from the roost and hit the wall, squawking and thrashing in the straw, I caught a glimpse of the intruder. He seemed to be even bigger than Greg, hunched over in highboy overalls and holding a flashlight in one hand with a *croker* sack* in the other.

"Not you or you. . ."

The light fixed suddenly on Jo, who cowered against the coop's back wall.

"Run!" she shrieked as she shrank back, then decided to follow her own advice, scuttling first one way, then another as Amy spun sideways, leaping up, colliding awkwardly with Beth. They both got swatted to the floor.

"That leaves just two," the voice observed. "And one of you. . . this one of you. . ." His light examined Thorazine, her *hackles* raised and her beak like a sword, curling her claws as if ready to fight. ". . . has longer legs," the voice resumed, "than what I saw in the paper."

The light threw her shadow on the wall as, turning to me, the man moved closer.

"So that leaves only you, my beauty! The one who's managed to stay so calm."

Holding the flashlight in one hand, he reached with the other towards my perch.

"Thaaat's right," he soothingly muttered. "Just come to daddy."

I sat transfixed, but what could I do? That he wasn't my father, I was sure. But cornered so helplessly there in the coop, too frozen with indecision to think, I understood in a terrible flash how numbly resigned most creatures must feel when the ruthlessly cunning come to call. I studied the hair on the back of his wrist as, wedging the flashlight under his arm, he freed both hands to grapple with me.

I heard a sudden piercing shriek, and then an angry yelp of pain. The light went flying across the coop. The man's arms flailed, and, in the dim reflected light, I glimpsed my dear friend Thorazine attacking the monster on my behalf as, dropping me, he wheeled towards her.

"You wanna be a dust mop, huh? We can arrange that right away!"

He'd managed to grab her by one leg and was smashing her head against the wall. Her body went limp as he raged on, and all I could do to make him stop was cause him to think I was getting away.

"HENPECKERRRR!" I screeched like a chicken from hell* hurling myself claws-first at his head, then diving and scurrying towards the door as, dropping Thorazine in the straw, he twisted around to head me off. Before I was close to getting away, he'd pinned my wings and was scooping me up. In a second, he'd dumped me in his sack, and then. . . what happened is all a blur.

I heard his footsteps hurrying, the opening of a door or lid, and then, while getting dumped in a cage, a disconcerting jumble of sounds—quacks and mews and rustling about. An engine coughed and started up. Some sort of vehicle lurched and moved, as, battered, bruised, and traumatized, I entered a new phase of my life far from the only family I'd known and worse than anything I'd imagined.

I tried to summon up what I'd learned that could help me out of my present jam, but nothing I'd read seemed relevant. So I thought instead about Thorazine and her lifeless body in the straw, regretting how easily in my mind I'd sold her and our species short. Even if Thorazine was unique for courage and loyalty to her friends, her example would give me cause to hope for better and braver chickens to come. I'd remember her all my life, I thought*—though, given my present circumstance, that might not be so long.

46

Chapter 7

I'd only traveled once before without knowing where the trip would end, and that was when I was headed towards what would soon become my first real home—unless you count my trip in an egg prior to stumbling into this world. Now I was speeding towards who-knew-what and couldn't help wondering to myself if I was on my way out of it, but that was a thought I didn't pursue, trying to concentrate instead on whether a human in his right mind would kidnap a so-called "Eye-in-stein" only to send her to the fryer, and if the answer was what I hoped, what other motive could there be other than asking for ransom money. . . though what sort of price could I command that would satisfy a criminal mind?* Believing in what was rational was harder than I'd naively supposed, so I waited the way you have to wait when snow starts sifting down at night—we'd see when we could see, I thought, while vaguely aware that, comforting though that thought might be, I'd never seen snow before either.

Whatever conveyance I was in went rattling along for several hours, and, after we'd stopped and the driver had left, I waited silently at first to hear from whatever had briefly quacked and mewed when I'd been dumped into the cage. Then, after several minutes had passed, I heard a raspy voice ring out, "So where's J.J. offloading us now? Back in Lexington County I'll bet!"

I was startled to hear the speaker so close—and so fluent in Chicken from what I'd heard, though I couldn't quite make his accent out.

"I hate it in the sticks," he carped. "Is everybody still okay?"

After a pause I heard a quack.

"Pennzoil*. . . that you?" the speaker asked.

The quacker replied with an Old Duckish drawl that he was still where he'd always been, thanks to the Big Duck in the sky—though, given his druthers he confessed, he'd much rather be almost any place else.

"Better here than in a *pâté*. You still with us too, Calliope*?"

I heard a sort of purring noise like a rag rubbed over a tabletop.

"I take it that's a yes, okay? And Frank, of course, has nothing to say. Hang in there, Frank. We're in this together, count on that—though, even if I say so myself, you're lucky old Runnymede's still in charge. That goes without saying for all of you. . ." Here he paused and gave a cough, and I understood that his roll-call review was merely by way of letting me know that he was the big shot in that group. "So, then. . ." he rasped and paused again. "Unless I'm mistaken, we've got a rookie who's joined our troupe who's probably, as we all were once, a little unsure about what comes next and a wee bit shy about speaking up—am I right so far?"

I held my peace.

"That sounds like a yes. . . so let me clarify where we are. My professional name is Runnymede*, and I'm the star of this little show. Do you think you'll have any problem with that?"

Again, there was nothing for me to say.

"Well, that's just fine," said Runnymede. "I take it your answer is *tacit* consent. . . and, if I may ask this candidly, an assurance you're not a rooster too?"

"Gimme a break," I muttered out loud.

"No or *nyet*?" he said with a snort. "You do speak Chicken, don't you, toots?"

"At least as well as you," I said, replying as calmly as I could.

He cackled at my retort in an oddly strangled way. "I love these feisty southern belles! As soon as we get out of here. . ."

But before he could finish his macho rant, I heard the rattling of a lock and the grating of levers being flipped as the doors of our trailer opened up, admitting a sudden flood of light that, once I'd adjusted to the glare, gave me a glimpse of where we were. Four cages were stacked up next to mine, and each of them was occupied but squeezed by poles and a canvas pile that I'd soon see converted into a tent.

I twisted to get a better look and saw, preening no more than a foot away, a red-and-black bantam rooster—not all that big but stretching his neck as if he was getting ready to fight. Then, cocking his head, he nodded and winked.

"Listen up, hot-wings, as I said. . . just stick with Runnymede, okay? and maybe you'll see your name in lights!"

"Pipe down in there, you prima donnas!" A man in overalls banged on the door. "You'll sing for your supper soon enough." He lifted Runnymede's cage with a grunt and carried it towards a patch of shade.

"Yeah! Yeah!" croaked Runnymede in mid-air.

I studied the man as he returned—Thorazine's murderer, I was sure. His voice was one I wouldn't forget.

"Ooof!" he chuckled, "a big fat hen!" lifting my cage and putting it down next to Runnymede's on the ground, then fetching the others one by one. They were, as I learned, descending in size, Pennzoil, the easily-rattled duck, who continued to quack at this and that in a *melodramatic* old-fashioned way; Calliope, a bashfully passive-aggressive rabbit who silently crouched and wrinkled her nose; and then the enigma known as Frank, a hamster or maybe a guinea pig who might have been taken for a shoe except for the fact that, now and then, he'd lift his muzzle to sniff the air. A rooster, a hen, a rabbit, a duck—two boys, two girls, plus something else that could have been either, it seemed, had anyone thought to inquire. I couldn't imagine what we would share but learned as soon as the man came back.

"So, listen up good!" he growled to the rest. "This here is Sunshine—say hello. She's auditioning for our talent show, and, though her drumsticks ain't that great, they say she's a sure-enough brainiac, which is what we're gonna see for ourselves. I'm aimin' to start her out today a'tween Pennzoil and Calliope—but, let me remind you Hollywood types, we jess' got room fer four o' you." He glared down at the guinea pig, if that's in fact what poor Frank was, who trembled and buried his quivering nose amid the wood chips in his cage. "Y'all go ahead now and get acquainted—and hydrate 'fore you go onstage. No more keelin' over while you work."

I wasn't sure what he meant by that, but I spotted the plastic water trays that he was about to slide in our cages, and I was feeling so parched by then that I started to cluck in spite of myself.

"Well, then, Miss Sunshine, I'll tell you whut. You jess' go ahead and babble there, but we better get one thing straight right now—nobody eats here 'less she works." As he started to leave, he snickered and said, "Ask Frank how come he's losin' weight."

Having said that, he finished unloading. Next came the canvas and the poles, and, after he'd emptied the trailer out, he closed its door and I could read what the words on it said: J.J. BIGELOW THEATRICALS in fancy big flowing cursive letters and, under that in red, white, and blue, "World Famous A-Bomb Menagerie" and then, in a banner underneath, "Show Your Dominion Over the Earth!" and "As in Genesis 1:28." The license plate was from Alabama.

"Hey, Sunshine!" rasped out Runnymede—he'd listened in and learned my name. "Still ready for the Bigg time now? Don't think it's gonna be Broadway, though—it's closer to the Coliseum. . . don't guess you've ever heard of that?"

"In Ancient Rome, I have,"* I said, thinking that sounded ominous.

"Well, now," Runnymede clucked to himself in a slightly less conceited way. "I'm talkin' 'bout tag-team at the Omni. Can't say I've seen any Romans there, but some of the wrasslers look right old, an' if they're in masks it's hard to tell. But I'm warning you, bright eyes, listen up. With Mister Bigg running this show of ours, either you win or. . . ga-ga-gghhh!" He made a ghastly choking sound. "Know what I mean? You lose for good."

Oddly enough, for all his strut—and despite a growing suspicion of mine that his accent was a stagey invention since it kept changing as he talked—I had a sort of comforting feeling that he was somebody I could trust. . . until or unless we had to compete in whatever Bigelow's contest was, and, even then, Mister Bigg had said there was room for four. But what about whoever lost out?

I saw Runnymede was appraising me, first with one eye, then the other, dipping his head affectedly as if he was coming on to me—and, despite his boorish hotshot *bravado*, I felt flattered by so much attention from him. I was still a very young hen, you see.

"What exactly are we talking about?"

"Using our noggins, get my drift?"

I shook my head. I didn't, no—though I started to wish I'd mastered chess if that was what he was going to say.

"Oh, come on, Sunshine!" Runnymede clucked, shaking his handsome gold-plumed tail. "J.J.'s a hardnosed talent scout. You must've been scoring big at the game."

"What game?" I asked, all innocence.

"What game? Sweet cakes, there's only one." He looked for a glimmer of recognition but, failing to see it, cackled on. "You've heard, I assume, of tic-tac-toe*?"

I nodded, "Yes, but. . ."

Raising his claw, he cut me off. "But nothing," he said. "We're talking high stakes, honey bunch! You think I'd play for *chickenfeed?*" He crowed as if he'd cracked a joke, stamping his foot and shaking his head. "You make this team, you gotta win—and Frank's been on a losing streak. Which is why J.J. recruited you."

"Recruited?" I squawked. "He *kidnapped* me!"

"Yeah, right, okay. That's what I said. But it's life or death in Mister Bigg's game. You gotta look out for number one. . . and sometimes, maybe, number two." He was waiting for me to answer him, but, when I didn't, he brrk-brrrkkked at me with a boastful leer, "Trust me, babe—I'm from Atlanta."

I was trying to guess why that would matter when I glimpsed some movement off to my right and saw more structures going up while trucks and vans came wheeling in and people got busy erecting things like booths and stands and merry-go-rounds—a portable city out of thin air surrounding our tawdry little arena.

"Show biz," shrugged Runnymede, acting cool, though I saw him flinch when J.J. returned and, after checking the ropes and poles, began to lug us into our tent—including Frank who, though looking *morose* and possibly going unfed that night, stayed as doggedly mute as before. I knew my presence meant trouble for him and hated what Runnymede had implied—that, sooner or later, whatever the game, it was every animal for herself. Not necessarily though, I thought, reminding myself of Thorazine and suddenly feeling sad and alone.

"Just stay on your toes, kid!" Runnymede winked, puffing his chest out, acting brave.

Chapter 8

It was easy to see as darkness fell and music and colored lights came on nearby that, whatever delusions Runnymede had about being some sort of game-show star, Bigelow's smalltime operation had attached itself like a mite or a flea* to a far bigger traveling enterprise making its way from state to state and fair to fair with rides and other high-flying attractions. Our tent was out on the edge of things and woefully lacking in razzmatazz with nothing explaining what to expect but a sign on an easel where people came in that initially made no sense to me.

It was a *rebus*, Runnymede said, containing what I called *hieroglyphics* consisting of pictures that stood for words—a skimpy two-piece bathing suit, a blob with legs resembling a tick, a big-headed nail that looked like a tack, and what I assumed was a human toe. For those who couldn't figure that out, a translation was written underneath: BIKINI, then TICK and TACK and TOE, a curious spelling for the game you've probably played a thousand times. I'd watched Zan playing it with Jones, but not while either was in a bikini.

Grander amusements weren't far off in places more crowded and better lit. But next to us was the back of a van from which customers bought the sorts of snacks they wouldn't consider anywhere else—deep-fried lumps of this and that that made me tremble to think about or cotton candy, elephant ears, syrupy drinks, and other stuff that, according to what I've since been told, are the reason most people flock to a fair: to eat, see, and do outlandish stuff that's corny, exciting, weird, and cheap like the magazines at a grocery store. So, if that's what a fair's supposed to be, Mister Bigelow's set-up fit right in by hinting at something truly bizarre, maybe even a little *illicit*—which means forbidden by custom or law, and therefore in some foolish minds more tempting than what's considered okay.

But foolish isn't the same as mean. I've noticed some humans like to act bad without necessarily being so, while others like J.J. Bigelow are really and truly what they seem. He liked to loiter outside the tent, briefly *detaining* passersby to tell them confidentially that, on top of having a little fun, there were curious things to see inside much weirder than a dog-faced boy or a cannibal lady with a beard. He'd open a flap to give them a peek but close it back quickly to explain he had animals there with human-like brains created in an experiment conducted on the Bikini Atoll, famous for scanty bathing suits as well as for the atomic bomb which had made his menagerie super-smart. "No admission fee at all," he'd wink. "You only pay if you choose to play" and, as the sign on his truck had said, confirm what he used to rope them in—their "rightful dominion over the earth."

Runnymede tried to fill me in. Every so often, according to him, somebody would stop and get intrigued and, with one person hooked, whole families came in, blinking as they got used to the gloom. There wasn't much there for them to see but four large booths that stood in a row, six feet tall and three feet wide with their top halves consisting of Plexiglas cubes with a circle of air holes on their lids while the bottoms were plywood pedestals.

Before he'd let any customers in, Mister Bigg would open all four lids and each of us in that night's "cast" would be lowered onto "the darkened stage" lit by an eerie blue-green light that made us seem to glow in the dark—which made for "a very dramatic effect" when somebody chose to start the show by pumping four quarters into a slot, and then a spotlight would come on revealing how brilliant our plumage was.

"Speak for yourself!" I said with a shrug.

"You'll be surprised," he encouraged me, "no matter how drab you think you are," adding that even Frank looked good before he started flubbing his moves. Our board would also be lit up with two sets of lines in either direction creating our tic-tac-toe arena—still empty of any X's and O's, but, "This is where the drama begins. . . with each of us making our first move" by pecking or prodding one of the squares to which the customer would respond by using a keyboard mounted outside. The squares would light up with every move.

He paused to turn one eye toward me. "You still with me, kid?"

I clucked and nodded that I was.

"So you wanna guess what's on those cards that are pasted up on each of the cubes?"

I said I could read them.

"Oh, yeah? You can?" He seemed a little taken aback. "Well, I guess you're ready for your debut."

What they said was more of Mister Bigg's *spiel*, advising whoever decided to play that what they were going to undertake was more than just an idle amusement because, in a very meaningful way, it was pitting everyday humans like them against a mutant-animal threat—of opponents possessing what it described as "extreme and unnaturally high IQs resulting from secret A-bomb tests" on that faraway island of Bikini. Beneath those truly *preposterous* lies was a customized pep talk on each cube with a brief reminder of the rules. "BEAT THE ROOSTER," it urged on one, "FOR THE MODEST SUM OF $1.00 A GAME! TIE GOES TO THE ROOSTER & ROOSTER GOES FIRST."

Those last two points were crucial, of course, because they stacked the odds in our favor—and that wasn't all that gave us an edge, for placed at the back of each of our booths was what was designed as a major *incentive.* . . a chute down which, if we racked up a win, would tumble whatever rations we'd get like bits of lettuce or grains of corn. As Bigelow had said with a snarl, we'd each of us have to sing for our supper, including poor Frank who couldn't sing.

Regarding that fellow creature's fate, the card on the cube that was third in line had just been altered to "BEAT THE CHICKEN." I don't know why it didn't say hen, but the card on the cube after Runnymede's also said simply "BEAT THE DUCK", and, last of all on the booth after mine, players were goaded to "BEAT THE RABBIT." Whatever questions I might have had, it was clear the booths had been arranged to rank how tough we'd be to beat with Runnymede as the current champ and Calliope as the mere *palooka*. Pennzoil was slotted as second-best, and, though I felt a little miffed to be rated no higher than I was, I knew there must have been a card for "BEAT THE GUINEA PIG - AT LEAST!" and it pained me to think what might happen to Frank if I happened to go on a winning streak. . . as it seemed I was going to have to do.

Mister Bigelow's face was expressionless as he opened our cages one by one, examining each of us in turn while humming a show tune to himself and slipping our legs through elastic bands that held some sort of costume up. He called it a "howdy doo-doo suit," but, as soon as I saw the polka dots, I knew it was just some sort of bikini—a joke for the customers to enjoy. Even Runnymede had to submit, and all of us looked ridiculous. But Bigelow flashed a satisfied smile, and after a while he clomped outside in order to hustle the passers-by.

Still, *rinky-dink* though our staging was, I was feeling a bit of pre-game jitters, partly because of Mister Bigg's threats but also because it really did seem a lot like the Roman Colosseum, pitting four smaller creatures like us against larger and more ferocious foes for what in the end would be nothing more than a cat-and-mouse amusement. And yet, as I came to realize, our opponents stood to lose something too—not just the money they'd paid to play but their blandly arrogant pride and conceit in being, at least as they assumed, the rightful lords of all creation. . . an increasingly flimsy claim to me as I remembered Thorazine and how bravely she'd defended me. For *kith* and kin, I told myself.

So, vowing to win in honor of her as well as for chickens everywhere, I waited with growing anticipation for our first customers to appear—though I knew that, once inside the tent, they'd *deduce* from how the booths were arranged as well as from Runnymede's confident swagger that he'd be the biggest challenge they'd face. So only after losing to him, not once but usually several times, would they work down the food chain closer to me, nursing their wounded vanity by trying to outdo Pennzoil next. I'd get to play if they lost to him and didn't skip me to get to the rabbit—for the trick lay not only in roping them in but in keeping them playing until they won without letting them know that they'd been fleeced. . . though beating a bunny in a bikini apparently wasn't quite enough since, after the victory hooter went off, there'd be a face-saving payoff too that didn't reduce Bigg's profit much.

But even Calliope sometimes won despite her heart not being in it, and, whenever that happened, my spirits rose because the message it conveyed was one that all of us ought to applaud—don't ever sell anybody short. It also eased my conscience a bit because it meant that, no matter what, Frank would have to be kept in reserve while making me wonder what sort of jerk would boast of outthinking a guinea pig.

To answer that question, let me explain.

Most of the actual players were men who, just as Runnymede had said, would sometimes enter by themselves but generally with a wife and kids. They'd usually saunter into the tent and right away start sizing us up, too amused to see us wearing bikinis to worry about our souped-up brains. I noticed that, while they were fishing for quarters, they liked to talk defiant trash like, "Batter up in there, doodle-do!" or "Hare today an' gone tomorrow!" But as soon as they'd shoved their money in and the board lit up with the sound of a bell, they'd suddenly get all businesslike as one of us fowls would peck at a square or the rabbit would nudge it with her nose lighting an X up on the board—always in a corner, of course, because our surefire strategy lay in having two different ways to win of which our opponents could only block one.

I came close to feeling sorry for many of them when noting how often they'd hesitate and stare despairingly at the board as if trying to solve some intricate riddle, relying too much on intellect alone without using all parts of their brains including their *intuition*. I'm not talking about a mindless approach. . . I mean using our minds creatively* and knowing which ways of thinking are best for any particular task, something we tend to overlook in our "counsels of perfection." You don't need a computer to tie your shoe—not that I've got any use for a shoe—and perfection itself has a downside too when it gets in the way of solutions.

Chapter 9

I quickly compiled an unblemished record, winning outright more often than not which, as I'd correctly anticipated, was generally after Runnymede had beaten his challengers once or twice and Pennzoil, whose quacks had distracted their brains, would pass the losers on to me. A bell would be ringing in their ears, and a neon sign unlit before would rub their embarrassing losses in by pulsing out atop the booth: "ROOSTER WINS!" Bing! Bing! A-Bing! or "DUCK WINS TOO!" Bing! Bing! A-Bing!

So, rattled by their successive defeats, they'd *glower* at the Atomic Hen—the stage name Bigelow chose for me since my real name was kept under wraps—and, just as I'd been led to expect, my opponent would usually be a man with a wife and two or three kids looking on, and he'd probably make some snide remarks like "Looks like it's Fry-day, butterball!" or "No fowl play now, har-dee-har!" mixed in with phrases like "dumb luck" explaining his previous losses away. Often his family would urge him to quit, but he'd indignantly shake them off, insisting he'd figured out how to win.

I'd see the conviction in his eyes, and what I was thinking to myself was, "Thaaat's right, buster, come ahead! Come on to mama one more time!" Sometimes I'd even say it out loud since, not knowing any Chicken at all, the dupe would think it was meaningless clucks and feet more confident than before.

Remembering those encounters now, I'm *mortified* to realize how much I sounded like Runnymede—or, even worse, like Mister Bigg. I'm afraid it's quite disturbingly true that I soon had succumbed to acting like them, *reveling* in the loser's dismay, the lights, the bings, and the grains of corn that came tumbling down the victory chute. I wasn't as boastful as Runnymede who, having won, would strut back and forth across the board crowing as loudly as he could and prompting opponents to pound their fists frustratedly on the walls of his cube. Mister Bigg, who was there on ready alert for competitors totally losing their cool, would escort rowdy customers out. But I have to admit it gave me a thrill to put such high-handed humans down— they had it coming, I told myself, and maybe they'd even learn some respect for species other than their own.

If only, I think in retrospect.

The corn was mostly moldy, in fact, but that would be all we got to eat during a work-day dawn-to-dusk and often until 9 or 10— sweatshop hours that wore us out and had an effect on how we played, especially poor Calliope who, as I've noted once before, was never a keen competitor. Sometimes she'd get a little confused, X-ing an outside middle box as soon as she heard the bell go off, and it wouldn't be long before we'd hear a hooter instead and see her pulsing sign proclaim that "RABBIT LOSES!" Oooga-oog! "RABBIT LOSES!" Oooga-oog!

Mister Bigg would then come stalking in to pat the winner on the back while trying to get him to play again and glaring at poor Calliope because the customer, once he'd won, would, after the *furtive* payoff was made, march out of the tent with money in hand and almost always that was that. I never saw what the payoff was because I never lost a match, and payoffs couldn't be advertised since they were strictly against the law. But after the tent was empty again, Mister Bigg, who'd told her to win before she lost, would make some sort of caustic remark like, "Rabbit stew might pay me back!" For the moment, at least, that was all he'd say, but Calliope was terrified while I began merely biding my time.

And then, late on a Saturday afternoon, a three-time loser to Runnymede played Pennzoil twice and lost both times. He was turning towards me to play again when his badgering wife led him away along with their two obnoxious kids who'd beat on the sides of each of the cubes while their parents were squabbling back and forth over whether to waste more money and time.

"Attempting to what?" she'd fumed at him. "Outwit that stupid-looking hen?"

I was still seething at what she'd said when suddenly he reappeared trailed by his tightlipped sullen wife and hyperactive kids with a beady-eyed red-faced scowl on his face. None of them dared to utter a peep as he silently replayed Runnymede and, having made a hasty mistake, got trounced as he had three times before. He instantly wheeled to Pennzoil's cube, losing once and tying him twice before finally turning towards me again. His wife looked ready to urge him to quit but reconsidered and just looked on as he popped four quarters into the slot and, impatiently waiting for my first peck, banged out a carelessly *errant* 0. From there, I was simply mopping up. The bell went bing, the sign lit up.

"She beat you, dad!" the man's son said, then turned to his sister to explain. "She's only a hen, and she beat dad!"

"She must have cheated," the little brat said.

The man turned even redder then and pounded his fist into his palm while the woman quietly told the girl, "Your father was playing her just for fun. These animals do it for a living."

"Let's go!" their pinch-faced daughter whined.

They quickly left in a quarrelsome huff but soon were back with the woman *aghast* and the man apparently primed to explode. With very poor judgment as they came in, Pennzoil let loose some raucous quacks but stopped when the man walked up to his booth, daring him to repeat what he'd said. Pennzoil did, and the man replied by yelling all sorts of crazy stuff about "that Communist Daffy Duck!" and birdshot being too good for him. Bigelow soon had rushed back in and, assisted by a gratified wife, escorted the man outside again.

But Bigelow must have turned his back because in seconds the man returned, this time initially on his own. Trouble was brewing, that much was clear, though no one could guess what the wacko might do. His wife and kids slowly followed him in and stood near the tent flap looking concerned while the man, with a murderous glint in his eye, stood fuming like Yosemite Sam. The boy had cotton-candy clumps stuck like *scrofula* to his cheeks—scrofula's a skin disease that gets its name from the Latin for "sow," a word that means a female pig. . . which maybe should help you picture the kid. The girl was eating an elephant ear.

Alerted by Runnymede's cackled alarm, Pennzoil quacked as the man approached—exactly what he shouldn't have done for, without knowing a single word of Old Duckish, the man apparently understood that "Welcome back, sucker!" was what had been said. He answered with a maniacal grin, and, marching back up to Pennzoil's cube, he slammed four quarters into the slot. Then, just as the signal to start began and Pennzoil prepared to make a move, the man grabbed his daughter's elephant ear and, crumbling most of it into crumbs, began squeezing them through the holes on top.

Suddenly, bits of elephant ear were bouncing everywhere on the board and lying enticingly on each square. It was more than Pennzoil could resist as, hungrily, he started to peck, setting a chain reaction off with X's randomly on the board while the lunatic calmly pressed three O's lined up in a neat little Sunday-School row.

"Quack on that, you little twerp!"

But that was as far as the wacko could get because, in tricking the frenzied duck, he'd caused short circuits in the booth that made its lights flash on and off while the bell and hooter rang and screeched like all the poor wretches ever confined in Bigelow's sick menagerie. Dense smoke poured forth through cracks in the board, filling the cube and spreading like fog to every corner of the tent. As the man's wife tried to drag him away, their kids danced gleefully about yelling that "Daddy's smoked the duck!" while Pennzoil, trapped and unable to see, was gibbering nonsensically, "TIE GOES TO DUCK! TIE GOES TO DUCK! THE DUCK IS DOWN! SOMEBODY, HELP!"

Wherever Mister Bigg had gone, he now was quickly on the scene, shoving the crazed man back outside along with his wife and sniveling brood and trying to fasten the tent flaps shut as if to make sure nobody escaped. Then, turning his anger back on us, he focused it all on Pennzoil alone who, nearly delirious with alarm, was muttering wildly to himself, "JUST A DECOY. . . NEVER MIND. . . A DECOY WITH A DECOY'S BRAIN!"

"You idiot!" Mister Bigg exclaimed, unplugging a power cord from the cube—a line I'd never noticed before that, sending its tentacles to the cubes, snaked out beneath the back of the tent.

With Pennzoil suddenly silent and still, alone inside his darkened box, I felt a resentment only made worse by Bigelow's ugly curses and threats. "One duck down," he said with a sneer, repeating Pennzoil's hapless cry. "You wanna be a decoy, huh? You'll be sorry you ever said those words." He peered at Pennzoil with a nod. "Time for an oil change, yessiree!"

Whether he really meant it or not, the meaning for all of us was stark—no matter what Runnymede thought or said, we were prisoners not performers there and no hoopla could ever change that fact. For an instant I thought about the past and all my carefree youthful dreams with Jones and Zan in our bedroom at night and Boykin and Greg just down the hall and Bevin in college and Boyd nearby and Annie Rooney and old Pa Ben who came to visit whenever they could. Then I pictured the Rhode Island Red quartet—Amy, Beth, Jo, and one-eyed Meg. . . and poor courageous Thorazine. All seemed so precious to recall—though, as a great poet once observed, there's nothing worse than happy times brought back to mind when you're really sad.*

So I thought again of where I was—with Calliope, Runnymede, Pennzoil, and Frank—and knew it was basically up to me to bring this nightmare to an end. The time had come, I told myself, for Mister Bigg too to have to confront the wrath of an atomic hen.

Chapter 10

In settling accounts with Mister Bigg, I might have preferred a duel of wits but settled for what I thought I could do with silence, cunning, and exile too*—if what that meant was nothing more than leaving where I was behind.

The silence and cunning were easy enough. I'm sure you've heard of Frankenstein—that made-up patched-together man brought back to life though he'd been dead. I'd seen the movie on Jones' computer, and, as it suddenly came to mind, I knew exactly what to do. Mister Bigelow and his nightmarish game would get a visit from. . . *FRANKENHEN!*

Amid the smoke and general commotion of Pennzoil's meltdown in his cube, I threw myself forward on my beak trying to look like Thorazine when Bigelow dropped her in the straw. That memory strengthened my resolve as I tried to guess what his next move would be—attempting to salvage the damaged cube? Untying the flaps to clear the air? Or protecting his assets, such as we were, by putting each of us back in a cage? All three, I thought, but which one first?

I'd positioned my head so I could see while trying not to blink or sneeze. But even before he'd glanced at me, I found he was unpredictable. He decided to fasten the rest of the flaps—not just to keep the public out but shutting potential runaways in. I saw there'd be no easy escape, which meant there was just one way to win. . . and that would be to go on attack.

I waited as Bigelow came and went with a traumatized Pennzoil under his arm, presumably taking him to his cage and obliging me to change my plan to liberate everyone in the troupe. I'd do what I could for everyone else, waiting and watching through half-closed eyes while Bigelow tied the last flaps down and turned to check on Runnymede first, Calliope next, and finally me.

I held my breath as I waited to see if he'd be fooled by my improvised *ruse*—a *ruse* is just a clever trick, but it's also used for misleading one's prey. . . and that's the meaning I preferred because, in return for his bullying us, I hoped I was setting a trap for him. So I lay like a sleeping alligator, knowing his eyes were fastened on me.

"Dead as a doornail!" Bigelow growled. "That weasel must have poisoned her before going after that dumbo duck."

I heard him open the lid of my cube.

"So much for the genius chicken," he griped. "I'll get what I can for body parts at that griddle that's just across the way."

He reached to lift me out of the cube but, because of the angle, he loosened his grip and briefly held me with one hand—the very thing I was waiting for. Wriggling free with all my might, I launched myself at his plug-ugly face, pecking, clawing, and beating my wings. His angry howls were egging me on as my *banshee*-like shrieks kept pace with his, joined by Runnymede's joyous cries and a medley of raucous squeaks and squeals from Calliope and an elated Frank.

"Atta girl, Sunshine!"

"Smack him for us!"

"Give 'im a bushwhack and a peck!"

Needless to say, I was trying my best and, even when one of his *gyrating* arms managed to hammer me to the ground, I was back in an instant on the attack, only dimly hearing him sob, "I'll wring your sorry neck for this. . . roast your gizzard and eat your heart!"

My *adrenaline* burst was starting to fade, and, concluding I'd done what damage I could, I saw it was time to disengage—even though, with the flaps tied down, no route of escape seemed open to me. So, squawking and dashing around the tent, I wove elaborate figure eights, at one point watching as Bigelow, in doing his best to cut me off, banged headlong into Calliope's cube, sending it crashing to the ground and setting off sizzling showers of sparks while hooters and bells were making a din and neon letters flashed off and on "RABBIT WINS!" Bing! Oooga-oog! "RABBIT WINS!" Bing! Oooga-oog! I saw Calliope slowly creep out, wriggling her nose and hopping about indecisively this way and that.

Bigelow looked the worse for wear as, limping and bleeding but back on his feet with a viciously bloodthirsty look in his eye, he managed to drive me into a corner. Nearing exhaustion, I feared I was lost when, just at that moment I happened to glimpse the power line that I'd noticed before now coiled like a serpent in the air leading away from the overturned cube. Surely, I frantically told myself, it must have slithered like any snake to where it was from where it had been, from some energy source outside the tent. And wherever it entered must be a gap that, if I squeezed as hard as I could, I might just manage to wriggle through.

But Mister Bigg had spotted it too and was headed once more to cut me off as, half-running half-flying over the grass, I scrambled to follow the power line. I found the gap, but quickly judged that, because it was smaller than I'd hoped, there wasn't much chance of squeezing through before he'd gotten his hands on me. He'd guessed my aim and concluded the same, and I froze for a second in dismay, shrinking back against the tent as he drew closer with every step.

But suddenly his arms were flung out like a diver about to plunge in a pool, and he was flying like Superman some two or three feet above the ground. It took me a moment to comprehend that Calliope, super-shy though she was, had won me a precious bit of time by tripping Mister Bigelow up. They both went caroming through the air with one soft landing out of two. Bigelow hit the deck with a thud, rolling into Runnymede's cube and knocking it to the ground as well before, gasping and groaning, back on his knees, he was crawling on all fours after me. I knew he was only inches away as I struggled to get my head through the gap and, thrashing and waggling as hard as I could, finally popped like a newly hatched chick into a vast, calm world beyond.

I shook my head to gather my wits. It was dark and gloomy behind the tent, and, as I was stumbling blindly about, I startled a man relieving himself, supposing nobody would see him there. He jerked around as I raced past, cursing at me for wetting his foot. I kept on running willy-nilly until I was in a brightly lit crowd of whooping and laughing passers-by who caused me to realize with dismay that I couldn't be *inconspicuous*. A frantic chicken on the lam was just the sort of off-beat thing most people go to a fair to see. So some chuckled and dodged to let me get by while others made a half-hearted lunge, trying to grab me as I wove around and under them, over and through.

"Hey, Pa!" I heard a shrill voice yell, and I recognized one of those sulky kids and then the whole obnoxious bunch, including the nasty weasel-faced man who'd gone so loco in our tent. "Ain't that one of them smarty-pants chickens there?"

The man looked up and started to turn as if to make a move towards me when somebody else got in his way, pushing and shoving people aside. It was Mister Bigg, who was bloody and crazed like something out of a horror film determined to get some awful revenge.

"HEY, YOU! McNUGGET!" he bellowed at me, stiff-arming one of the passers-by who just happened to be the weasel-faced man— who also had revenge in mind. . . an unexpected break for me.

He swiveled and launched a mule-like kick, catching Bigelow in the gut. "You want some McNuggets? Chew on that!"

They started to grapple. Both went down while I for the first time in my life, summoning all the strength I had, soared for once just like a bird up over the booths and people's heads as I heard more voices shouting out.

"What's going on?"

"Two guys in a fight, tussling over some chicken McNuggets."

"Here comes a trooper to settle 'em down."

I too at that moment was settling down in a shadowy, mostly deserted place with a handful of stragglers headed home meandering through a parking lot. I knew how far I was from home but told myself two things were true—I needed to find a getaway car, and, assuming good luck was with me still, I'd find one with a license plate that said it had come from North Carolina. My exile might be very brief.

Chapter 11

S ome people think luck runs in threes, which is more or less how it worked for me. I'd escaped from Bigelow's clutches twice, inside his tent and outside too, and then, while prowling the parking lot, I spotted a driverless poultry truck in which, I thought, if I took the risk, I could probably hide and hitch a ride while blending in with the rest of the load. . . and luckier still was its license plate— "North Carolina – First in Flight." Since I was in headlong flight myself, that seemed an *auspicious* sign, and, so long as it took me in that direction, the truck ought to get me most of the way. . . after which, I assured myself, I'd continue to improvise until I reached Birch Circle.

It was parked behind a 4-H shed which struck me as yet another good sign because, among the many things 4-H does is help get animals kids have raised to competitions at state fairs, and then, I supposed, back home again, exactly what I wanted to do. I was too relieved by my narrow escape to wonder why all those roosters and hens who must have been there for a poultry show would be loaded together in one big truck, just as I felt such pangs of remorse at having to leave my teammates behind that I focused instead on the forlorn hope that Calliope might have gotten away and Runnymede too might have somehow escaped. At least two of the cubes had been broken to bits and having seen Mister Bigg brought low was reason enough to celebrate.

Still, taking such pleasure in somebody's pain was also very troubling to me, especially when I called to mind what Runnymede had so cynically said—that "You gotta look out for number one!" I'd hoped to live in a more generous world and, wanting to keep that hope alive, I'd bet that no one else in the truck would spitefully try to give me away. It was only the driver I worried about because, as I'd learned so far on the road, animals tend to be as safe as the humans around them let them be, and I feared that, if he found me out, he'd be likely to see me as nothing more than a couple of drumsticks on the run decked out in a silly bikini. . . which, while making sure the coast was clear, I managed to wriggle down to my feet and quickly peck into shreds.

Then, peering more closely into the truck, I saw crates stacked on either side with a narrow gap down the middle along the bottom tier. A tarpaulin atop the load prevented me from seeing more, but, hearing a couple of sleepy clucks that sounded as if they'd come from hens, I thought it was prudent to question one before the driver returned.

I moved to within a couple of feet. "Are all of you heading home?" I asked. "Back to the Tar Heel* state, I mean?"

"Who says we're Tar Heels?" grumbled a hen, confirming what I most wanted to know—that it really was a poultry truck fully loaded and ready to leave. "And who told you we're heading home?"

"So where're you from?" I asked again, noting her accent wasn't like mine.

"Gamecock country!* Where do you think?"

Just then, I heard a human cough and footsteps headed towards the truck. Knowing my time for deciding was up, I flapped and sprang between the crates, hoping the load was well secured.

A raucous chorus greeted me.

"Freeloader!"

"Who do you think you are?"

"She's like that other illegal guy."

"A Tarheel's what she said she was!"

"Not one of us! Not one of us!"

In an instant, that last complaint caught on, and the whole truck started to cackle it. "Not one of us! Not one of us!"

'STIFLE IT BACK THERE, SOUTHERN FRIED! You'll be spilling your giblets soon enough."

It wasn't exactly Mister Bigg, but I recognized the brutal tone and guessed what those withering words implied. Had none of the others understood, or were they that ignorant of the world? The tailgate banged as it was shut, and I realized that my fate would be sealed if I elected to stay aboard. . . unless at some point down the line I could pull another Houdini.* After thinking about it for less than a minute, I decided I ought to take the risk, but as soon as the engine started up, the hostility aimed at me resumed.

"No room! No Room!"

"No moochers allowed!"

"We're way too crowded as it is!"

I got a peck on the side of my head from whoever was in the crate on my right. Then somebody on the other side stretched out her neck to peck me too. There wasn't much use in fighting back—they were waiting their turns all down the gap. So I tried to reason.

"Listen," I said, as the lights of the fairground were slipping away. "I've just lit out from a really bad scene. But where we're now headed might be much worse."

A long pause followed, then a sob. I was startled to think they already knew.

"Worse!" a frightened voice started to wail. "You've heard of TYSON?"

I'd heard, of course, but I didn't know what or how to reply. Tyson owned lots of processing plants. I knew there was one in Fayetteville. I thought its name was Lickety Split.

The chorus of chickens started to keen, but, suddenly, seemingly inches away, I heard a baritone voice in my ear, unnervingly *suave*— and not a hen's.

"Welcome to zuh *tumbrel, chérie. . .*"[4] His accent made my feathers stir without my knowing where it was from—though whatever he was, it seemed a good bet that he wasn't much of a Tarheel fan. And yet he knew what a *tumbrel* was—a word for a sort of two-wheeled cart I'd found in one of Jones' books about a terrible time in France when prisoners who'd been condemned to die were taken in one to the *guillotine.* But who else there would know such a thing? Somebody like me, I told myself.

I wanted to hear the voice again but waited in vain for a minute or two until, in a quavering, resonant tone, it crooned melodically in my ear, "*Allons enfants de la patreee-ee-uh. . .!* "[5] then paused to add, "*Tu parles français?*"[6]

---

[4] "dear" as in "my dear" (French)

[5] "Let's go, children of the fatherland. . ." It's the opening line of the French national anthem or "La Marseillaise" which calls on the people of France to rise and defend their country.

[6] "Do you speak French?" The question is posed in a way one would speak to a child, close friend, or sweetheart.

"Foreigners!" sneered a scornful hen.

"Not one of us! Not one of us!"

"A pair of left-wing reds I'll bet!"

"What's wrong with that?" asked a Rhode Island Red.

"Forget it—they're just not one of us!"

"NOT ONE OF US!" the chorus resumed.

Whatever they might have meant by that, two things seemed perfectly clear to me as I swayed with the motion of the truck—first, that those catty provincial hens were stupidly *xenophobic*, and second, that, unseen in the dark, a broad warm chest was pressed against mine. He was definitely not inside a crate.

"*Tu peux comprendre?*"[7]

"*Oui, un peu!*"[8] That wasn't quite true. I'd sometimes listened in at night when Jones had practiced his French for school, but I hardly knew the language at all. When asked if I could understand, I'd answered, "Yes, a little bit" with a hint of a tremble in my voice. Jones' big sister, Bevin Bell, had spent a year of college in France, and I wished I'd spent more time with her. This was the first time in my life a fellow chicken had showed me up. I swallowed hard and gathered my wits.

When I got up my nerve, it was English I spoke. "What do they mean, 'not one of them'?"

"Zey are *Dominiques*," he said in a voice that flowed like honey from a spoon, though something about the way he drawled implied he was also putting them down—not just the ones attacking me, but all the others trapped in crates who hadn't uttered a single cluck.

So I spoke up on their behalf. "The best friend I've ever had was also Dominicker."

He paused as if, having gotten my point, he wanted to make some sort of amends. "You were lucky," he purred, "to have had a friend. Most of us are alone in this world."

No doubt, in French, that would sound even better. But, merely in English, hearing those words sent a series of shivers up my spine. He seemed so tragic and full of regret.

---

[7] "Do you understand?" (French)

[8] "Yes, a little." (French)

As if he'd read my very thought, he lowered his voice still further and said, "I too have befriended many hens. You must excuse zeese unfortunate ones—zey are understandably terrified. In zuh end, we must depend on each uzzer."

I let his words sink in again, and the clamor around us seemed to *subside* as if our detractors were reassured, though I doubted they'd even understood.

"What breed are you?" I quietly asked just as the truck rolled over a bump and he was either jostled about or moved deliberately closer to me, laying his neck against my own. I felt confused but gratified.

"I am. . ." he paused dramatically, "a Cinq-Doights Faverolle by birth. And you, my sweet?"

His head was very close to mine.

"A true Scots Dumpy," I managed to gasp, feeling myself go slightly faint.

"Zen, of course, you are varry beautiful. . . in a fetching if somewhat short-legged way. My true name, which I use no more, is Monsieur le Coq[9] Jean-Marie Le Parc de Faverolle. But I have taken an American name. I hope you will call me Rodney."

"Rodney!" I exclaimed, struggling not to laugh.

He seemed offended. "What is wrong wiz Rodney?" he inquired.

"Nothing at all," I hastened to say. "It's just. . . not very romantic."

"And you are called. . ."

"Sunshine," I said. "It's not very romantic either."

"Ah, *ma chérie*," he mournfully said, and again I felt a little shiver. "Romantic is as romantic does. And zuh problem we share here—do we not?—is how to refuse an urgent request to visit zis Tyson fellow's *abode*?"

A groan went up from the nearby crates, reminding me forcefully once again that what Rodney and I and all in that truck might have to face in Fayetteville was only an echo of the grief that most of the species on this earth have suffered since their creation. I wondered how chickens might have behaved if we'd been told to multiply and hold dominion over the earth. . . as, in fact, you know, we formerly

---

[9] "Mister Rooster" (French)

did when birds were actually dinosaurs. I guess you could say we'd had our shot, but because of the weather or who knows what, we'd managed to blow it in the end—though like lizards and other cousins of ours, it seems we're still just hanging around waiting to see how humans will fare because, as I'm told the cockroaches say, the final verdict's not in.

Such gloomy thoughts made perfect sense given the grim mess we were in. And yet for reasons I couldn't explain, my thoughts went back to multiplying and, more specifically at that moment, to Rodney—or, as he might put it, "the rooster formerly known as Jean-Marie"*—and on from there back to myself who might have been truly called at that moment "She Who Was Totally Losing Her Wits to An Accent & A fancy Name," otherwise known as Sunshine Bell.

We stood there together, mile after mile, rocking as the truck rolled on, hearing the highway under the wheels and, after a giddy couple of hours, watching a full moon rise in the sky and glint on the tailgate's metal rim as if it was turning to silver. But how to explain my giddy confusion except to admit, as I probably should, that Scots have a weakness for Frenchmen* and to note that, at certain points in our lives, especially when danger's present as well—like dangling from a *precipice* or escaping together in a truck—romance and a tight *predicament* can easily get confused, often to our misfortune. That's one of the times when, despite what I've said, reason's much better than instinct. . . at least till you're back on solid ground.

Chapter 12

It was, I admit, a heedless extravagant folly. There's a word for that as well—*infatuation*, involving a lesson that can't be taught but is learned by making willful mistakes. In my case, it had come about because of details I've mentioned already plus a handsome and dashing Faverolle and my own bewildered moonstruck self. There's not a lot more to say about that but a much longer story to tell.

My reaction to Rodney slowly changed. Though I wasn't exactly competing with him, it didn't take all that long to discover he knew far less than I'd supposed. He was a *swashbuckler* right enough, though wise and reflective, definitely not. So the basic question confronting me was if gallantry might make up for the rest. Initially, I thought it could, though the problem was, as I've tried to explain, I wasn't really thinking at all and completely ignored my intuition.

On the other hand, consider my actual situation. I'd learned a lot from what I'd read but had too little experience. I'd only met one rooster before and never one like Rodney, so I was totally unprepared for the captivating appeal of his beard-like wattle* and scarlet comb or the jauntiness of his upswept tail, so assertively dramatic compared to any hen's. His chest and tail and part of his face had a very beguiling ebony sheen while his neck resembled a snowy cloak and his powerful wings were bronze and black with tips like a gentleman's gloves. Even his legs were strikingly sheathed in feathery leggings down to his claws. . . and he had a most elegant strut.

No wonder I felt so overcome, but was what I was feeling love at first sight? I guess in a way it must have been, though I've since realized that such heady allure resembles most cafeteria food— whatever you see put out on display looks better than it's going to taste. I vaguely assumed our meeting was fate, and that, given my luck so far that day, I must have been on an unstoppable roll. . . which is said to be how most gamblers think, though more often than not they'll find they're wrong.

Still, the bottom line is that I succumbed, requesting the story of his career, and, after some teasing and witty *bon mots*—a phrase in French for clever remarks—he unloaded a history too far-fetched to suppose he'd merely made it up. His parents had been transported from France for a breeding program at Clemson, a university not far off from where we were traveling that night. It had once been mainly for farmers, it seems, before it became better known for football than for husbandry—the study of crops and animals—and the professor in charge of the poultry lab just happened to have a nine-year-old niece who lived in nearby Spartanburg, the town where Boykin's father, Pa Ben, was president of that little college that had last beaten Clemson in football more than seventy years before but would upset the Tarheels in basketball not once but several times in the course of the next few years, living up to its mascot, a terrier.

Then, when Easter came along in the year before I was born, the little girl wanted a chick, and her uncle, the professor, had a brand new hatchling at hand that was Jean-Marie de Faverolle, re-christened Rodney by the girl when she received him as a gift along with some chocolate eggs with multicolored sprinkles. Rodney was the professor's name.

So it was as Rodney, then, that he'd begun a prize-winning tour of 4-H shows throughout the state with a string of successes capped that day by a Blue-Ribbon Best-in-Show award for poultry at the big State Fair which was held a hundred miles away in Columbia, the capital city, instead of in Lexington County as Runnymede had supposed. In other words, just shortly before we met, Rodney had reached what many would have considered the pinnacle of a chicken's career. . . and yet he'd thrown it all away. Just after the prizes had been announced, while winners were being congratulated and losers were moping and being consoled, Rodney had left the podium and, strutting unnoticed through the crowd, slipped out through an open side door and into the parking lot. Then, like me a short time afterwards, he'd stumbled upon the unattended truck seemingly bound for North Carolina and, throwing all caution to the winds, hopped in with dreams of the open road.

But why had he done it? I wanted to know, impressed that he'd shown such *derring-do*.

Rodney shrugged. "Zere must be more to life," he said, "than winning awards and wooing hens."

That seemed so adventurous and romantic—though I wasn't entirely comfortable with how he spoke about wooing hens, which should have sounded a warning bell. But I naively told myself that, because of his looks and brilliant success, they must have been literally flocking to him, and, though I didn't mention it, my own very modest celebrity made it easier to guess how hard it might have been for him to deal with that as well. Besides, I thought, he was French.

"You know, *mon petit rayon de soleil*,"[10] he said, nuzzling me with his beak, "I have a destiny to fulfill."

His boldness was irresistible.

Before we knew it, the sun was up—though, if there were other roosters in the truck, none of them had the slightest incentive to crow, and Rodney's mind was on something else as, according to his reckoning, the state line shouldn't be far away. No sooner had he told me that than, peering through crates and under the tarp we saw a sign ahead saying Welcome to North Carolina, and, just a short while after that, the truck turned off the Interstate and into a Waffle House parking lot. Without so much as a glance at us, the driver got out and locked the cab and walked into the restaurant.

As soon as he was out of sight, Rodney said with an amorous nudge, "*Allons y, petite!*[11] It's time to go."

I looked at him uncertainly as he peeked up over the tailgate's rim and quietly brrkkked, "'Ow would you say—'we now check out'?"

I nodded without answering him, but tripped and stumbled against a crate, waking a Dominicker hen who guessed at once what we were doing.

"Don't leave!" she clucked. "It's you and us."

This caused a sudden wild chorus of squawks. "DON'T GO! DON'T GO! IT'S YOU AND US! YOU AND US!"

---

[10] "my little ray of sunshine." (French)

[11] "Let's go, little one!" (French)

Buffeted by their cackles and cries, we were clambering onto the tailgate's edge when, glancing towards the Waffle House, we saw numerous faces staring at us while a waitress was pointing at the truck. A customer rose and looked our way, then turned and started for the door.

"Must be zuh driver," Rodney said. "*Dépêche-toi!*"[12] he yelled at me, followed by, "Zhay-RON-eemo!"*

We leapt together from the truck, then scrambled across the parking lot and onto a two-lane asphalt road.

"Zis way!" he screeched at me again, sidestepping a swerving SUV with bicycles strapped across its back and, weirdly enough, a cage of some sort affixed to its roof containing a wildly barking dog. Some sleepy children inside the van were gazing out at the parking lot, not knowing they'd covered our getaway by cutting off the driver's view.

It was also lucky for our escape that the Waffle House stood at the edge of a very small town called Columbus, and there was a nearby overgrown field towards which we darted as fast as we could, assuming we'd have to run for our lives. But the driver, once halfway to the truck, just stopped and stood with his hands on his hips watching us as we raced away. Then he turned to check the rest of his load and, after tightening up his tarps, returned to finish his meal inside.

So far so good, we told ourselves, though we'd only gone a few hundred feet. Still, pausing a moment to catch our breath and confirm that we really were in the clear, we shared an emotion of great relief, flapping our wings and nuzzling beaks like flighty young wood ducks out on a tear. Then I remembered Chapel Hill, fearing how far we'd have to go but telling Rodney how nice it was and how certain I was he'd like the Bells. But he just shook his waddles and said most towns won't welcome a rooster in, to which I replied that rules can be changed. But once again he shook his head and asked me if perhaps I'd heard of a book called *Paul et Virginie**?"

I confessed that I hadn't, so he explained that, though he hadn't exactly read it, it was a very moving story of two young lovers in what

---

[12] "Hurry up!" (French)

he called *l'état de nature*—"*Pardon*,"[13] he added, "A state of nah-toor. . ." I assumed he meant a state of nature. "Like where we are at zis moment," he said, "with no need for uzzer people."

Not understanding why romance should have to exclude my family, I asked if maybe Tarzan and Jane were closer to what he had in mind.

"*Peut-être*,"[14] he answered thoughtfully, though I'd meant it as a playful reproach. "Or Faverolle and Dumpy, eh? So we must find some little nest where you can become a good little wife. But, *hélas*,"[15] he added with a shrug, "there're no monkeys here to help us out."

Mon-*kees*, he said, and 'eer, and 'elp, and I was so charmed by how he spoke that I never considered what he meant. A moment later he shrugged again, and, noting how well his accent had worked, repeatedly urged me to 'urry up!

"And go where?" I asked a bit *testily*. I thought we needed to have a plan.

"Why do you want to quarrel?" he asked me in return, and, just like that—because, it seemed, I'd questioned his taking the lead—we were having a peevish little spat about which direction to take.

I could tell by the sun that we'd come from the west and the truck had been headed towards the north and the mountains looming up ahead which meant, whatever its destination, it wasn't bound for Lickety Split or anyplace close to Chapel Hill. So somewhat relieved for the chickens still caged aboard it, I reasoned my home must lie a long way to the east. But Rodney opposed our going in that direction, insisting that, no matter how small the neighboring town might be, our chances of being caught made would make taking that route too risky. He thought they were probably chasing us now. I told him I thought that sounded absurd.

He stretched his neck and gazed around as if trying to be very patient. "Listen, *ma choupinette*,"[16] he said as he glared back over the

---

[13] "Excuse me" (French) preceded by what he translates as "a state of nature."

[14] "Perhaps." (French)

[15] "alas!" (French)

[16] Affectionate slang—in effect, "my cute little cabbage!" (French)

way we'd come, bitterly brrkking his words. "No 'uman can ever be trusted, especially zose who pretend to be so friendly. Zey're just as ferocious at 'art as all zuh uzzer *predators*." He stopped to reflect a bit further, then told me in a confidential way, "I think my destiny lies to zuh west, where a chicken can be a chicken," sounding as if what he had in mind was scratching across the open range. "Not 'ere in zuh east where one of your former presidents said zuh people would 'ave 'a chicken in every pot.'* He really told zem zat, you know—not a duck or a pig or a cow." He paused before he shrugged again and added, "Besides, little funny face, in matters like where to go, a hen should follow a rooster's advice."

I struggled with that but let it go. "So you want to return to the Interstate?" I asked as he started in that direction with me reluctantly trailing behind.

"Only zuh fearless are truly free!" he crowed.

"If road-kill counts as freedom," I snapped as we made our way through the underbrush behind a filling station, and I thought about trucks and SUVs cruising along the I-26 much faster than we could run. "Why would any sensible chicken. . .?"

"Want to cross zuh road?" With his accent and *condescending* charm and the all-too-familiar riddle, he tried to dismiss our argument by treating me like a chick. "But, *écoute*,[17] my precious little stumpy legs, you might as well want to know why zuh fireman wears red suspenders. Zuh answer is obvious," he smiled.

"But that question is dumb," I objected, "whereas crossing the Interstate. . ."

"Ah, but you know, *ma petite*, the fireman wears zose suspenders because he got zem from 'is muzzer—for Christmas, you see—and 'ee wants to make 'er 'ap-pee." He meant happy, of course, but his accent had now become so strong that he seemed to be speaking in baby-talk as he nuzzled my neck and said, "Which is also why zuh chicken you ask about would want to cross zuh Interstate. . . to lead 'is sweetheart towards 'appiness."

---

[17] "listen" (French)

He clucked with a sort of self-satisfied nod as if he'd settled the matter for good, though his accent seemed less charming than before. By then, we'd arrived where the undergrowth stopped and stood at the edge of the Interstate where I could hardly stay on my feet because of the gusts of passing cars.

Rodney dropped his voice down low. "Watch me," he said, "so you'll see 'ow it's done."

Then, not waiting for a reply, he puffed up his chest and, glancing at the oncoming cars, fell forward like a bungee jumper, propelling himself with rapid strides while stretching his neck out towards his goal, running and soaring in squawking bursts as he vanished into a honking storm only to briefly reappear amid a din of screeching brakes. I watched him as he ducked and bobbed, evading a swerving pickup truck, scuttling beneath an oncoming car, and then, as an 18-wheeler loomed, I shut my eyes. . . not wanting to see, but looking again and finding him on the other side, shaking his wattle and tossing his head, gazing triumphantly back at me.

He'd made it somehow—what about me? He was beckoning me to do the same, and, whatever my "genius chicken" claim, I was nonetheless a lovesick hen that also had a competitive streak.

I waited for a gap to appear, then recklessly made a dash of my own, dodging a couple of motorcycles while prompting some frightful skidding and yells but somehow making it safely across.

"*Magnifique!*"[18] Rodney applauded, emitting an admiring cluck.

He looked so vibrant and *debonair*. I ruffled my feathers and preened a bit, feeling elated at my success—though somewhere inside me I think I knew cheap thrills and lasting happiness aren't likely to be the same. At that moment I guess I didn't care.

I looked at Rodney lifting his wing and pointing away from the morning sun which glittered behind us through some trees. "A new life waits ahead!" he crowed.

I was eager to learn what that might mean. We shuddered and stamped expectantly, and then the two of us set out. . . into the wild, as it were.

---

[18] "Magnificent!" (French)

Chapter 13

Like every Scot, I've come to suppose—even those hatched in far off climes—I've got in me a wanderer's soul, and the rolling hills where we were then, sparsely inhabited as they were, must have struck its first settlers centuries ago as so like the auld sod[19] left behind that many of them had decided to stay and their descendants were living there still. . . so I should have felt completely at home. But, by nature and experience, I was a *domestic* chicken at heart, which meant I was used to household affairs, to fences and roosts and chickenfeed trays. I missed my family in Chapel Hill as Rodney with his footloose ways apparently couldn't comprehend— and yet, I honestly had to admit that, after our mad dash moments before, I'd never felt so fully alive or so ready to deal with whatever might come.

What came, however, in three or four minutes, appeared like some sort of nightmarish mirage as we found ourselves once more on the brink of a traffic-glutted interstate. Rodney seemed dumbfounded at first, though it occurred to me at once that everything on the one we'd crossed had been traveling in the same direction while on the one confronting us now it was headed back the other way—from which I could only *infer* one thing: we were on an island between the two. . . and furthermore and even worse, there were buildings across from where we stood, including one with a dreadful sign bearing the letters KFC.

Rodney *morosely* shook his head. "Is zere no safe haven for chickens?" he asked. His tail feathers drooped, his eyes were sad.

---

[19] Scottish dialect for "the old sod" or place where one's people are from.

I tried to console him by suggesting—as opposed to demanding or declaring—that maybe we should at least consider returning to where we'd been before and striking off to the south from there. I told him I'd noticed from the truck that, for quite a long way before we'd pulled off, I'd seen no houses lit up at all. Did he think that might be worth a try? But, before he could respond to me, I meekly added I wasn't sure I could make it across the Interstate again, a confession that seemed to perk him up.

"We must be brave," he brrrkkked in reply. "It takes more courage"—he said koor-rahjj—"to suffer zan to die. Do you know who said zat, *ma petite peureuse?*[20] Napoléon Bonaparte. . . *l'Empereur!*"[21] He whispered the title with great emotion, then lifted his head and cried, "Follow me!" as if he was leading an army.

I did just that, doing my best to march in step until we were back at the Interstate exactly where we'd crossed it before, pausing for him to check it out as if returning to a battlefield and then, when a gap in the traffic occurred, scampering back across without any further incident.

"Forward!" Rodney urged with resolve, and, after mounting a short steep hill, turned towards neither east nor west but in a generally southwards direction where we entered a meadow with grass so high that, in order to find our way, we had to bounce at intervals as if we were riding on pogo sticks—first Rodney, then me, then Rodney again. But, after his third or fourth bounce, Rodney said anyone watching us would think we looked ridiculous.

"Like who?" I asked.

"Like anyone. . . like uzzer roosters," he explained. Besides, he clucked, he'd seen enough on his previous bounce to felt quite certain that he could cope with whatever we might encounter next. But after proceeding five minutes or so through tangles of densely matted grass, he squawked as if he'd spotted a snake, stamping his feet and turning his head until he'd identified what it was—a field mouse gibbering in despair, cringing and wringing her tiny paws.

"Oh, no! Oh, no!" she wept aloud, shuddering like a wind-up toy.

---

[20] "my little fearful one." (French)

[21] "the Emperor!" (French)

I'd run into mice on several occasions invading our coop in Chapel Hill, and, though we hadn't much liked each other, I could see that the one we'd happened upon was merely what a fellow Scot had once addressed as a "wee, *sleekit*, cow'rin, tim'rous beastie"*—by which he'd meant in his down to earth way a sly but timid little creature—and I tried to calm her fear by using a couple of squeaks I'd learned from watching Animal Planet. . . but hearing me speak to her in Mouse only seemed to alarm her more.

"Better watch out! Watch out! Watch out!" she wailed in a pitifully shrill and frightened voice, looking anxiously all around.

I repeated to Rodney what she'd said while he uneasily turned his head.

"Watch out?" He jabbed his beak in the air. "For what?" he sternly told me to ask.

She shook her head despondently, twitching her whiskers as she squeaked. "For. . . for *everything*," she whimpered and quaked. "Especially things like you that fly—buzzards and owls. . . and chicken hawks!"

"But we're just chickens," I told her in Mouse, *aghast* at how miserable it must be to feel so small and insecure. "And as for flying, we really can't. . . no matter how hard we try."

"Just chickens?" she trembled, twitching again. "I've never met just a chicken before."

I thought that sounded ominous—not only for Rodney's safe-haven hope but for wondering if what had terrified her might prove to be as threatening to us. . . especially the so-called chicken hawks, something I'd never heard of before. But I wanted to calm her fraying nerves, so, noting a seed she'd dropped at her feet, I did my best to explain to her that, except for eating bugs and worms, I wasn't much of a *carnivore*—a word I didn't know in Mouse and one she didn't understand. So I nodded at the seed she'd dropped. "Are there plenty of things like that to eat?"

She blinked as if I meant her toes.

"Here in the meadow," I explained. "We haven't eaten for quite a while."

She widened her eyes and started to snivel. "Oh, no! Oh, no! I knew you both were desperados! My poor little babies! Sad, sad, sad!" But then she got a *sleekit* look. "Watch out behind you! Eeeeeek!" she squeaked. "A fox! A fox. . . who'll eat you too!"

She pointed a paw and, when we looked, it was only to see her scurry away as soon as we'd started to turn our heads. There wasn't a fox—only that seed to mark the spot where she'd just been.

"No need to waste it," Rodney observed, darting his beak to gobble it up. "If she hadn't looked so withered and gaunt, I might have given her a try. It's been a while since I've eaten a mouse."

I must have looked as shocked as I felt.

"What?" he asked. "You don't like mice? All chickens eat mice!"

"Not me," I said, though I wondered about the hens at home who'd been so vicious in a way. Had they feasted on meat when I wasn't there?

"And mice nibble on us too," Rodney said, "when we're trying to get a good night's sleep."

"A nuisance and murder aren't the same," I muttered quietly to myself, vowing that, as an adopted Bell, I'd stick to plants and seeds along with bugs now and then and scraps and chickenfeed whenever they could be had—though none of them seemed to lie at hand until we reached a newly ploughed field with rich brown furrows teeming with snacks. But no sooner had I started to peck than my thoughts returned to chicken hawks and how, if the mouse's warning was true, they'd be looking about for snacks of their own. . . a concern that I was about to share before thinking I'd hold my tongue for a bit and, while glancing nervously at the sky, fill up my *craw* instead.

Midway through accomplishing that, I noticed a road not far ahead, much narrower than the Interstate, and just past it a split-rail fence that bordered the edges of a field with dozens of silently grazing cows. I bided my time for dignity's sake before saying that, after we'd eaten enough, I'd feel safer there among the cows.

Rodney replied with a confident nod. "But, of course," he said. "We'll cross to zuh uzzer side, if you like, to stroll among zuh dull-witted cows."

Then, flashing his plumage, he led the way over the lukewarm asphalt road and along a driveway towards a barn, passing through the uninterested cows and scrambling under another fence to get to a gently sloping field where all the grass was vividly green but cropped back almost to stubble. We discovered why when, farther on, we spotted four elegant thoroughbred horses with one little pinto looking serene in the company of his regal friends—rather like me with Rodney, I thought. I'd never encountered live horses before and found it thrilling in a way, knowing they too were herbivores, which means they never eat meat.

The thoroughbreds raised their heads to watch as we entered their field like well-mannered guests, ducking and mincing step by step— though, delighted to have our stomachs full and our sense of adventure newly restored, we were both as blithe as newlyweds. The sun was warm, and a light breeze blew, and what was uppermost in my mind as the horses quickly grew bored with us was in keeping with Rodney's bold *aplomb*. "As big and beautiful as they are," I looked at the horses and told myself, "they're fenced-in in a way we're not. . . I'd so much rather be me!" For the moment at least, it seems, I'd decided the mouse's warning was grossly exaggerated.

I grew even happier with my lot when, after leaving the pasture, we happened upon an overturned log with delectable tidbits crawling about looking like *bonbons* on a tray, a perfect dessert for both of us— though from the tidbits' point of view, no doubt, we were *ravenous* monsters gobbling them up. But we both were simply *insatiable* as, spurred by feelings of greedy joy, we shared an *impromptu nuptial* feast. It occurred to me as I bolted it down that, rather than eating feed from sacks or pecking about in a combed over run, *foraging* in the wild was immensely satisfying.

Chapter 14

It's tempting to think that falling in love is so special that it must be unique for everyone, but even a moment's reflection should cause us to realize that keeping a species humming along is such a serious business that there're going to be certain rules of thumb—or spurs* or fins, whatever you've got—among which one that's often been cited is that, if you're truly *infatuated*, you don't have any appetite. . . at least, nothing approaching *gluttony*.

But for Rodney and me, gorging ourselves as we did was a definite confidence booster and renewed our flagging stamina because, by late that afternoon, we'd stumbled through woods and down dirt roads for what I guessed was more than ten hours. By then, I was verging once again on the brink of total exhaustion, and, though still aglow with giddy emotion, I'd begun to feel a spooky sense of something following in our tracks—though, whenever I turned to peer behind, whatever it was appeared to have stopped as if we were playing a game of freeze, the sort of tag I'd watched Zan play.

I tried to share this creepy notion, but Rodney merely clucked some advice that I should try harder to relax and that, no matter how clever I might appear in showing off my "language thing," I was acting like a typical hen. That raised my *hackles* quite a bit, and I replied indignantly that, even beyond what the fieldmouse had said, there were plenty of things to worry about—like foxes and bobcats for a start and maybe, for all that he or I knew, grizzlies and boa constrictors too.

I knew I'd overstated my case, and he cackled at my anxiety. "There aren't any grizzlies 'ere," he brrkkked.

"There're lots of bears, though," I protested.

"Zey don't eat chickens," he declared. "And zer're not any boa constrictors either.

"If bears could catch chickens, they'd eat them," I said, "there're plenty of other snakes in the woods—not to mention coyotes, possums, raccoons. . ."

"Calm down, *ma effrayée poupette!*"[22] he said in his self-important way. "Zuh world is full of dangers, I know, but fortune will always favor zuh bold!"

He complacently gave his feathers a shake, and, almost literally just like that, on top of my worry and fatigue, I'd had it up to my wishbone with his know-it-all habit of putting me down.

"Well, you weren't so bold with that mouse," I clucked.

My comment clearly caught him off-guard, but he quickly recovered by cocking his head and telling me with a haughty look, "I was waiting to see what the danger was and choosing my angle of attack."

"Of course, you were," I dryly replied, but he appeared so reproachfully stung that I instantly felt apologetic, blaming myself for losing my cool and thinking that maybe, in a way, it wasn't so far-fetched after all to describe me as a nervous hen. . . if prudence and caution are what that means as opposed to tying yourself in knots by supposing that what you haven't seen keeps hiding because you're looking for it. Such thinking can sometimes be profound,* but not this time I had to admit.

As far as what we actually saw, I glimpsed three or four rabbits along the way and lots of squirrels that were up in the trees or prowling about for nuts on the ground. But the rabbits couldn't be bothered to speak while most of the squirrels seemed very put out as if we'd come to pilfer their hoards. The rabbits merely stopped and stared when, recalling some words that Calliope used, I mumbled out a Rabbit hello, and the squirrels, whose language was hard to pronounce, kept chiding and jabbering overhead until we'd moved on through the woods.

Once we startled some white-tailed deer who shifted about uneasily, flicking their tails and snorting alarms as if to warn a trio of fawns, one of whom simply stood where he was while the other two skittishly scurried away with a comical sort of rocking-horse gait—

---

[22] "My frightened little doll!" (French)

but only to gradually reappear when their mothers took no notice of us and went on calmly munching grass. Then, pluckily curious, one of the fawns, who'd probably never seen chickens before, approached us in a Bambi-like* way, at which Rodney began to amuse himself by suddenly rushing in its direction while hopping and flapping and uttering squawks. All three at first leapt back in alarm, but soon they were treating it like a game with the bravest ones prancing fearlessly up to see if Rodney would charge again.

At that point, Rodney tossed his head as if resuming his dignity and led us farther into the woods where we wandered about for several hours, discovering more things to nibble on and skirting several quiet farms from which it was easy to steer clear—though from one of them came a rooster's crow that warned us in a quarrelsome way that, "This is my yard, you hear what I say? And these are my hens, so keep away!"

On hearing that bit of boastful rant, it was Rodney's turn for his *hackles* to rise, but I begged him not to answer back. He fretted about it for a while, but then, as the sun was about to sink, we happened upon a pleasant place—a grassy clearing surrounded by trees, located above a slow-moving stream—and Rodney gallantly served as a guard while I went down to have a gulp before he followed me over the bank to grab a guzzle of his own. We were looking about for a light-supper snack when suddenly a voice rang out in a lilting but guttural dialect that, though I understood passably well, had an odd sort of accent I couldn't quite place.

"Are you two out of your pea-picking minds?"

The voice was clearly addressing us, but I couldn't tell where it was coming from or if, as I'd at first supposed, it was speaking to us in Old Loonish or possibly Turkolet—which eventually I guessed it must be because, though the languages are alike, most turkeys tend to gobble their words where loons prefer to screech. . . and what I heard when it spoke again was definitely a gobble. If you've ever happened to overhear an irritated Scot complaining in broken Chinese with a slight Bulgarian accent, you've got the general idea, but I waited to make sure.

"Eloping, huh?" it said. "You must be a pair of runaways."

It seemed to come from some bushes nearby, but I didn't know how to answer that, and only after a lengthy pause did we see a peculiar head emerge—bald and bluish with oversized eyes, a crimson wattle under his chin, red eyebrows and a curving beak. He looked like an overgrown rooster of sorts or an otherwise dignified human wearing a costume for Halloween. . . which is to say, imposing and even intimidating while more than a little absurd.

Warily, he peered about, then *sashayed* out where we could see.

Not knowing the language, Rodney was stumped. "What is it?" he asked me under his breath.

"Wild turkey," I whispered.

"Wild, my foot!" the turkey exclaimed. His hearing was better than I'd supposed. "You *domestics* don't last so long out here for exactly the reason you just revealed—you've no idea what you're up against. Bobcat dumplings, if you ask me!"

He didn't suppose we'd understand.

"I'm Sunshine Bell," I answered him, ignoring his impolite remarks. "And this is Rodney, my good friend." The word for friend in Turkolet implied that we were sweethearts too. It made me blush to tell him that.

"Oh, ho!" the turkey *burbled* back. "You speak a little Turkolet—quite unexpected, I must say!"

He strutted up closer, cocking his head. "You two are really runaways?"

"What's that he's saying?" Rodney blustered, mistaking the turkey's gobbles for threats. "He wants a fight, he'll get one from me!"

The turkey was more than twice his size.

"No, he's okay," I hastened to say. "I think he's trying to let us know that this is a dodgy neighborhood. We probably ought to hear him out."

Rodney looked a little relieved, though he kept glaring and ramping up in a way that reminded me of those fawns. . . and yet he was protecting me, which struck me as very *chivalric*. The turkey took it all in stride.

"I'm Mel," he told me, wagging his wattle. "Your boyfriend looks a bit nervous to me."

"Your gobbles sound so ferocious, I guess."

"Think so?" he sniffed. He gobbled again, and, as he did, his head grew more and more *iridescent*—meaning it took on rainbow hues, though mostly in shades of red, white, and blue. "Mel's short for

Melchior, you know. Named for a wise old turkey I'm told, though nobody seems to know just who."

"One of the Magi* I suppose. . . the one who carried myrrh, I think." Even in halting Turkolet, Magi and myrrh were a mouthful for me.

Mel looked baffled and impressed. "Say what, little lady?" he gobbled at me, turning his head for a better look.

"Part of the Christmas story," I said.

"So long as it's not Thanksgiving!" he whooped. "Know what I'm saying? Har-de-har, but that's no joke. Black Thursday for us when that rolls around!" He gobbled indignantly to himself while his head turned brownish-blue again. "But, as I was getting ready to say, you tell your antsy friend over there that some scary dudes hang out in these parts. Take my advice and perch in the trees. Move to a different tree each night. Otherwise. . . szluuuuusczh!" He made a gruesome sort of sound while drawing a wing across his throat.

"Now, see 'ere!" Rodney bristled again, though Mel, who'd been ignoring him, swiveled to look him in the eye.

"Szluuuuusczh!" he repeated, nodding his head. "You won't last long out here like that."

I nodded too while Rodney scowled. "That sounds like good advice," I said. I'd read somewhere on the internet that jungle fowl, as a general rule, prefer for the most part roosting in trees, and I knew that they're close cousins of ours. "But," as I pointed out to Mel, "you can't lay eggs when you're out on a limb."

"Or in a fox's stomach," he shrugged. "Everything's up to you, of course. I'm warning you, though. . . and, I must say, I'm extremely impressed by just how well you're speaking to me in Turkolet. Almost nobody can but turkeys, you know. You know the call I'm waiting for?"

"Keow keow!"

He dipped his head admiringly. "You're one smart chicken, Miss. . .?"

". . . Sunshine Bell," I nodded again, adding a sweet little curtsy as well and smiling while pronouncing my name. In Turkolet, it came across as "Zun-shay'en," which I rather liked the music of despite the fact that I had to add, "It's generous of you to tip us off, but, if it's as dangerous as you say, what are you doing out here by yourself?"

"Well," he said with a crestfallen look, "I and my hens were happy here, just gobbling and fooling around, you know. But now. . ." he *forlornly* dipped his head. "Now every one of them is gone," he groaned.

"How awful!" I *commiserated*—which means I tried to comfort him. "Some *predator*. . ."

"No," he shook his beak. "They got this idea in their heads of having a nest off on their own—'just hens,' they said—and left me cold. Like poof! Without any warning at all, one morning I found they were up and gone—I've looked and looked but don't know where, though they're probably not so far from here." He peered at me appealingly. "I gobble and call, but. . . well, you see. . ." He choked on what sounded like a sob. "Nobody remembers Good Times Mel."

"They flee from me that sometime did me seek."* I was quoting from a poem I'd read.

"They do?" asked Mel distractedly. "You want to know who's after their eggs? Foxes and bobcats, skunks, raccoons. . . plus buzzards, owls, and even crows—and I'd protect them if I could."

Rodney had noticed Mel's change of tone. "What's he rattling on about so long?"

"He's sort of traumatized," I said. But, seeing Rodney's face go blank, I tried to put it in simpler terms. "He's so lonely that he'll take a chance by coming out in the open like this. He must have hoped we were two of his hens."

"He'd better back off from that idea!"

"Don't worry. He has."

Mel looked at Rodney, holding his peace but guessing what we were talking about. "Your boyfriend thinks he's tough," he said. "Tell him there's a bloodthirsty fox that prowls around here in these woods, and plenty of others you'll never see until they've gotten you in their jaws. Last warning for you, Miss Sunshine Bell—go back to your farm while you still can."

And, with that, Mel quickly disappeared into the bushes from which he'd come.

What farm? I wondered.

"Creepy guy. . . what else did he tell you?" Rodney preened.

"To roost in a tree as soon as we can."

"On our honeymoon, we should roost in a tree?"

Rodney's *ardor* was part of his charm, but, as the old Dumpy saying goes, "Don't cackle while you're still in the woods!"* I was already choosing a limb.

Chapter 15

J ust before dawn, I was jolted awake from my dreams, not knowing at first where I was but quickly aware of my perch on an ancient but leafy beech tree limb—with Rodney beside me snoozing away despite my impression while looking about that sunrise was only minutes away. I peered below in the eerie dim light, but what I saw sent a tremor of fear all through me.

A large red bushy-tailed black-legged fox was crouched at the bottom of the tree, grinning up *sardonically*—which is to say, with a scornful and mocking expression.

"*Comment?*"[23] brrrkked Rodney sleepily, awakened by my shudder.

He followed my gaze and saw the fox who, now that he had our joint attention, spoke slowly and distinctly to us in faultless but sinister Chicken. "I'll be back to visit," he purred. "Don't think you can hide. We have much that we need to discuss."

Neither of us said a word, but, though he'd quickly disappeared, his presence seemed to linger behind as we clung to our perches and listened. I'd been ignoring the chatter of squirrels, but now I tuned them in again as they railed at the fox from overhead and tracked him while he slipped away.

"Get off the ground while that jerk's around!" I heard one cry from a nearby tree, and "We've got a hunch he's looking for lunch!" as another one passed the warning along. "Well, say what you please—he can't climb trees!" came a retort from farther off, and then, as the din grew fainter and fainter, "There he goes—old needle-nose!"

---

[23] A word in French meaning "how" or "what"—in this case, "What?"

I never heard the fox reply, but I guessed he'd store the insults up until he could answer them closer at hand—as he was planning to do with us. . . or, as they'd say in the Squirrelish tongue, "while on the prowl for two citified fowl."

Still, for all the terror I'd felt at first, I'd learned a truly important lesson about getting along in the wild, something you ought to know as well. It's not just a matter of watching-out as the mouse had so frantically squeaked to us—we also have to keep listening-in to that jumbled but constantly busy commotion we tend to overlook in the woods, especially the buzzing undertone of those in danger of being eaten. . . and their sudden silences too.

We'll know when a fox is on the prowl if we listen more closely to the squirrels and be told by the birds when hawks are around—for, as I'd discovered from that scare, all small and defenseless living things are parts of a wood-wide *predator*-watch, including even crickets and frogs and most of their outgoing cousins as well, leaving aside some slithering mutes and turtles who either don't hear very well or simply prefer to lumber about muttering nonsense to themselves.

I'm sure many humans have learned this as well—though, as far as languages are concerned, I've noticed how many know only one or, if they happen to learn another, it's likely to be a human one too which, though they seem content with that, can drastically limit what they know and even what they can comprehend. I hope you'll believe me when I say how much I love and admire your truly remarkable species, but isn't it odd that creatures who're really quite clever at building and inventing things can be so simple in other ways? They can't see as acutely as a bird or hear as well as a deer. They can't smell like a dog or run as fast as all sorts of animals I could name. . . and yet, as I learned from Mister Bigg, they consider themselves "the lords of creation" because they've gotten so good at things that cause such harm to others. As I've said so often before, some of my very best friends are human, but a lot of us would feel better if somebody else had a turn at running the show. Like elephants, for example.

I'm sorry to be so *garrulous*—which means I'm talking too much—but I sometimes get wound up just clucking to myself. Please also note, however, that I didn't suggest that chickens should be in charge. . . for the very simple reason that, for all our occasional smarts

,

we can sometimes seem as blind as worms and totally unaware of what's staring us in the face.

Take my handsome friend Rodney, for instance, who'd also heard the squirrels and gotten at least the gist of what they were telling each other. But, instead of concluding that he'd do well to pipe down and listen awhile, he got all blustery again—bragging that he wasn't scared of any jabber-mouth fox, and. . . what did they call him? he wanted to know.

"Needle-nose," I told him. "There he goes—old needle-nose."

"Right, Needle-nose! If Needle-nose shows up," he said, "I'll treat him like I treated those deer. . . you saw how I handled them, I guess?"

I assured him that I had, and he responded by demonstrating exactly how he'd flap and peck, dancing about on our beech-tree branch with a truly ferocious look.

"*Regarde, ma douce poussine,*" he said as he struck a heroic pose while clinging to his perch. "*Je suis sans peur et sans brioche.*"[24]

I held my peace until he was done, then told him very quietly that I thought I'd be getting down from our roost while the fox was off prowling somewhere else—that is, while I dearly hoped he was. Then I'd start wading in that stream in order to leave no scent behind while heading the way the water was flowing, which was back the way we'd come before. Then I'd look for the safest place I could find. . . in order to lay an egg.

At this point in my declaration, I gave him a significant look to let him know it was going to be a very special egg, the first I'd ever laid that would hatch into a chick.

Rodney, who'd been puffing up his chest to pooh-pooh my concern, softened in an instant. "*Our* chick?" he earnestly asked.

I nodded and clucked.

"*Really?*" He seemed quite pleased with himself. "Ah, well, *chérie*. . . that changes everything!" What he actually said was "Zat

---

[24] "Look, my sweet chick. I am without fear and without a bread roll." Rodney has gotten confused in likening himself to a famous French knight named Bayard, who was said to have been "*sans peur et sans reproche*"— without fear and beyond reproach.

changes *every-zing*," to which he added, flapping his way to the ground and strutting about impressively, "*C'est vrai, mes amis*. . . It's true, you know: *travail, famille, patrie*[25]—zeez are what we live for—work, family, and farzerland*. . . which eez to say, my task as a rooster born to lead, my pride as a five-toed Faverolle, and zis land of ours right 'ere zat I've come to love so well!"

At first, I thought he was just saving face after being unnerved by the fox. But then, as he waxed so eloquent, ruffling his wings and stretching his neck, I saw he was thinking much bigger than that. I have to confess that, lovesick though I was, he struck me as somewhat pompous too. But roosters tend to act that way, and I could take comfort in the thought that he'd boasted of having a family too—even if it's sometimes easier understanding another species than the opposite gender of one's own. From where I sat, his blustery talk, which sounded to me like a campaign speech, was utterly beside the point compared to hatching one's egg.

But it all worked out eventually, for what we agreed to in the end was backtracking towards the Interstate, aiming to go just far enough to elude the fox's pursuit while keeping in mind, as we both would do, that the woods held other dangers too. Life's always full of dangers, of course, as Rodney himself had proclaimed, but the trick of avoiding constant fear lies in choosing which risks we're willing to take, not just in being bold. Some creatures take every precaution, it seems, while others appear to take none at all. I've learned to favor hedging my bets with careful preparation—which initially for us that day meant finding a way to cover our tracks as I'd already said I'd do.

We were helped a good bit by a thunderstorm that blew right through as we started out, buffeting us with gusts of wind and drenching us nearly to the bone. But we made good time as soon as it stopped, not glimpsing anyone at all but serenaded much of the way by tree frogs singing with delight.

By lunchtime I was feeling pooped, though Rodney favored pressing on. I gestured towards a tree-shaded grove with a thicket of close-knit bushes and shrubs. The stream we'd followed was still

---

[25] "It's true, my friends. . . work, family, country" (literally "fatherland," as in the first line of "La Marseillaise"). Rodney speaks as if he's addressing a crowd.

close by, and it looked like a perfect hideaway, especially for hatching a brood. But Rodney firmly shook his head, declaring we'd be too isolated. It would be a potential trap, he said where we could be cornered too easily.

When I reminded him that, the day before, he'd wanted to get to a place just like where we were then—"where a chicken can be a chicken," was how he'd put it—he nodded but amended what he'd said.

"What is one chicken alone?" he asked. "Or even two or three in dealing wiz foxes and humans alike? Zuh only strength that counts must be in larger numbers—a family, a flock. . . even hundreds, you see? And absolute *unanimity!*" He stood unmoving for a while, gazing fixedly down the stream, seemingly listening for applause and muttering to himself, "It will take an iron will."

There may have been some truth to what he said, but I was so taken aback by his sudden turnaround that I simply stood there where I was at the entrance to the grove.

"I must 'ave followers!" he brrkkked as much to himself as to me, which clearly wasn't the same as declaring *e pluribus unum**.

"Well, I must lay an egg," I said, though that seemed to have little effect as, once again as he'd done before, he started strutting off as if he knew where he was going—though he might have been, for all I knew, headed blindly towards the fox.

"Follow me!" he cackled, repeating his words from yesterday without looking back even once.

But I had more than myself to think about, and my instincts— plus my stubbornness too—caused me to stay right where I was. He was almost completely out of sight when I heard a low, dismissive voice softly emitting some "purrs" and "cutts" just a couple of inches away.

"Let him go, my dear. You're welcome to join my friends and me."

I feared at first that it was the fox who'd spoken Chicken so fluently, but it dawned on me that the words I'd heard had been uttered instead in Turkolet—not gobbled and *burbled* as Mel had done but murmured and chirped like a purling stream.

"Where are you?" I addressed the voice, replying to it in Turkolet.
"In here. Step in."

The voice was warm, but I was wary. "Would you let me have just a glimpse?" I asked.

"Look a bit harder," she told me.

So I turned my head this way and that in order to peer with either eye and gradually saw a turkey hen who—though perfectly camouflaged in the brush with light-tipped plumage for a coat, a long lithe neck, and expressive eyes—was big but a good bit smaller than Mel.

"I can see you now," I answered her, adding with some uneasiness, "but my friend's apparently disappeared!" I hoped that meant he'd simply stalked off as opposed to having been snatched away by something lurking in the woods.

"Don't worry," answered the turkey hen before adding in a more negative tone, "All toms are much alike I fear."

"He's a rooster, though."

"Same thing," she sniffed. "My name is Enid."

"And mine is Sunshine. . . Sunshine Bell."

She paused a while to take that in. "Well, tell me then," she purred in a friendly but slightly teasing way, "what's brought a nice little hen like you to an iffy place like this?"

"It's a very long story. . ." I started to say, but then confessed the simple truth that I needed a place to lay an egg even if I was by myself. "It'll be my first to hatch, I think."

"Trust me, honey," Enid said. "Alone is better in your case. Same for us as you can see. Come on, step in! My roomies are *foraging* up some grub, but you might as well take a little peek."

She seemed to sort of melt from view as I stepped towards where I thought she'd gone, finding a leafy corridor with different pathways branching off.

Then Enid suddenly reappeared. "This way! This way!" she beckoned me on.

I followed her on a narrow path to a roomy ingeniously hollowed-out space that, no matter how safe and snug it seemed, did not appear to contain any eggs.

"A lovely apartment, Enid," I said. "But, really, I've got to find a nest, a place where I can. . ."

Enid smiled, "Of course, you do, my dear! Of course!" and, plucking some leaves and grass aside, revealed a dozen cream-colored eggs spotted with lilac and reddish-brown and bigger than any I'd ever seen. "We're taking turns guarding them," she said, nodding with protective pride, "and we'll hatch them together, too, in time. We've never had chickens visit before, but we've rarely seen them anywhere and nary a single one like you who speaks such fluent Turkolet. . . and with such a charming accent too! Please make yourself at home, my dear. . . and, if perchance you feel inclined, just lay your eggs here with the rest."

I remembered an old Dutch saying I'd read that a hen prefers to lay her egg where others have laid their eggs as well, and maybe that's true I told myself—but, given the urgency I now felt, I didn't appear to have much choice. So, carefully stepping into the nest, I clucked and fluttered as all hens do and waited to see what happened next. To my relief and satisfaction, what happened, of course, was a smaller but beautifully cream-colored egg, nestled in with the others.

I felt a maternal affection of sorts for all the eggs that mine had joined, but I must admit it seemed quite weird to have laid my very first hatchable egg in a turkey hens' nest so far from home or from anybody I really knew. But then I thought of the perilous things that had happened over the past few days and felt an enormous gratitude towards Enid and her turkey friends who'd yet to lay their eyes on me.

Enid was smiling and dipping her head.

"That's right, that's right," she cackled approval. "Just twenty-eight days from now," she said, "you'll have a strong young *poult* of your own."

"Biddy," I corrected her, "because, I guess, compared to yours, our chicks must look so itty-bitty—though I think there's a chance it'll hatch much sooner."

"Oh, really? Are you sure?" she asked as if this disconcerted her. "I mean. . . unaccustomed as you are. . ."

But I was sure. I'd read about it on Jones' computer. "A biddy takes only twenty-one."

"Well, that's perfect, isn't it then? They'll be hatching together, yours and ours!"

I heard some rustling on the path through which we'd come just minutes before, then leisurely greetings of clucks and purrs as Enid's friends strolled into view.

"Ernestine!" Enid cackled back. "You'll never guess what's happened here. This is our new friend Sunshine Bell."

"Two names? I never!" someone huffed in a good-natured way that I didn't resent.

I saw another baldish head, then one behind her crowding in, prompting some "cutt-cutts" all around while fussing politely over me and reporting to Enid on what they'd found—an over-dressed rooster on the loose crowing his heart out in the woods.

"Sunshinnnne!" a hen named Ethel screeched, not knowing yet that the name was mine, and "Sunshinnnne!" shrieked another in turn sounding, even in Turkolet, like an actor in a movie I'd seen in which a man in his undershirt stood in a steamy street at night yelling a woman's name out loud.* They laughed until the hen I'd met—Ernestine, as I'd *inferred*—widened her eyes and looked at me.

"But that's your name!" she said with concern. "I didn't know chickens. . ."

"What?" I asked.

". . . were so emotional," she explained. "Our toms can kick up such a fuss, and we. . ."

"We're used to it, you see." Enid took me under her wing as Ernestine tried to apologize.

"Dreadfully sorry. Really, my dear. I'm sure your breed, whatever it is, has very deep feelings in its way. . . but is, ah, very practical too."

"The hens, at least," Enid chipped in.

"He's a different breed from me," I said, "if he's who I think you must have seen. He's French. . . and somewhat *melodramatic.*"

"Well, there you have it, I suppose!" Ernestine *burbled* with some relief.

"The truth is," Ethel also said by way of further apology, "there's not much drama in our lives—not at the moment, as you can see—and if you'd seen this woebegone rooster. . ."

"Heartbroken," added Ernestine.

I needed no further description, of course, and felt ashamed of having supposed that Rodney had simply wandered off leaving me there to fend for myself. I told the hens I should probably try to let him know that I'd be brooding in their nest. "But I'll be right back," I promised them, though Enid had a dubious look.

"Don't bring him with you," Ernestine said.

"I won't," I said and wandered outside, carefully noting where I was.

I hadn't gone far when Rodney's crow rang out reproachfully through the trees. He looked half-crazy with concern which made me love him all over again.

"Where *were* you?" he cackled, seeing me. "After everyzing I've done for you, how *could* you?" he sputtered, shaking his head.

I soothed him with a cluck or two, recounting all that had happened to me—including the *momentous* news that Rodney Junior was on the way. He never asked to see the egg but wanted to know when it would hatch. "Three weeks from now. . . in the turkey hens' nest."

That seemed to annoy him. "Fine for you," he said with a frown. "But what am I supposed to do while you're gobbling with zose weirdo hens? Zey look like aliens to me."

"The hens don't gobble," I answered him, "and they're totally American. . . unlike some others I could name."

"Like who?" he cackled, meaning me. "You're like zuh—how do you say?—zuh haggis* while I'm zuh *haute cuisne*[26] in zis country's razzer crude melting pot!"

"Listen," I answered impatiently. "It doesn't really matter what you or I might be. Our egg will be safe in that nest, and that's where it's got to stay until it hatches. You know I love you, Rodney, but, without a *coed* option here, you'll have to find a place nearby to roost on your own for a while, and, soon enough, we'll be together again. . . with Rodney Junior joining us."

He glared at me accusingly.

"What if it's a hen?" he asked.

"That'll be okay too," I said, "and maybe even better."

"You see," he complained, "zey're starting to influence you."

I let that go while he rambled on, insisting if only I'd followed him after he'd told me to, he wouldn't be in this pickle now.

---

[26] "grand cooking method," the most carefully prepared and artfully served dishes in the French culinary tradition. It was popularized in the United States by a very tall and very clever author, chef, and television personality named Julia Child who, while serving in World War II had invented a shark repellant that's still in use today. [The editor of this book used to see her on a regular basis in the Star Market in Cambridge, Massachusetts, during the 1960s.]

"There can be uzzer eggs," he snapped. "Zat one is not so special."

"It is to me," I told him, and, just then, hulking Enid appeared.

"I'm off to grab a bite to eat," she clucked to me somewhat breezily. "Don't suppose you'd care to join me?"

That sounded very enticing, but Rodney looked so miserably glum that I thanked her and declined.

Chapter 16

The next three weeks of guarding the nest while tending to Rodney's ego too flew by like June bugs in July. The fox gave up on catching us—at least, so far as I was aware—and, though Rodney kept sulking and mooning about, he'd leave each day on some errand or other, returning late in the afternoon to share whatever I'd found to eat and repeat that my newfound plus-size friends were dangerous radical feminist freaks whose family values needed work.

But summer's lovely in the woods, especially in that foothills terrain, and, though I dreaded his grumpy moods, I relished my interludes with the girls that felt at times like a sitting hens' *spree*.

Ethel had a boisterous wit and kept us in stitches with her quips, especially when Mel came stumbling by, bawling for them to socialize.

"Come out and party, girls!" he'd sob. "Remember what fun we used to have?"

Ethel would wink at us and wait until he'd wandered off again before she'd start her mimicry, mock-gobbling in a Mel-like voice. "Dear little Enid, where'd you go? And, Ethel, don't you want to dance? And Ernestine, you sweet little birdie, remember how we pitched some woo?" Then she'd perform some comical steps that she described as Mel's "turkey trot." Enid would shriek and clap her wings while Ernestine laughed until she choked.

Though not subjected to ridicule, Rodney's exclusion from the nest ruffled his feathers more and more. During our brief *trysts* in the woods, he'd always have some snide remarks about "that homely bunch of hens" and ask me how I was going to feel if Rodney Junior got confused and started to gobble instead of crow. I said we'd have to take that chance—though, hearing how vain some toms could be, I told him I guessed it was probably true that roosters make better husbands by far, a tactful fib that settled him down. He'd stretch his neck and shake his head and say as he struck a stately pose, "Without roosters there'd be no hens, you know."

But often I'd find, when I got a break, that he still wasn't back from wherever he'd gone, so I'd go *foraging* on my own, becoming increasingly self-reliant. Then, just as I'd started feeling bold, I learned how foolishly rash I'd been.

It was mid-afternoon on a hot summer day, and, while scratching about in search of bugs, I'd wandered a little too far from the nest when I spotted a clearing up ahead that held a couple of rotting logs.

"Ideal!" I chuckled to myself, not listening out for squirrel-alarms or hearing the gossiping birds go shrill. I was pecking away at bits of wood and cocking my head from side to side when suddenly, from a giant pine, I heard a heavy swoosh of wings and turned to see a chilling sight—the outstretched talons of a hawk swooping down towards me through the air.

I'll never forget its dagger-like beak and merciless glare or understand why I froze again as I'd done in the henhouse with Mister Bigg. But I know how quickly I'd have been hash if something miraculous hadn't occurred as, with an angry raspy "cutt-cutt-cutt" a feathered avenger rose from the ground and soared like a rocket towards the hawk, thudding against it in mid-air.

It was Ethel, my "easy-going" friend, who'd appeared out of nowhere just in time. For a moment the hawk lay stunned on the ground, screeching and thrashing with one hurt wing. Then, righting itself, it shrieked with rage and threw itself at Ethel's chest while Ethel stabbed back at it with her beak.

"Get out of here!" she ordered me as I tried wildly to comply.

As if startled by Ethel's counterattack and nursing its badly damaged wing, the hawk went scuttling in retreat, then, yawping indignantly, took to the air. It lit on a pine limb overhead, glaring angrily down at us while shifting its weight from foot to foot. I was cowering under a wild cherry tree when I heard a creak from the branch it was on and watched it as, veering awkwardly in its flight, it squalled and seethed and flew away.

Ethel was bloody from head to toe, but, ruffling her wings exultantly, she lumbered over to where I crouched to lecture me as a grown-up would.

"Extremely careless of you, my dear! You'd leave your poor chick motherless."

Which had happened to me, I thought to myself—my mother had been an incubator.

But Ethel wasn't finished yet. "That's what '*domestic*' means they say," she grumbled as she checked her wounds, "deprived of any mother wit."

She had every right to lambast me. She'd saved my life at the risk of her own, exactly as Thorazine had done, and I murmured my thanks shamefacedly, thinking it's true of us chickens too that, no matter how smart we think we are, it's easy to be appallingly dumb.

"Thank you," I mumbled. "You're stupendously brave."

"Impulsive, I fear, like all us birds." She ruffled her feathers and smoothed them down. "We're cousins, you know."

"Lucky for me."

"I'd say so, yes," she purred in return. "But no more of that. . . let's toddle back home."

Enid and Ernestine made a fuss when we rejoined them in the nest, but I could tell how proud they were of Ethel and what she'd done for me. For my part I was overcome to think they'd been protecting me while I was mostly oblivious and that what they'd felt towards me as a friend they'd feel towards their young poults as well—as would I, of course, for my own little chick, something both fierce and tender at once. I was lucky I'd live to see the day.

As it happened, such happy maternal thoughts were even more apt than I could have guessed—for at just that moment, as if hearing a signal beamed only to us, we all grew perfectly silent and still, turning our eyes towards the slumbering eggs. . . one of which, almost *imperceptibly*, seemed fleetingly to quiver.

We breathlessly waited for something more, riveted on that single egg. Then it shook and quickly shook again, prompting us all to talk at once—not just about the *precocious* egg, but expressing concern for Ethel's wound while she pooh-poohed what she had done, and we anxiously watched the other eggs, clucking and cheering as, one by one, almost all of them bumped about in turn, pausing and starting up again.

For the longest time my egg was still, though, after a while, it started to quiver. It shook and bobbed like a cork in a stream, but then, alarmingly, it stopped, and I waited with increasing dread until suddenly, like a summer rain, I heard a tiny pattering sound and saw a jagged crack appear in one of the lilac-speckled eggs and then, heart-stoppingly, in my own as if they were somehow dancing together to music too faint for us hear, barely audible scratches and pecks that grew like a little percussion band as holes grew bigger and shell bits started to fall away, revealing brownish patches of fuzz and. . . finally, in my own sweet egg, a glimpse of precious golden fluff!

How could I ever convey to you how wondrous that moment truly was? I shared the excitement and jubilation, nuzzling their gawky featherless poults named Clem and Jed and one named Bal—short, I'd learn, for Balthasar*—then Edith, Edna, and Emmerline. But, even amidst such festive delight, I was waiting on pins and needles it seemed for that tuft of yellow-white fluff in my egg to turn itself into a chick.

What I should have kept in mind, of course, is that miracles when they do occur, are always right on time it seems, and so it was, at long last, when I saw a drowsy little face wondrously peering up at me from what little remained of his former shell as, shivering with anticipation, he bravely stepped into the world—my own, my precious little chick, not speckled black-and-white like me or rainbow-hued like Rodney, but a pale and buttery yellow like the sun!

I was simply so full of pride and relief that, at first, I failed to notice that two of the lilac-spotted eggs remained as still as they'd been before, like unlit light bulbs on a shelf. They hadn't hatched, which seemed so sad. . . though happily all the others had, and each of us had cause to rejoice with beautiful offspring of our own with still more names I'd never forget like Bric and Brac, and Mick and Mac, and a bright and bubbly little girl whom Ethel proclaimed was *Effervescent*, shortened to Effie almost at once. It was Effie who made our commune complete with a dozen strapping new-born poults and a single chirpily handsome chick.

Needless to say, I was greatly pleased that, along with the vigorous peeps and chirps that came so easily to Rodney Junior, he was joining the chorus of purrs and cutts the poults were busily trying out. Our brood would be truly *bilingual* it seemed, which means they'd speak two languages—though, to any outsider listening in, it might have seemed full of *gobbledygook,* a word that sounds like what it means. . . inspired by listening to turkeys, I'd guess, by humans who don't speak Turkolet.

In any case, it didn't take long for everyone in our nest to be chatting away with everyone else, and, when Rodney Junior crept under my wing to hear me repeat what mother hens must always tell their chicks, if only instinctively like me—that "in the beginning was the egg"—I saw the whole nest tuning in. And when Enid observed that, in Turkolet, the word for egg is "gobble-kee-cluck" Rodney Junior chimed right in with "In the beginning was. . . gobbledygook!"*—at which the rest of us yelped and cheered before attempting to straighten him out while he just beamed like the sun.

Chapter 17

O ne lesson no biddy of mine would ever fail to learn is where to find a courageous friend. "You can always trust a gobbler," I've said, and, "No matter what they might do or say, don't ever call losers a turkey." I'm hardly the first to feel that way, especially here in the United States where, when the founding fathers met, Ben Franklin thought our national bird should be the brave and peaceable turkey. But, after a somewhat heated debate, his colleagues preferred a *predator*, one whom Franklin later described as "a bird of bad moral character."

In my humble if slightly biased opinion, I think Franklin probably had it right, though Rodney Senior always insisted a rooster should have been chosen instead because, he said, "It's what this country ought to be. . . *debonair*, bold, and *prolific*," sharing his image of himself. *Prolific* to him meant lots of hens and, incidentally, many chicks—though Rodney had never laid an egg. When I ventured to point this out one day, he answered me disdainfully, declaring his countryman Lafayette* would surely have agreed with him if someone had only thought to ask.

But something else was on Rodney's mind, which soon became more evident because, in only two or three days, the much bigger poults were ready to roam under their mothers' watchful eyes while Rodney Junior went tagging along, though it was a major feat for him merely to stay on his feet. He kept blinking as if he was falling asleep and teetering with every step, but, at the start of his second day out, just after emerging from the nest and discovering how far he'd fallen behind both Enid and the scrambling poults, he saw a shadow fall over the path. . . and there was his father looming ahead with his chest puffed out and his head askance.

Rodney Junior straightened up, then took a deep breath and cheeped hello.

"Good evening, Sonny," Rodney clucked as if he was emperor of the woods.

Rodney Junior cheeped again, and "Sunny," I thought, "the perfect name!" Calling him Junior seemed somehow wrong, so Sunny it was from that moment on.

Rodney meanwhile strutted and preened. I knew that he'd resented my friends, but I didn't expect so sudden a change—as if he'd just won another big prize and had to be off to the next competition, wasting no time on chicks or hens. He crowed as if addressing a crowd, proclaiming what he called Chicken Power—"*la puissance de poulet*," he cackled in French to Sunny's utter bewilderment, and, gesturing at the gawky poults hobnobbing together under a tree, he brrrkkked with a resentful sneer that it's only your own who really count—"*les oiseaux de même plumage*,"[27] he said—"not zose gawky oddball misfits zat your muzzer's so taken with."

I stood like a tree stump where I was, at the entrance to our nest where I thought I couldn't be seen. Some screw had come loose in Rodney's head as if, while he'd wandered alone in the woods, his resentment and vanity from before had grown grotesquely *virulent*, and I wondered if I myself was to blame for moving in with the hens. I watched him glare and stretch his neck, appalled by what he was spewing forth but feeling responsible in a way and ashamed in front of my friends. I knew what sharp hearing turkeys have and worried when I saw Enid raising her head as if to listen in.

"Whatever your muzzer's been teaching you," Rodney continued his tirade, "it's every species for itself, and when you grow up to roosterhood. . ." He paused as if to clear his *craw*. ". . . keep counting your chickens *after* zey hatch because you'll find zey're fewer and fewer—and you know why?" He glowered at Enid who merely shrugged as if she'd heard all that before while Sunny shrank back onto his heels recoiling from such spiteful words. "Because someone

---

[27] "birds of a feather" (French) as in the old proverb "birds of a feather flock together."

or uzzer, Sonny boy, has persuaded all zose *gullible* humans zat chickens are somezing good to eat. . . and who do think would do such a thing?" Again, he seemed to clear his throat as, waving one claw, he ranted on. "You don't see ads for Honey-Fried Crow or Egg McMuffins wiz woodpecker yolks. Am I right? Speak up!"

Sunny peeped weakly from a crouch.

"So, you look for who stands to gain zuh most," Rodney resumed maniacally, "zuh edible alternatives, zuh ones who get roasted once a year instead of battered up every day. . . and you've got to know zem for what zey are. Don't trust 'em, my boy! They'll sell you out." With that, he crowed at the top of his lungs, "*DIE PUTER SINT UNSER UNGLÜCK!*"*—or "Turkeys are our misery," the only German I'd ever hear him speak.

But I'd heard enough by then and didn't want Sunny browbeat any further, especially by such vile ideas. It was in one sense, I suppose, an important moment for me because it was then I promised myself that, whatever else might befall my chick, he'd soon grow up to become a different sort of rooster.

"We're going for a dust bath," I said, stepping into Rodney's view while addressing myself to Sunny. "Wouldn't you like to join us?"

Sunny blinked as he straightened back up, and, giving himself a vigorous shake, hopped over to join the burbling poults while Rodney haughtily declined, shaking his wattle and stalking off.

"Come on, then, Sunny. Let's join the others."

We caught up with Enid. "Sorry," I said.

"Good thing we've all got gizzards," she clucked, herding the stragglers back into line. "Some things are not so easy to swallow."

I dipped my head in the turkey hen way as the poults began thrashing in the dirt, laughing and tossing dust about. Sunny rushed in and was knocked off his feet, but two of the poults helped him onto his feet and he cheeped with excitement, joining in. I resisted my own desire for a bath.

"Enid," I said in a serious voice. "What happens in the next few weeks?"

"I'll tell you, honey," Enid replied. "We'll be teaching the poults to run and swim. We run as fast as most horses, you know, and swim about as well as ducks. Do you guys swim?"

"Not hardly, no."

"And then," she continued, "they'll learn to fly."

"How far and fast?"

"Oh, nearly as fast as cars on the road. . . and more than a mile sometimes," she said as modestly as she could. She knew no chicken could do the same.

"Then, after the poults can swim and fly. . .?"

"We'll hunt Mel up," she said with a smile.

"*Mel?*"

She shrugged. "He's really not so bad, you know. . . when he's back in his right mind, at least. We drive him crazy in the spring, but, in the fall, he'll more or less settle down for a while. That's when two or three dozen of us will get all our families together in one big flock again." She purred and clucked. "To everything there's a season, you know. And there'll be plenty of room for you and Sunny as well. . ."

"But not for Signor Mussolini?* No, that's okay. He wouldn't go. He's got some weird ideas in his head."

"Roosters or toms," said Ernestine, who'd caught up and heard that last exchange. "Most of the time what they've got in their heads shouldn't be called ideas. . . if you happen to get my drift."

"Still, some of the time," Ethel sighed, arriving to watch the youngsters' fun, "let's just admit that's not so bad."

We cackled together, hen to hen. Then, shifting to a somber note, I put a question to all three. "Can Sunny and I—and Rodney too—get through the winter on our own? Out here all by ourselves, I mean?"

They traded looks. Nobody spoke, then Enid nodded with a frown. "But it'll be tough."

"It's harder to hide that time of year," admitted Ernestine.

"And there's less to eat," Ethel chimed in, "for everyone. . . so there're foxes and raccoons on the prowl."

"Coyotes and bobcats too," said Enid.

"Plus hawks and buzzards in the sky," Ernestine added.

"And humans," said Ethel, shuddering.

"Which humans? Where?" asked Ernestine.

"On that hill up there," was Ethel's reply as she ducked and pointed towards the east. "There's a house up there above the pond. A man and woman who seem okay. . . but you never can tell. They don't seem to hunt, that much I know, and sometimes they'll scatter things you can eat."

"It could be poison," Enid warned.

"It wasn't. I ate it."

All of us gasped, but headstrong Ethel merely shrugged.

"I waited until they'd gone, of course, and it was really delicious."

"With humans, though, you never know."

"That's what I said a minute ago."

"I'm part of a human family," I said.

They looked at me blankly. What could they say?

"Same as with you," I tried to explain. "The kindness of strangers, know what I mean?"

"Not sure I do," said Ernestine.

"But humans. . ." Enid started to say when Ethel stopped her with a frown.

"Sometimes they're very nice," she said, and nobody spoke for a minute or two until Enid asked Ethel which pond she meant—the one just downstream from their nest?

I hadn't known about the pond, but then, I hadn't wandered far.

"That's right," said Ethel.

"You found a fawn there—didn't you, Ethel?" Ernestine asked.

Ethel nodded but said nothing more, and everyone fell silent again, leaving me to guess for myself what she'd meant for her silence to imply.

"Picked clean," said Ernestine at last.

Enid repeated what she'd said, "Coyote. . . bobcat. . ."

"They move on."

"And sometimes they come back again."

Another silence as we watched our innocent babies stirring the dust. They all regretted scaring me, but it's a hard life in the woods. Ethel lowered her head towards mine to say in a quiet, gravelly voice, "You must be very careful, my dear."

I nodded, not knowing what else to say except how much it meant to me to have such friends who really cared. After a while, we traipsed back, herding our little ones into the nest.

That evening I spoke with Rodney again just as it was growing dark.

"What are we going to do?" I asked, having repeated what I'd learned and thinking, despite my qualms about him, we'd be safer if we stuck together.

He was still in his self-important mode but nervously shifting from foot to foot while peering about the surrounding woods as if daunted by what I'd just reported. *"Tu sais, ma chérie,"*[28] he eventually said, wagging his wattle semaphore-like and gesturing towards the turkey nest, "while you've been *lollygagging* here, I've been busily *reconnoitering* for 'ow we can best address zuh dangers you describe." He was talking like Napoleon again and paused to let his words sink in, though all he actually meant to say was that he'd been looking around a bit while I was engaged in hatching our egg.

He clearly had some message for me but couldn't decide how to put it. *"Eh, bien,"*[29] he finally shrugged and said, "you remember zose farms zat we passed by on zuh day we left zuh truck? One of zem has a beautiful spacious fenced-in run, some five-star coops, and endless banquets of feed." He paused before proceeding. "In short, *tu vois, ma bien-aimée,*[30] it's a true Club Med* for chickens. . . and it led me to think again zat what I have dreamed of for us and for chickens everywhere is not—how do you say—a *gateau*[31] in zuh sky."

He blinked and leaned his head towards mine. I knew he was turning on the charm, but I steeled myself when he nibbled my neck and murmured softly into my ear, *"Enfin, ma belle dodue. . ."*[32] he flapped his wings dramatically, "it is time to be ourselves again."

Maybe so, I told myself but thought it more likely that what he meant was he wanted to be in charge again, which certainly wouldn't be the case as intruders into a poultry farm—and yet I knew we couldn't delay in coming up with some sort of plan "Oh, Rodney," I said by way of reply, "if we could just get to Chapel Hill!"

"What?" he replied derisively. "To live in a tiny provincial pen wiz zose screwball human friends of yours? In zat town where you say I can't even crow? I'd rather roost alone in a tree."

---

[28] "You know, my dear. . ." (French)

[29] "Well. . ." (French)

[30] "you see, my beloved," (French)

[31] "cake" (French)—what Rodney means, however, is "a pie in the sky." He meant to say *"une tarte."*

[32] "At last, my lovely plump one. . ." (French)

"That may be what we have to do," I clucked at him resignedly.

We said our good-byes the following day. To my relief and surprise, Rodney's manners appeared to return when we parted from my turkey friends. He was very polite to them, in fact, and also very *suave*, which simply means he knew how to act—nearly all Frenchmen are *suave*, I think, though there's clearly no guarantee.

Reverting to speaking French again, he gallantly thanked the three of them, *"Alors, adieu, nos tres chères amies. . . et merci beaucoup pour la belle salle d'accouchement!"*[33] I doubted if they could understand, so I translated what he'd said.

Sunny got teary-eyed as did I while still wondering if Rodney was sincere. Enid said maybe we'd meet in the spring, and I said, yes, I hoped we would—and, at just that moment, what should we hear but Mel's crazed gobbling headed our way.

"Lover boy!" clucked Ernestine.

Everyone laughed, and Ethel said, "We might as well see what's on his mind."

At that there were cackles all around. But Rodney, unable to share in the joke, said that was enough and we needed to go.

So Rodney, Sunny, and I set off, bound once more for "who knew what?"

---

[33] "Then good-bye, our very dear friends, and many thanks for the beautiful delivery room!"

Chapter 18

Though Rodney thought the pace was too slow, we tramped through the woods for more than an hour until Sunny, who'd given it all he had, was tottering on the verge of collapse. When it started to rain, we came to a halt under some bushes near a stream to let him get a little rest. I was worried once more about the fox and asked if perhaps, when we resumed, he thought we should walk in the stream a bit to hide our tracks and cancel our scent. But Rodney, in his lordly way as if moving battalions across a map, said he, of course, had considered that, but Sunny wouldn't be up to it and the best of the options open to us was moving as rapidly as we could. Towards what, exactly, he didn't say—though I guessed it involved some impractical scheme that he'd be forced to abandon soon while each step towards the east took us closer to home.

After a while the rain let up, so we scratched and pecked about for some lunch, then walked again until mid-afternoon, when I insisted we had to stop before poor Sunny fainted away.

Rodney looked exasperated. "Again?" he groused, but then, with a slightly shifty look, he agreed to our taking a weak-kneed break while he once more would *reconnoiter*.

At last, when evening was coming on, he returned to say the farm he'd described was close enough to where we were.

"Close enough for what?" I asked.

Again, he assumed a *furtive* look. He'd been studying every angle, he said. It looked as alluring as he'd thought. It wasn't at all like the *camps de la mort*[34] where chickens could scarcely spread their

---

[34] Using a phrase applied to concentration camps during the German occupation of France, Rodney means "holding pens," in effect, of the sort employed by slaughterhouses.

wings like those he'd heard were near Fayetteville—"not far from Chapel Hill," he cracked while I tugged Sunny under my wing to muffle his father's grim account of the "Colonel" this and "Tyson" that in a diatribe aimed at "Frank Perdue*," the poultry magnate on TV.

His harangue broke off like the earlier rain, and Rodney began to gush instead about lavish "free range" poultry resorts where chickens could roam like chickens again and the bill for as long as you wanted to stay could be paid with nothing more than eggs.

"Practically free" was how he put it. "And what matters most about such a place is zat uzzer animals aren't allowed, it's only for zose like us," he said, "*et tu sais bien, ma douce petite. . .* "[35] He looked at Sunny and shrugged again as Frenchman are often wont to do. ". . . zuh young ones zere don't live in fear."

I saw what he had overlooked. "If the bill is paid in eggs. . ." I said.

"*Oui, my chérie?*"[36] He nuzzled my neck.

". . . how many roosters do they need?"

"*Attends!*"[37] he warned. "We're getting close. "We must be quiet from now on."

Cautiously, he parted some leaves, and there was his glittering Shangri-la* some forty or fifty yards away. There was netting to ward any chicken hawks off and a high wire fence enclosing the yard, inside which there were condo coops and hundreds of chickens roaming about, scratching and gossiping, looking fit. I saw no chicks but lots of hens. No Dumpies, of course, but Rhode Island Reds mixed in with hordes of Dominickers—though there wasn't a single rooster in sight until, to my astonishment, I saw a Rodney-lookalike come stalking around the nearest coop looking as if he owned the place. A Faverolle. . . and a big one too!

"*Strutter!*" brrrkkked Rodney with a scowl, and much that had been just slightly obscure was suddenly making far more sense. One rooster ruled the whole resort, at least the portion that I could see, and,

---

[35] "and you know well, my sweet little one. . ." (French)

[36] "Yes, my dear?" (French)

[37] "Wait!" (French)

though I couldn't yet guess his plan, Rodney had hatched one, I felt sure, to somehow grab that role for himself. But why and how? I asked myself. He'd have to get rid of Strutter first, if that was the other Faverolle's name, along with a lot of other ifs—if he could smuggle us under the fence, if he could successfully launch a *putsch*, if the humans who must be running the place would let him rule the yard instead. A *putsch* is simply an overthrow, but what would become of Sunny and me while Rodney became the Rooster King?

I wasn't convinced by what I'd *surmised* and asked if he'd really thought things through, whatever it was he was hoping to do. He said that he'd been roosting nearby, watching what happened inside at night while I and my friends were lolling about. He'd seen a fox dig under the fence—the fox who'd paid a visit to us—but, just as it started to slip inside, a woman had come down from the house apparently on a random patrol. She'd had a flashlight and a gun, and faster than you could peck at a bug, the fox had pulled a vanishing act, leaving the hole still ready for use. Nobody inside had spotted it yet— not even Strutter, Rodney sneered—and, when it was dark, the three of us could slip right in and join the rest. . . to be fed and protected all winter long.

"Zuh three of us," he said again and clucked as paternally as he could, putting me even more on guard. Then, noting how skeptical I appeared and supposing me mainly concerned for myself, he pointed out that, "Zuh *Dominiques* look a lot like you. . . with zat sultry salt-and-pepper look."

But I objected, "No, they don't—they don't resemble me at all."

"You're a little short-legged," he agreed. "But who will care? You'll fit right in."

"But what if they do?"

"Do what?" he asked.

"Object to a couple of *interlopers*."

He didn't seem to know the word, so "intruders" I said. "And what about Sunny?"

"Just act like he belongs, and he will. Zey'll all love having a biddy around."

Though I wasn't persuaded, "Maybe," I said, "and what about that other one?"

"Who? Strutter?" he smiled with a humorless snigger, giving his wattle a confident shake and crouching while cocking his head to the side as if reviewing some master scheme. "You leave zat simpleton to me!"

So we waited there until evening began and the last of the season's lightning bugs came floating about like gourmet snacks—though like a lot of glittery stuff, their packaging's better than their taste. Then Rodney led us to the hole that, according to him, the fox had dug—half-hidden by vines and underbrush but *capacious* enough for us it seemed. He slipped through first and beckoned us in. Sunny went next, and I came last.

"Wait over there," Rodney advised, pointing behind the nearest coop while stealthily skulking off on his own.

But almost at once I heard him cluck in an urgent and confidential way, "*Viens, viens, mon frère! Mais je m'excuse*[38]. . . I forget you don't speak French so well. But you will soon see what you've been missing."

"Brrrrkkk?" cackled the other Faverolle, who cautiously approached the hole the three of us had just scrambled through. "This is the secret passageway to what you call a 'pleasure dome'?"

I strained to make out Rodney's words, something about unforgettable sights, delectable bugs, and "bevies of very hot Faverolle hens" all merely for the asking, he said, in the Free French portion of the woods.

I heard what sounded like skepticism as Strutter appeared to hesitate, saying he couldn't think of much that wasn't at hand for him already.

"*Déjà,*[39] you say? Oh, no, my friend. Being born in zis country as you were, you can't begin to see in your mind what's waiting for you in Pa-ree!" He meant the city of Paris, of course, pronouncing it as a Frenchman would to make it sound more enticing.

"And you say it's really as close as that?

---

[38] "Come, come, my brother! But I apologize. . ." (French)

[39] "Already" (French)

"Just over zuh border," Rodney lied. "Go under zuh fence and through zuh woods. . . by early morning you'll be there. But youmustn't forget zuh password when you get to zuh *douanes*[40]."

Strutter said something I couldn't hear, but Rodney patiently told him in French, "*C'est 'puissance de poulet,' n'est-ce pas?*"[41] then asked him to repeat it.

Rodney's plan was horribly clear, though some details remained *abstruse*. Apparently, Strutter's main concern was not being caught going *AWOL*, using the term a soldier would use for leaving one's post without permission and suggesting that Rodney had shrewdly guessed that Strutter would be a sucker too for things Napoleonic*.

"Call it a furlough," Rodney said. "You and I look enough alike for me to cover awhile for you, but promise zat you'll come back again after you've had a taste of Pa-ree. Oh, how I miss it, *mon ami. . . zuh* frogs' legs, snails, zuh dancing hens. But I'm willing to do it for just zis once in order to smuggle my family inside. Zank you for admitting zem." He gestured towards us with his wing, and Strutter, who gawked as we stepped forth, appeared surprised to see a chick.

"Ah, *ma famille!*"[42] Rodney said, embracing us with apparent emotion. "We must eat zuh bread of exile here."

I wanted to expose his ruse, but, detecting how appalled I was, Rodney urged Strutter towards the hole. They lowered their voices, and, after a while, I heard a scratchy, scrambling sound that must have been Strutter leaving the pen. Rodney was whispering, "*Bon voyage! À bientôt!*"[43] Then Strutter brrrkkked, and he was gone while Rodney lingered by the fence as if waiting for something to occur.

I heard what he'd been listening for—a sudden, choked-off, strangled cry. No point in mincing words, I guess. One king was dead, a new one reigned. . . and the fox had gotten his dinner.

---

[40] "customs" (French). Rodney's referring to the agents at the border.

[41] "It's 'chicken Power,' is it not?" (French—a phrase that Rodney had used before, see page 107)

[42] "my family!" (French)

[43] "Have a nice trip! See you soon!" (French)

Chapter 19

I felt a bit like Lady Macbeth*—who, according to Shakespeare's play at least, was a Scottish queen with blood on her hands—as we crept into one of several coops, a shadowy well-constructed place filled with muted murmurs and clucks from two or three dozen dozing hens, all of whom must have gone to sleep expecting to wake as they had every day with Strutter commanding the sun to rise. I knew that wouldn't happen, of course, as Sunny and I unobtrusively climbed to a mostly empty lower perch. Sunny sagged heavily under my wing, nodding off almost at once, and, despite my discomforting burden of guilt, I joined him in a minute or two.

When I opened my eyes, it was still half-light, but, though the coop was immersed in gloom, I heard a cluck from one rung up.

"You're new here, aren't you?" asked a hen.

I thought she might be challenging me, so I squinted to see her in the *murk*—a pleasant-looking Rhode Island Red.

"Uh-huh," I answered warily. "We snuck in last night after dark."

"So you've come from one of the pullet coops? Can't blame you much for leaving there—I hear they're a fairly raucous lot. . . but, oh my word, what have we here?" She craned her neck to peer at my chick, whose yellowish little sleep-sozzled head had just emerged from under my wing. "How in the world. . .?"

I guessed at once why she was surprised—the bills for staying in this resort were paid with eggs before they hatched. "A human mistake," I improvised. "An oversight, I guess you'd say. But, ah, you know. . . we all pay our way."

"Riiiight," she clucked. "How old is she now?"

"Just a couple of weeks." That much was true, but what she wanted to know, of course, was whether or not it was truly a she. On egg-farms hens are much in demand, but future roosters very much not.

"Cute!" prrrked a hen on my other side, a Dominicker with a wing that seemed to hang limply by her side. "What do you call her?"

"Sunny," I said.

Just then we heard a clamorous noise, a crowing and squawking from the yard.

"Strutter," the first hen said with a shrug.

The second one looked exasperated. "Every morning, we get the same routine! Why does he have to make such a fuss?"

"We'd better go pump his ego up."

All the hens who'd slept in the coop were scrambling out through a little door.

"Stay close to me," I cautioned Sunny as we trooped outside along with the rest.

Something novel was going on, prompting a hubbub in the yard. Elated to have a morning diversion, swarms were scurrying towards the noise while out of the house a woman came running, trailed by a girl in a pinafore.

"What is it, Strutter?" the woman called.

It was Rodney, of course, who stood by the hole, stamping and crowing with all his might.

"Why look at that!" the woman exclaimed. "You've found where that fox is sneaking in. Good going, Strutter! Good for you!"

The little girl trilled and clapped her hands as "Strutter" preened and crowed again. A hen beside me brrrkkked and said, "He's really quite dashing, don't you think?"

"And seems he's taken a turn for the better," another hen sarcastically clucked.

"Oh, definitely," I said to her, as dozens of young attractive hens were scuttling excitedly in his path, twitching their tails and ducking their heads.

"Mama, look here!" the little girl cried.

To my dismay, she pointed at me—or not at me, at poor little Sunny, who crept for protection under my wing.

"What is it, Alyssa?"

"A biddy! Look! It's over there!"

"How does it happen? Not again!"

The woman was clearly very put out, but Alyssa, her daughter, leaned down to see and, as Sunny recoiled, she picked him up.

"I want him, Mama! For a pet!"

"Rodney!" I called in a panicky voice.

But Rodney was over by the fence, surrounded by bevies of new admirers.

"Please!" I begged the woman and girl. But they ignored me, standing up and cradling my frightened chick in their hands. He'd never seen a human before.

"It must have come from an egg we missed. . . probably laid there in those weeds that have definitely needed some cutting back."

"It looks real healthy. Is it a girl?" The girl held Sunny upside down.

"I wonder who its mother is."

I frantically scratched out words in the dust: "ME! ME!" But Alyssa, determined to get her way, kept scuffing and kicking up the dirt, erasing my marks *obliviously.*

"Mama, *please!* It looks so cute."

"We'll see. We'll see. Higgins will have to fix that fence. Higgins!" she called.

"Yessum, Miz Betjeman," croaked a man who came shuffling up from behind a barn with tufts of red hair poking out from under his old railroader's cap.

"How come that fox is smarter than us?"

"I reckon tha'ss all he's got on his mind—gittin' them hens 'n' gittin' away."

"Huh!" said the woman. "Well, be as it may, let's fill up that hole. And look here at what Alyssa found."

The girl was nuzzling Sunny's face as he shrank back from her with alarm. The woman watched, then gave a nod, and she and the girl went back inside with my precious but panicky little chick whose plaintive peeps flew through the air, stinging like buckshot into my heart. I rushed to Rodney by the fence and shoved my way through the doting throng. He looked at me with mild surprise, as if, for just a second or two, he couldn't remember who I was.

"They've taken Sunny!" I managed to gasp. "Into the house. . . that little girl. . ."

The hens stepped back uncertainly but lingered just a short distance away to watch the *domestic* drama unfold.

"Rodney, please! You've got to help!"

"Are you confused?" he dismissively asked.

"Strutter!" I corrected myself. "Our biddy. . . *your* biddy. . ."

He turned his head towards his admirers as if to say he'd attend to their needs as soon as he'd dealt with the oddball hen who'd popped up screeching about a chick. Then, looking at me with *condescension*, he told me in a lofty way, "He'll be just fine—what better good fortune could he have?"

"She!" I quickly reminded him, knowing the risk that any boy ran. "Sunny's a she." I tried to wink.

He stared at me blankly, then at his hens. "As I was saying," he resumed, "I've been outside to hassle the fox. I doubt if he'll dare come back again."

"Bodacious!" cackled a nitwit hen.

"Higgins is back with that thing on a stick," a Dominicker nervously said. She seemed more sensible than the rest, though "shovel" was not a word she'd learned. "He's back already to fill the hole."

"I'd better make certain he does it right," said Rodney, now the counterfeit Strutter, tossing his comb and sauntering off.

As if the world had been dropped like an egg and was oozing its yolk out under my feet, I wandered about the hen-filled run and back into our five-star coop, where I roosted and closed my eyes to think. But almost at once I heard the voice of someone I thought I'd heard before—the hen I'd talked to earlier, clucking indignantly by my side.

"I saw what happened. It's a crime. They take our eggs, they take our chicks. They'd take our feathers if they could."

"They can," clucked someone else in the gloom.

The same two whom I'd met before—they'd followed me out and now back in.

"Strutter's an *egomaniac*."

That's what you call a pompous ass, somebody who's so obsessed with himself that he can't really think of anything else. But how, I wondered to myself, had anyone in that *fatuous* harem picked up that sort of vocabulary? Despite myself, I cackled out loud, "But where'd you learn a word like that?"

"Honey, I think you'd be surprised. I'm Anastasia. . . Anna," she said.

"And Henriette," her sidekick clucked. "Both of us saw. . ."

"My biddy!" I cried, forgetting my manners. "They took him away."

"Ah, so it's a boy!" they clucked to each other, nodding their heads. "Your secret's safe with the two of us."

"At least. . ." and "Until. . ." they said and stopped.

"*Until*?" I croaked.

"In this place, hon, it's all *until*," clucked Henriette despairingly. "That's how we're forced to live in here—*until* the fox digs under the fence, *until* we're done with laying eggs, *until* it's time for *coq au vin**. . ."

I knew what she meant, though that startled me too. *Coq au vin* means "rooster with wine," but mostly they make it using hens. Rooster or hen, it's not much fun if you're the one who's bound for a platter. In a way, that knowledge helped me think instead of merely feeling fear.

"Excuse my asking again," I said, "but how do you know such things as that?"

They both fell silent for a bit. "House Chickens," answered Henriette.

Then, moving closer, Anna revealed, "Both of us had a stint inside. That little girl—Alyssa's her name—gets what she wants no matter what. . . though whatever it is, it won't last long."

"As we both found out."

They looked at each other. Then Anna clucked, "As soon as she thinks you're not so cute, she dumps you back here in the yard. . . where the others won't be so happy to see you." She nodded at her injured wing.

"If Anna hadn't stuck up for me. . ."

"I knew what it was like," she shrugged. "But while you're there inside the house, so long as you keep your wits about you, it's possible to learn a lot."

"There's a talking box that's called tee vee. . ."

"I know," I said to Henriette, glad that my sort of education had happened to other chickens too—though neither of them mentioned books or computers or public radio. . . how much I'd learned from NPR!*

"Your biddy will be all right, I'm sure."

"At least until. . ." said Henriette, repeating that disturbing word.

"*Until* we all escape?" I blurted, sharing a half-formed thought in my mind.

They answered together in a rush.

"But Higgins would catch us!"

"Foxes!"

"Hawks!"

"There're scary things loose all through the woods. . ."

"Weasels and bobcats."

"Humans too."

"Yes," Anna said. "And humans too."

They sighed and pondered what they'd said while I debated with myself which side of the fence was really worse. Was it better safely imprisoned there than free and forever insecure? Had I ever actually been free? Is it truly the truth that makes us free?

"Strutter," said Anna, reading my mind. "His job's to keep us all in line."

"*Pacified!*" squawked Henriette. "A kapo's* what he ought to be called"—though that was a word I didn't know. "Just one of us who's one of them."

"Strutter's not Strutter," I burst out, then suddenly feared I'd said too much.

"Of course. We know. And neither was Strutter."

"They come and go. . ."

". . . but they're all the same. A strutter's a strutter," Anna clucked, ruffling her wings and settling down. "If only they weren't so full of themselves, they'd almost be endurable."

The three of us laughed, and we were friends. Though I'd been surprised by how much they knew, I was reassured to realize that there must be many more like us, a lot of them just as smart as I. . . so, whatever else I'd learned that day, I knew I wasn't alone.

But that night as the coop filled up again and I was brooding by myself, Sunny was so much on my mind that it became useless trying to sleep. I tried to reason my fears away, thinking that maybe, despite what I'd heard, Alyssa was more like Jones or Zan and Sunny would find things *hunky-dory*—though I knew in my heart that wasn't the case. What Rodney had called a poultry resort was really a fenced-in zombie farm, and, except for Anna and Henriette, the place was full of *nincompoops*—mindlessly silly and shallow hens content to merely

peck and poop, frantic to capture Strutter's attention and deaf to anyone else's distress. "Eggheads!"* was Anna's term for them, and I didn't bother correcting her, knowing that, as I'd sadly learned, we're all at our worst in a mob.

And as for the Rooster Who Would Be King, the *pseudo*-Strutter understudy, I'd finally come to realize that, natural imposter though he was, he'd fallen so much for his own deceit that now, to my regret and contempt, he meant even less to me than Sunny and I had meant to him. "As vain as Nero*," I told myself, seeing a little bit less of him with every passing day and soon not seeing him at all except when, heady with self-importance, he'd mount the roof of one of the coops, preening and crowing as loud as he could.

Once he got so carried away that he blasted out the very same song with which he'd formerly wooed me too during our night-long ride in the truck—the national anthem of France, of course, which was now just a *paean* to himself. It earned him such ecstatic applause from his fan base of adoring hens that, whenever they flocked in response to his call, he'd serenade them with his *chanson d'amour*[44] just slightly adjusting the first line's words to "*Allons enfants des pou-leh-eh-eh-eh-yay. . .!*"[45]

They couldn't make heads or tails of it while he, puffed up with vanity, was completely unaware of the fact that most of them were onto his game, knowing he wasn't Strutter at all. But why should that matter to any of them? He was like an Elvis* impersonator just pretending to be a superstar—a joker who was himself the joke.

---

[44] "love song" (French)

[45] Rodney is singing "Let's go, children of the chicken coops. . .!" [The last word in French is *poulaillers*.]

Chapter 20

Meanwhile, life in the yard went on—though, grateful as I was for Anna and Henriette, I could never for even a second stop yearning to see my Sunny. Every morning and many afternoons, the woman would come to collect our eggs. Sometimes Alyssa would be there too and, whenever I saw her in the yard, I'd try to overhear what they said, hoping for word of my kidnapped chick. But I never heard them mention him, and often, for maybe a week or more, Alyssa wouldn't appear at all and I'd sink into bleak anxiety, fearing what might have happened to him. Then two things occurred to change my life again.

The first took place on a typical day. The woman had just collected our eggs and taken her *plunder* back to the house. I was moping about by myself in the yard when the door to the house flew open again and the woman came quickly down the steps.

"Look!" cackled Anna racing towards me—she'd been scratching about on her own as well.

I could tell from her excited tone that something unusual was underway, but it wasn't until I looked for myself that I felt a mingled joy and dismay that hit me like a raccoon's paw.

The woman had something in her hands that she tossed to the ground disdainfully. I saw it was Sunny, my source of joy—but, instead of his buttery golden hue, he was garishly purple from head to toe. I stared uncomprehendingly.

"Mama!" cried Sunny, spotting me.

"Sunny! Sunny!" I replied, rushing to greet him as he stopped, looking embarrassed and ashamed, and stood there trembling, eyes on the ground.

"Oh, darling child, are you okay?"

His wretched expression wrung my heart. He looked bedraggled and scrawny too.

"She must have dyed him," Anna observed. "She didn't do that to either of us, but she's done it to others—sometimes pink, sometimes green, sometimes something in between. Then, when she's bored, she tosses them out."

"Into the yard," warned Henriette, "where they're bullied and pecked for looking so odd." She didn't need to show me her wing, but she stretched out her neck and gave me a look that promised they'd have to deal with her before poor Sunny could be hurt.

Anna clucked and nodded her head, helping me shield him from the stares as more and more hens came over to gawk, uttering insults as they came, calling Sunny an ugly freak whose presence alone was polluting their run. I saw the bewildered hurt in his eyes.

We'd already started for the coop when the heckling throng began to part, and Rodney, the king of his Club-Med yard, confronted us with an *imperious* air. He sized the situation up before proclaiming with a scowl, "That eggplant is illegal here! There's no room for the likes of him. You understand. . . whatever he is?"

I didn't deign to answer him. Not only had he betrayed his son, he'd told them that Sunny was a boy—which, power-mad as he'd become, might mean in some ruthless, twisted way he'd brook no rivals in the yard, not even from his own flesh and blood. But what he'd done made one thing clear: Sunny and I would have to leave for somewhere, somehow, right away.

Stay calm, I tried to counsel myself as, once I'd gotten him into the coop along with Anna and Henriette, I checked in order to know for sure that, other than making him look absurd, the little girl hadn't injured him. The next step, while I planned an escape, was to shield him from those bigoted hens insisting that everyone must *conform*, and I knew my two friends would help me there. Then I'd lift his spirits if I could by finding some tasty treats for him, reminding myself that, leaving aside what Alyssa had done, my dearest hope had been realized. I had my precious Sunny back and, no matter how glum and scraggly he seemed, he'd actually grown much bigger and stronger. That much, at least, I could celebrate—though, regarding the much worse peril we faced, I needed to find a solution quick before he instinctively tried to crow.

Here's what's really strange about such dilemmas. I reported just a few minutes ago that two things had happened that changed my life. The first was grief at losing my chick and then the joy of getting him back, though only to find he'd become a *pariah*—an outcast nearly everyone shuns and some, for that reason, are eager to harm. The second came equally out of the blue but forced me to solve both problems at once without ever devising an actual plan as if, instead of freezing up, my brain had revved up in a panic. . . but, once again, at a heart-rending cost.

I remember it all so vividly—a moonlit evening in the yard with a touch of autumn in the air, though inside the henhouse it was warm and much too dark to see a thing. We'd settled together for the night, I roosting with Sunny under my wing and Anna and Henriette next to us, one of them on either side. I hadn't intended to sleep at all, but, after a lot of futile thought, I must have snoozed off as before during our first night in the woods, probably out of sheer fatigue. Then suddenly I was yanked awake as if there'd been some sort of alarm warning of danger in the coop that neither my eyes nor ears could confirm. Such instincts can often serve us well if we learn to trust them when we should—which something inside me urged me to do.

Without moving a muscle on my perch, I opened my eyes and tried to guess what stealthy menace was loose in the dark. Then I managed to catch the faintest glimpse of something just halfway through the door, pausing for a second or two like somebody in an ice cream shop trying to choose which flavor to get. I knew at once what that something was and also somehow understood that others were equally wide awake and aware that all of us were trapped. A hush had descended on the coop as if a great actor had appeared but hadn't yet spoken his first line.

But then he did.

"Hell-lohhh there, ladies!" he softly crooned in a nastily soft and silky voice, speaking in faultless Chicken too. "Don't anybody make a fuss, and all but one will be quite safe." I smelled his rancid gamey breath as he slid his hindquarters through the door. "There's a lovely big full moon tonight, so I've come to choose a dancing partner. . . somebody to be the belle of the ball."

As if he'd cast a hypnotic spell, not one of us ventured to budge an inch. His yellow eyes shone as, otherwise still, he moved them slowly about the coop. For a moment they seemed to rest on me with maybe a flicker of recognition, but then they moved on through the roost until, with a squint and a twist of his head, they swiveled to focus on Sunny's face as he peeked out from under my wing.

"What have we here? I do declare—a Little Debbie just for me!" Lifting his nose, he sniffed and grinned. "Well, now," he purred as if to himself, "my dance card still has one place left—a foxtrot for this little snack and then a waltz with some nice fat hen."

He looked around to hold us in check, but, as he was savoring his control, Henriette took a long deep breath and cut loose with an outraged scream. "I'VE HAD ENOUGH OF YOU!" she shrieked and flung herself at him like a hawk, aiming her claws at those insolent eyes.

I did the same while Anna, beside me, flapped her wings, scratching and clawing as she dived. With *consternation* matched by pride, I thought I heard Sunny's ninja cheep as he too joined us in the fray, and, in less than a second or so it seemed, the coop was a riotous *brouhaha* with some who'd merely tried to escape now jamming the fox's only retreat, though retreating was far from his first thought. He savagely lunged towards Henriette, and, as Sunny and I got slammed to the wall, I saw her neck was locked in his jaws. Her body went limp, and I shouted her name as explosions erupted next to the door.

Henriette plummeted with a thud. The fox had suddenly disappeared, but there were lights outside in the yard and more explosions—Boom! Boom! Boom!—as humans went running and shouting about. I tried to nuzzle Henriette, but she was bravely, tragically dead. Anna, beside me, clucked and grieved.

"Listen to me, Anna!" I brrrkkked, and everything seemed clear in my mind. "That killer's way in is our way out. I've got some good friends in the woods."

She looked at me and shook her head.

"Anything's better than this," I said. "There're always foxes in this world. Those who're free don't live in fear."

"I can't," she said, still shaking her head.

"You can," I insisted. "He must have tunneled in somewhere. We'll find it together and get away."

More lights were on at the back of the house with flashlights darting in all directions. Hens were hysterically milling about as one of the humans yelled to another, "You got him, Miz Betjeman! Over here!"

A flashlight shone on a reddish heap that lay like a dust-bag in the yard, appearing much smaller than I'd supposed. I stared and saw the snout was ripped where Henriette had raked her claws, though I noticed the mouth was still in a grin. While I was looking, Rodney appeared and, climbing atop it, struck a pose. As the woman drew near, he started to crow.

"Shoo!" said the woman with a kick.

"I'll help you," Anna clucked in my ear, and the three of us frantically started to search, trying to follow the fence's edge. Anna went one way and I the other with Sunny following in my tracks. I noticed how strong his legs had become.

The woman was bending over the fox while Rodney looked resentfully on and two men brushed him farther aside. She jabbed at the carcass with her gun. A crowd of curious hens drew near, approaching and retreating in waves, causing the woman to tell the men to get those ninnies back in their coops. "That rooster too!" she yelled at them. "He must have been sleeping on the job."

The two men started waving their arms, and, knowing they'd get to us in turn, we realized time was running out. Then, just by chance, I stumbled and fell. . . and, looking more closely, saw the hole.

"Found it!" I cackled.

Anna ran over.

"You go through first," I said to her.

She hesitated. No time to lose.

"Sunny, squeeze under!"

Sunny did.

"Now you," I said and gestured to Anna.

She gave me a sad despairing look. "I can't," she told me once again. "I love you both. I hope. . ." But that was all she managed to say as one of the men came stomping our way.

"Good-bye!" I dove into the hole, wriggling and squirming as best I could but, finding myself hung up midway, I feared I wouldn't make it through.

What if I'd chosen the wrong hole?

"Hey!" shouted the man as Anna squawked, diverting his attention to her instead.

I flattened myself against the dirt, digging and flailing with my wings. But I was snagged on some sagging wire.

"Hurry up, Mama!" Sunny begged.

The man's boots seemed to shake the ground as he yelled to the others, "Over here! These two are fixin' to escape!"

But suddenly, nonsensically, I thought how humans like to say that cowards must be "chicken-hearted," and then I remembered Thorazine and Ethel and one-winged Henriette, and I suddenly gained a surge of new strength. In between two thumps of the boots, as if there'd been an *abracadabra**, I magically came unhooked from the wire and was slipping through to the other side.

"Dadgummit!" I heard the man cry out.

"Way to go, Mama!" Sunny exclaimed as we scurried together into the woods.

Chapter 21

Apparently, no one followed us. My guess is that, on a farm that big, it didn't really matter much if one or two chickens slipped away so long as it wasn't a regular thing—like foxes marauding night after night or the little girl's chicks evading her clutches before she'd dumped them back in the yard. It pained me to think of Anna alone and, whatever they truly thought of him, of Rodney *bamboozling* all those hens. . . though his status had clearly taken a dip, and Anna could surely fend for herself.

Among the useful things I'd learned was that chickens and humans are much alike in how they behave when the pressure's on— some good, some bad, most in between. But we ought to take pride in those that are brave and share their stories whenever we can, especially with youngsters like Jones and Zan—and Sunny and the poults as well—who'll make a difference when they're grown. Like you, dear reader, whoever you are, whatever your age, however you came across this book. I hope against hope we too connect.

Something of me is in this tale, and, if you've stuck with me this far, I think I can catch a glimmer in you of what I've encountered among my friends like Thorazine, Ethel, and Henriette along with all my family of Bells. . . and Sunny, of course, my brave little Sunny who, as we made our way through the woods appeared to be cotton candy with legs. He glanced at me as I thought of that. I winked at him, and he winked back, hardly aware of how he looked.

We were more or less where we'd been before, backtracking along that winding stream with no notion of what we were headed towards. In the chatter I heard from overhead, some birds and squirrels were asking each other who in the world we thought we were—two feathered pedestrians on the prowl, one gaudy as a cockatoo and the other a dowdy mother hen. I did my best to tune them out but couldn't help hearing some of their guff.

"Weirdos on the loose down there!"

"Looks like one of 'em's dressed for Mardi Gras!"*

"What's he hoping to get decked out like that?"

"Some peace and quiet!" I yelled back, surprising them when I squawked in Squirrel. They muttered, but the razzing stopped.

We soon arrived at our former nest. It was empty, of course, but, revisiting it, I felt a wave of melancholy. We seemed so totally on our own as we tramped through the tunnel of underbrush and found the spot where Sunny was born, our interspecies hatchery. In another week or two at most, the flattened grass would straighten up, erasing all signs we'd ever been there.

We made our way still farther upstream, and, with a little searching about, discovered the pond that Ethel described nestled amid some gentle hills. On three sides stood tall clusters of trees with thick-branched beeches, cedars, and pines, and seeing them made me think of some lines I'd read while living in Chapel Hill. "The waters stand in the hills," it said, predicting the place we'd stumbled upon, and "beside them shall the fowls of the air have their habitation."*

I wasn't so sure about "of the air," but, without any question, we were fowls—and, with that in mind, we decided to roost in a beech tree's limbs beside the pond until we could find a more suitable spot for Sunny to spend his cockerel stage, which meant until he was really grown up.

There was water at hand and we'd forage for food, assuming we'd find enough to survive, though I'd no idea how cold it would get or how hard it might be for us to pull through with all the hazards of the woods. Still, one of the local foxes was gone, and how many *predators* could there be. . . a couple of hawks? A raccoon or two? There were plenty of harmless turtles and frogs, and, somewhere not so far from there, my turkey friends' flock was settling down, roosting and gobbling in the trees, though I doubted if we could track them down. So, except for two humans up on a hill—the couple that Ethel had told us about—it seemed a safe enough place to choose as our refuge for a week or two. . . or possibly longer, who could say?

But we had to be on constant alert, sleeping at night with an open eye. As it happened, every now and then, the man or woman on the hill—and sometimes both of them at once—came down to the dam on our side of the pond. But mostly they seemed to hum as they walked or talk to each other on the way, so, whenever we heard their feet on the path, it was easy to lie low out of sight.

Once or twice they put out feed, which I insisted we avoid until at last I gave it a try and pronounced it safe for Sunny as well. I wondered if they'd spotted us, though they might have been merely feeding the birds. Either way, it was generous of them.

So, other than keeping to ourselves and wondering how we'd cope with the cold, there wasn't a lot to worry about. Sunny grew bigger every day despite his outlandish purple hue, and, after only three weeks or so, his fluff appeared to be giving way to feathers that closely resembled mine. One sunny cool morning as I awoke, I heard him distinctly trying to crow—which, though it was reckless in a way, filled my heart with motherly pride.

We talked a lot about everything, including my days in Chapel Hill, but he hardly ever uttered a cluck about the farmhouse where he'd been—except to say the little girl had never done much but watch tee vee or act as if she was on it herself, preening and posing while brushing her hair and imagining fans applauding her. It sounded fairly strange to me, and Sunny confessed he'd merely been bored until one day she'd giggled at him and called him her little Easter egg. Remembering that, he choked back tears.

Though nights were gradually growing cooler, the days took on a balmy feel. One afternoon while the two of us were lazily scratching near our roost, we heard a clamor in the sky like angels performing on trombones as they descended towards our pond. I'd seen pictures of angels in Jones' books—though, except for a few with harps or horns, I thought they'd sing instead of honk.

"What is it, Mama?" Sunny asked, trying to look as brave as he could.

"Honky-tonk angels, I suppose."

"I see them, Mama, over the trees!"

I saw them too as they swooped down. Like creatures hatched from fabulous eggs, they looked so glorious in the sky, so powerful and superb to watch that they literally took my breath away as they braked and glided onto our pond, calling and chortling to each other. I thought I'd been hardened by the road, but I felt awed by what I saw —a majestic sort of heavenly blend of turkey, chicken, and supersized duck—and, summoning memories of my friends, I stood there gazing from the dam repeating a word that came back to mind from the book I'd quoted once before.

"Behold!" I mused again and again, and then, to Sunny, finished the phrase. "Behold the fowls of the air!" I said.

After a while, they noticed us and several swam over in our direction, questioning us in a language of honks that made no earthly sense to me. I could tell that, in their rarified minds, we were bumpkins who couldn't have travelled much with Sunny in such outlandish duds of fluff and feathers intermixed and me so squat and low to the ground. For my part, I was casting about through every language I'd run across, seeking some way to understand as they hooted and honked repeatedly.

The most I could fathom of what they said was a question about what people there were and whether we'd seen them carrying guns. I tried to discover where they were from and where it was they were planning to go, but all I could learn was "Cann-a-dahh" and "from far away to far away" to a place, they said, that wasn't so cold. I didn't ask "so cold as what?" but thought that sounded ominous. Finally, one of them swam up close and clambered out heavily onto the bank. I saw he was much less graceful on land and waddled in an ungainly way.

A couple of others followed the first, and one of them, nodding curtly at both of us, spoke in a curious dialect that sounded vaguely Russian to me. "I do. . . BIG business. . . in this world."

As I smiled to show I'd understood, he began to relieve himself on the bank. "BIG business. . . da!"

Then all of them were relieving themselves amid a chorus of "Da! Da! Da!"

Sunny and I were both amazed at the volume of guano they produced—you remember, of course, what "guano" is, and "da" is just how Russians say yes.

"I thought you came from Canada!"

They looked at each other as I spoke, surprised to be addressed in Goose despite how little I'd pieced together.

"NYET!" the biggest goose declared, but then they all honked, "CANADA! DA! We love our Mounties and our Moose!"

"Meese!" one of them hissed, correcting him.

"Mooses!*" The biggest one stretched his neck and pecked the other one on his back, which caused more honking all around with a flapping of wings and milling about while Sunny was stumbling out of the way and I revised my initial view.

Not angels after all, I thought—more like a traveling circus troupe with glitzy high-flyers overhead and red-nosed clowns that toddle about without a serious thought in their heads. Life's full of illusions, I realize. There's a beautiful "seems" and an everyday "is," but I was surprised by the turn of events.

The racket produced another result. It brought the two humans down the hill, and the instant the man and woman appeared, the geese leapt wildly from the bank, honking indignantly into the air with wing-beats thudding like horses' hooves. In a matter of seconds, they were gone, leaving us startled and face-to-face with the couple who'd watched the geese depart and saw two chickens staring back as if we'd fallen from the sky.

"Totally weird!" the man exclaimed. "Was that chicken just talking to those geese? And how in the world did they get here—two chickens wandering in the woods?"

"A single mother and her chick? And the little one's half-way *purple* too!"

"I never saw a purple chick. . ."

And both sang out in unison, "I never hope to see one!"—which struck me as nonsensical.*

A minute later the woman said she thought we must be runaways from the poultry farm just down the road.

"You think?" The man looked unconvinced. "But that's a couple of miles away."

"You don't turn purple in the woods! Besides, they'll freeze when it turns cold."

I looked at her more closely now, noting her gray hair, kindly face, and half-familiar tone of voice. But those weren't why I felt such a thrill. If you keep reading as you are now but delve into fiction as well as fact, you'll discover a lot of bad writing depends on coincidence and far-fetched events that'll make you protest, "That's all too neat. . . it couldn't have happened. . . we all know life's too messy for that!"

But the funny thing is—and here I go, in keeping with my upbeat name—sometimes such marvels do occur, and, after they do, we think it was fate for, if they hadn't, our lives would have changed. We'd be lost or dead or alone in the world, still seeking the rooster of our dreams or doubting that animals think and talk and feel and love and hope to grow wiser as all of us do, including you.

So, I ask you to believe me now when I report that, however unlikely it might seem, I recognized who the people were. They'd visited us in Chapel Hill and met me when I still lived there, and I'd been told when they arrived that they'd come from the other end of the state because they were Boykin's mother and father, Annie Rooney and Pa Ben. I looked again and knew for sure—it *was* Pa Ben and Annie Rooney!

As I started to cluck and flap my wings, Pa Ben stepped back and pensively said, "Just look how excited that chicken's become. Something peculiar's going on."

"They're frightened of us," said Annie Rooney.

"Of course, they are. I'll catch the hen, you grab the chick, and we'll return them to their farm."

My blood ran cold when I heard that. There were no bare spots nearby on the bank where I could scratch a message out. Sunny could sense that something was wrong, but his knowledge of English was still too scant for him to fully comprehend.

"It's me! It's me!" I shouted in Chicken. "Sunshine! Look! From Chapel Hill!"

Pa Ben reached down and picked me up. Annie Rooney had Sunny in her hands.

"Jones and Zan!" I squawked in despair. "Greg and Boykin! Baby Boyd. . . and Bevin, the sister I've hardly met!"

They looked as if they thought me deranged. I started to gobble, quack, and mew.

"Just listen to that!" said Annie Rooney. "She sounds like a ventriloquist."

"I swear. . . there's something. . ." Pa Ben said.

And then it hit me, what I should do. From the very beginning what I'd learned is there's music in all things everywhere—in wind and water, turkeys and birds, chattering squirrels and muttering fox. The poetry of the earth, I thought, the language that every creature speaks. I thought of the music Jones had played and songs that Pa Ben must have heard. If only I could bring it off, it would mean as much as the rest of our lives.

So, focusing every bit of my mind, not saying the words but catching the tune, I stretched my neck and started to sing, "I can't get no. . . satis-FAC-tion!"

As if stupefied, Pa Ben just gawked. Then I repeated what I'd sung and this time even stayed on key.

"I CAN'T GET NO. . . SATIS-FAC-TION!"

"I don't know how to account for this," said Pa Ben slowly to his wife. "But it's really no harder to believe than a chicken that's mastered rock 'n' roll." He turned me gently side to side so Annie Rooney could clearly see. "Rooney," he said in a slightly awed voice, "what we've got here is the prodigal hen. It's Sunshine, the genius chicken!"

Chapter 22

The rest of my story is quickly told. After calling the Bells to share the news, Pa Ben and Annie Rooney together drove Sunny and me the very next day all the way back to Chapel Hill—with both of us in a cardboard box, comfortably watching the trees flash by. Sunny had never been in a car and found it quite exciting at first, though after a while he went to sleep and woke with a start when we arrived.

"Where are we, Mama?"

"Sunny, we're home!"

That in itself was glorious. Both Jones and Zan looked older and bigger, but they welcomed me back with shouts and hugs and carried me proudly to our room which was full of new things to study and read. I nuzzled their necks and introduced Sunny, whose purple fluff was almost gone with grown-up plumage taking its place—more Dumpy, I thought, than Faverolle, though patches of bronze appeared on his wings. . . and I was pleased with how he looked, a little like Rodney but more like me.

I noticed that Jones' computer was on and hurriedly pecked out Sunny's name. "Sunny!" cried Zan, who'd learned by then to read quite well, while Jones just smiled and said, "That's neat!" while gently stroking Sunny's back. I'd worried that Sunny would be afraid—he'd only been in one house before and that had been a frightening ordeal—but he knew the difference right away, happily beaming and brrrkkking along.

All the Bells were truly thrilled with him, but there was that problem with roosters in town since crowing at dawn was not allowed. So Boykin's younger brother Ben, the father of little Baby Boyd and baby Mae who was yet to be, talked to a friend who had a friend who was looking to find an understudy for a mascot for a football team that used a rooster to proclaim its fighting spirit to its fans. As soon as Sunny could really crow, he'd go to live a pampered life—and we could visit him, Boykin said.

Maud Gonne was grayer than I'd recalled, but unmistakably overjoyed, perhaps the most excited of all, while Nellie managed to wag her tail, which was all I could have expected from her. My fellow chickens—Jo, Amy, and Meg—had been transformed into *corpulent* hens, a little frumpy and somewhat smug, but it was nice to see them again. Poor Beth had had an accident. . . or maybe, they said, she'd run away. Opinions differed, no one knew. But the big surprise was Thorazine, who I thought had been killed by Bigelow but was instead now Queen of the Coop—matronly, plump, and happy to see me. She greeted me like her very best friend, as I did her, dear Thorazine!

There wasn't much fanfare in the town, a fact that left me greatly relieved. Other details I managed to learn only as days and weeks went by. For example, I learned that Boykin and Greg had tracked me as far as Mister Bigg—I don't know how, but they'd figured it out from rumors about a fairground show with animals playing tic-tac-toe. Arriving just after my escape, they'd helped nail J.J. Bigelow for larceny (i.e., chicken theft), cruelty to animals (even poor Frank got foster care) and running a gambling operation. But after that my trail had gone cold, and they'd despaired of finding me.

There'd been a flurry of news reports, and my picture appeared on cartons of milk in towns throughout the Carolinas and even in parts of Nova Scotia—because, I gather, somebody there was claiming me as a native hen. But, as with all such tabloid fads, interest had waned as the narrative stalled, and my fame had quickly *evaporated**— which is to say, it disappeared.

That was for me a big relief, and it's not for fame I've written this book but simply to share the things I've learned—that most of us do the best we can, though some people cheat while others are mean, and sometimes we've got to take a stand regardless of what the outcome is. That every life is as special as ours, even the lives of insects and worms. . . and, yes, I know! You don't have to say it! I'm sorry I find them so delicious. I'm going to try a chickweed diet.

Some of those bugs live only a day, though they seem no sadder because of that, and that remains a mystery to me. For if you should ask how we differ the most—they from us or I from you—I wouldn't cite feathers, size, or brains or in which direction we bend our knees, but to how we measure out our lives. With the slightest good fortune on your side, you'll live maybe ten times longer than I, and I'm tempted to wonder what I might do with nine more lifespans than I'll have. But really, you know, that's not the point. It's instants that we should focus on in deciding whether a life is full and how often we make them meaningful because, in this gorgeously varied world, all lives will seem too short in the end. Or as a Prince of Denmark* said, being extremely fond of words but finding he'd have to cut them short, "Had I but time. . . O, I could tell you." What do you think he'd have wanted to tell? How precious his life had been, I'll bet.

With that in mind, I'll ask for a little bit more of your time to tell you something else I've learned. The ultimate secret of genius lies in how closely you pay attention—to others as well as to yourself and, above all, to this planet of ours which is, when all is said and done, as perfect and as fragile as an egg. It's really just that simple, you see, because what "all" in that last sentence means is nothing less than everything.

We should always stop when we think we've said whatever it was we had to say, so, to quote from a favorite book of mine, as Humpty Dumpty told Alice, though it seemed they'd hardly begun,*

That's all, Goodbye.

Appendix I:

CHARACTERS IDENTIFIED BY NAME & BREED IN ORDER OF APPEARANCE

Sunshine Bell	Scots Dumpy (*Gallus gallus domesticus*)
Boykin Bell, Greg Bell, Jones Bell, Zan Bell	Humans (Homo sapiens)
Maud Gonne	Labrador & English Spaniel mix (*Canis Linnaeus*)
Nellie	Uncertain Mixture (*Canis Linnaeus*)
Thorazine	Dominicker (*Gallus gallus domesticus*)
Jo, Meg, Beth, Amy	Rhode Island Reds (*Gallus gallus domesticus*)
J.J. Bigelow	Human (*homo sapiens*)
Runnymede	American Game Bantam (*Gallus Gallus domesticus*)
Rodney (Jean-Marie le Parc de Faverolle)	Cinq-Doights Faverolle (*Gallus gallus domesticus*)
Ethel, Enid, Ernestine, Emmerline, Effervescent (Effie), Melchior (Mel) Bric, Brac, Mick, Mac, Jed, Clem, Balthasar (Bal)	Eastern Wild Turkeys (*Dindon sauvage*)

Sunny Le Parc de Faverolle-Bell	Scots Dumpy/Cinq-Doights Faverolle (*Gallus gallus domesticus*)
Strutter	Cinq-Doights Faverolle (*Gallus gallus domesticus*)
Anna, Henriette	Buff Orpingtons (*Gallus gallus* domesticus)
Mrs. Betjeman, Alyssa, Higgins	Humans (*homo sapiens*)
Annie Rooney, Pa Ben	Humans (*homo sapiens*)

Appendix II:

AN INTERVIEW FROM *THE EPHESUS SCHOOL NEWS*

[Conducted in Chapel Hill, North Carolina, on April 10, 2009, by Alexander Boykin Bell with answers provided on a computer]

Reporter: First of all, I want to thank you for agreeing to this exclusive interview.

Sunshine Bell: I'm very happy to chat with you and hope I'll be able to meet some of your readers in person, especially since we're neighbors.

Reporter: I'm sure that can be arranged. In the meantime, how would you describe yourself?

Sunshine Bell: I'm a typical mature and fairly respectable Scots-Dumpy, somewhat plump, stumpy-legged, and speckled all over like salt-and-pepper. Like chickens everywhere, except for those in the jungle, I'm technically known as a *Gallus gallus domesticus*, but, since *gallus* means "rooster" in Latin, that's not an entirely accurate label for those of us who're hens. Also, in Scotland and especially in Glasgow, a "gallus" is a wild rascal, so some might question how domesticated we really are. On that matter, I should add that my breed is sometimes known by less flattering names like Bakies, Stumpies, and Creepies. But, among our more positive traits, we're gifted with such sharp hearing that, in ancient times, we were prized as ambush alarms by the Picts and Celts in Britain, who weren't so pretty themselves when they ran about without any feathers and their bodies painted blue.

Reporter: That's very interesting, especially since some of the fans for a neighboring basketball team do the very same thing when they're playing the Tar Heels. And, while we're on that subject, you mention in your book that you were born and raised in Chapel Hill. Would you elaborate on that?

Sunshine Bell: Well, as you know, for that sort of information we all have to rely on either our birth certificates or what our mothers tell us, and, in my case, I didn't get the former and never met the latter. So, although it's fairly clear that, at some point in the past, my kinfolk must have come from Scotland, I have to take it on faith that I myself was hatched in the spring of 2004 right here in Chapel Hill, which I'd describe as a picturesque little college town that, as you've just implied, is better known for its basketball than for its chickens. Maybe that's because, according to our detractors, we tend to double-dribble, but it's also because, until several years ago, as I was told by a visiting German *Krüper,* Chapel Hill was said to be totally *hühnchenfrei,* which means that it was against the law for us to live here anywhere in this town. In the interest of full disclosure, I should add that *Krüpers* are distant cousins of mine and that the law has now been changed, largely because of my family and friends and partly because of my story. Also, I apologize if some of my sentences seem to get tangled up. I sometimes write the way I peck at bugs. . . it's just the chicken in me coming out.

Reporter: I'm sure our readers can deal with that. Is basketball something that interests you?

Sunshine Bell: Yes, but mostly, I think, because in dunking a ball the players seem to be trying to fly, and, in general, I'd argue that learning anything new is in many ways the same sort of undertaking. Admittedly, those of us with wings would seem to have an advantage, but the best that I myself can manage is only about a dozen feet— which is paltry compared to an albatross but useful in tight spots on occasion. There are lots of ways to soar, you see. It's not just something you're born with.

Reporter: That's good to remember. But, speaking of being born, that's something you skip over fairly quickly in your book. Is there anything more you can tell us?

Sunshine Bell: Actually, I think I can, beginning with the fact that, whether you later remember it or not, it's something in which we chickens, at least, are obliged to play a very active part. For me, at the start, it was like an alarm clock going off. One second I simply wasn't, it seemed, and the next I almost was—as if I was being beckoned onto a stage by music that, though it didn't have words, was as clear to me as a Bell [*laughter here because of the pun*] telling me one thing over and over: "Live! Live! Live! Live!"

Reporter: That's very exciting. What did you do?

Sunshine Bell: Well, of course, I was still inside my egg when I suddenly found I had a beak and decided to figure out how to use it, jabbing it as far as I could. Nothing much seemed to happen at first, but I liked the way it made me feel, and, as soon as I'd done it only twice, I knew I wanted to do it again. . . and again and again, and the harder I tried, the better I got—and the better I got, the faster it went until it was just a matter of keeping the rhythm up—a *peccadillo* here, a *peccadillo* there—and then, to my utter amazement, a jagged crack appeared.

Reporter: That must have been a little frightening. What if you'd liked the way things were and wanted to stay inside the egg?

Sunshine Bell: Life's much too strong for that, I think. But, of course, that was all some time ago, and, if I have to explain it now, I feel inclined to point out that neither music nor life can ever quite stand still, and, with that tune repeating itself in my head, I realized instinctively that, since I'd first begun to tick, I'd been moving along through what we call time and felt I needed more space as well. . . because they go together, you see?

Reporter: I'm not sure that I do.

Sunshine Bell: Well, here's the thing, okay? I don't want to sound pretentious, and, really, you know, I'm not claiming to be an Einstein—it's just that others have said I am . . . mainly, I think, because, in some of the photos they've seen, they say we look a lot alike. But I've pondered this problem of space and time, and what I've concluded is simply this: they fit together like music and dance. Once you've gotten one, you'll get the other—first by tapping a toe, then by moving your feet, then by prancing about in what in a way resembles a sort of *hokey-pokey*.

Reporter: The *hokey-pokey*'s some kind of dance?

Sunshine Bell: That's right, and it comes very naturally too, especially if you're equipped with a beak and find yourself inside an egg—though, once I was finally out of my shell, the music *impelled* me into a jig with all sorts of hopping and flapping about and tossing my beak up high in the air. . . for that was the new dance I'd begun. In other words, I was dancing the Chicken—the chicken was me!— and what I was doing is what chickens do. I peck, therefore I am, you see?

Reporter: That's not the only thing you do.

Sunshine Bell: No, but I want to emphasize that I'm a chicken and proud of being what I am.

Reporter: Okay, and I'm sure you've made a lot of other chickens just as proud. But you said a little while ago that it was just one *peccadillo* after another, while actually. . .

Sunshine Bell: Excuse me for interrupting, but that's really clever of you! You're right again. I was trying to demonstrate something else that I hope we can discuss a little further. A *peccadillo* is actually a trifling sort of minor misdeed—in Spanish, it means "a little sin"— though wouldn't you think it could also be used to describe a wayward peck or two, especially since, if you didn't know better, that's what you'd probably think it meant? In other words, do we always have to obey the dictionary, or can't we be more inventive than that? We have to agree on some rules, of course—but languages are living things, growing and changing all the time. . . as we are too in our way.

Reporter: I think I see where we're going now—to what just inside the cover of your book is described as "easy to follow suggestions for becoming a genius too."

Sunshine Bell: That's mostly my editor's hype. But, yes, I believe how you talk can affect how smart people think you are—and the lower their expectations, the more impressed they'll be when you use a word that they don't expect you to know. It's the same with a lot of other things about which they'll often know much less than many will try to pretend, and, trust me, if you're a chicken—or a human between the ages of, say, three and seventeen—it's easy to surprise them. As for what I suggest in my book, the younger you are, the better it works, though there's really no limit on when to begin.

Reporter: So when did you begin?

Sunshine Bell: Well, Zan. . . is it okay if I call you Zan?

Reporter: Of course—why not? You always have.

Sunshine Bell: That's true. Well, Zan. . . as I think you remember, when I first made the news because I could read and write, a smart-aleck TV reporter asked me with a smirk why a chicken would want to cross the road. I blinked one eye a couple of times, then pecked out my reply: "I really can't say what might *impel* it, sir, though your question is one I've often *incurred* from those who rarely ask why a chicken would want to lay an egg!" That caused his smirk to disappear because he'd thought I knew nothing at all and was stunned by even a *smidgen* of sense. A smidgen's almost nothing, you know, and that's really all you'll need for what I recommend—a few unexpected words like several that I just used. Just tuck it away in your mind that skateboards *impel* us once they're shoved, and so does life once it's *incurred*. Then, if you need to apologize for something you shouldn't have done, try saying thoughtfully, "I don't know what *impelled* me to do it," or, if you haven't done something that you should, say in the same tone of voice, "I *incurred* a little difficulty." Neither answer will get you off the hook, but they'll move you one step closer to being considered a genius.

Reporter: Can you give us any more examples?

Sunshine Bell: I can, but let me say first that the most important thing is to really love the taste of words and the different shades of meaning with which they're so frequently stuffed. Words are really the stuff on which genius is raised—and numbers too, of course, along with images and sounds, but most especially words. They're sometimes hard to digest because, even when we know them well, they keep rhyming and combining or stringing themselves together to form a sort of richly seasoned *screed*. . . which is nothing more than a long-winded text that's crammed with endless jumbles of words. I'm sorry to get so carried away, but isn't it a delight to look a little closer and find that there's another word, *scree*, nestled inside *screed* like a chick just biding its time inside an egg? And what fun to then discover that *scree* is nothing more or less than piles of pebbles and rocks at the bottom of a cliff, looking like heaps of letters and words dumped out onto a page or some sort of bug-fest under a log!

Reporter: Uh, I guess so. That's really neat. But what I think our readers are most interested in is words that'll work for them like a sure-fire *abracadabra*.

Sunshine Bell: Where on earth did you learn that word?

Reporter: *Abracadabra*? It's in your book.

Sunshine Bell: Why, so it is. . . and good for you! Let's see, then. For a word all grownups use that they don't expect kids to know, how about *pistachio*? It's a green and improbable little nut that's got a flavor I can't describe, but the word itself will work like a charm, especially if you're younger than ten and find yourself in an ice cream shop where you're asked what your favorite flavor is. All you have to do is reply, "I'm very fond of *pistachio*" and then stand back to see the result. You may not like how it actually tastes, but you'll love the amazement you provoke. As I was saying a moment ago, there are lots of ways to dazzle the world, but words are among the easiest. Just be sure not to say "Pinocchio," which sounds very much the same.

Reporter: Got it! Thanks. That's the sort of thing that's useful for our readers. So, at the risk of wearing you out, I'd like you to comment on what to do if a grown-up on hearing you talk that way starts tossing out big words back at you.

Sunshine Bell: That's an excellent question, Zan, because it'll happen all the time once it gets around that you're a pretty smart kid. So, here's something you can try if somebody sees you're reading my book and asks you in a *condescending* way what can possibly have you so *engrossed*, which means "capturing all your attention." You should simply say, "A book about chickens," with a modest sort of shrug. "Oh, really?" he'll smile and widen his eyes. "And do you find it *edifying*?" He'll use that word expecting it to confuse you, though all it means is "enlightening." But you should just nod while wrinkling your brow and say in a grave but solemn way, "Yes, very, of course . . . though to tell you the truth, it's somewhat *esoteric*"—which simply means it's hard to explain.

Reporter: Could you repeat that word?

Sunshine Bell: Ess-oh-TERR-ick. . . with the TERR as if you're "tearing" something. It's an even better word than *pistachio*, I think, and it almost never fails. Once they hear you use it, they'll call you a prodigy or say you're quite *precocious* and stop badgering you to pick up your toys or asking you to act your age. Just try it—you'll see. And remember, with words it's the same as with bugs: the number of legs and feet helps determine the taste. *Esoteric* is a four-footed word like *pistachio* or *peccadillo*—more flavorful than a *monopede*, something with only a single foot, but bland compared to *lexicon* which, though merely a modest three-legged word that means the same as a "dictionary," contains that truly luscious x. X's are spicy, o's are not. But even gnat-sized words like scree can satisfy like *pistachios*—the more you eat, the more you want. I find that's true with dirt-daubers too.

Reporter: I'll have to try one sometime. Is there anything more you'd like to say to our readers?

Sunshine Bell: Maybe just one more thing. At the end of my book, I mention a Prince of Denmark. His name was Hamlet, and his mind was brimming with ideas, which is why everybody around him considered him so *precocious*. Among other things, he'd walk around with an open book in his hand, and, if anyone asked what caused him to be so *engrossed*, he was likely to shrug and say, "Words, words, words." Which was true enough, but not what they'd actually asked— no better than saying, "Scree, scree, scree"—though, because he was a prince and so obviously *esoteric*, nobody bothered to point that out. Still, as I'm sure you've figured out, things that are hard to explain can be meaningful anyhow and can even be understood by those who're willing to try. My book is, in some ways, hard to explain. So am I, so are you, and so was that Prince of Denmark.

Reporter: I'd like to thank you, Sunshine Bell, for a really informative and very ED-uh-fye-ing interview. I know typing your answers must have been a pain.

Sunshine Bell: You're more than welcome, Zan. Do you happen to have an aspirin?

Appendix III:

GLOSSARY

of words used in this book and selected by Sunshine Bell along with their meanings and often checkered backgrounds

This "vocabulary list," which is all that a glossary is, consists of 200 words for which guides to pronunciation and page numbers for their locations in the text are also included along with additional comments by the editor. For best results, the author recommends using at least one of these words in conversation every day as naturally and casually as you can. For anyone under the age of fourteen or so, recurrent usage is practically guaranteed to lead to a *supposition* that you're extremely bright and, for those under nine or ten, that you're a prodigy—at least in the eyes of those who haven't made a similar claim for themselves and haven't yet read this book. Double bonus words in this list are preceded by a bullet (•)—you may need to practice them a bit, but they'll be especially effective when used as recommended. To hear any of these words spoken, conduct an internet search and click on the audio icon.

•**Abated** (uh-BAIT-ed) pages 175, 188 = decreased or diminished. [As Ms. Bell once shared with me while working on this book, "May our pleasure in learning new words never abate!" The word that she'd just learned was *palooka*.]

•**Abode** (uh-BOAD) page 70 = a house or a home. [Most often used *ironically*, as in "my humble *abode*." Few have ever been heard to say, "*Abode*, sweet *abode*" or "There's no place like an *abode*."]

Abracadabra (AB-rah-ka-DAB-rah) pages 130, 148 = a magical incantation derived from a Hebrew phrase meaning "Let it be as I say" but best known today as a spell or incantation used by stage magicians. [In the Middle East, where it was thought to be of help in warding off diseases, it's as old as the second century of the Common Era while, in the West, it's as recent as the Harry Potter novels of J.

K. Rowling, who describes it as a "killing curse" spelled "Avada Kedavra." Though all such purported magic spells are merely hocus-pocus—which means just sleight-of-tongue—they're indicative of the power attributed to words, even when used ironically.]

•**Abstruse** (ab-TROOSE) page 117 = obscure or difficult to understand.

•**Adept** (uh-DEPT) page 177 = skilled or proficient.

Adrenaline (uh-DREN-uh-len) page 63 = an energizing hormone produced by the body and often triggered by fright. [As Ms. Bell has pointed out (on page 71), being frightened can also release a hormone known as dopamine that facilitates falling in love—which means that meeting someone to bungee jump or at a horror movie may be an excellent strategy for furthering a relationship.]

•**Aghast** (uh-GAST) pages 59, 81 = shocked, *appalled*, or horrified. [For a long time this word was spelled "agast," though it got modified along the way by the Flemish, Dutch, and Scots to suggest it was how you might feel after having seen a ghost.]

•**Alleged** (uh-LEDGED) page 18 = claimed but not proven. [It has been *alleged* by an author named Samuel Butler that "a hen is only an egg's way of making another egg." But he had it backwards, of course—an egg is a chicken's way of making another chicken.]

•**Appalled** (uh-PAWLED) pages 20, 103, 107, 117, 152 = greatly dismayed or horrified.

Appendix (uh-PEN-dicks) pages 13, 141, 143, 151 = something that hangs from something else. [It's interesting to note that, for the instances in this book, the correct plural is "appendices," but, for the mysterious and apparently somewhat useless organ appended to our intestines, the plural is "appendixes." Learning Latin is no longer required for physicians or, indeed, for most other people, so the following plurals are also on an endangered usage list: "gymnasia," "memoranda," "cacti," and "syllabi"—although using them at school should earn you some extra points. So will telling your science teacher that some very recent research has concluded that our *appendixes* are actually very useful.]

•**Aplomb** (ah-PLOMM) page 83 = confidence or self-assurance, especially in a difficult situation. [From the French phrase *á plomb* meaning poised or upright—related to what in English is called a "plumb line" or a weight suspended on a cord to determine whether something's straight up or perfectly perpendicular. So a person who shows *aplomb* is self-assured, poised, and squared away.]

Ardor (ARE-dor) pages 90, 199 = passion or zeal. [Ms. Bell once observed in passing that, "It's not *ardor* itself that's good or bad, but what we're ardent about."]

•**Auspicious** (aw-SPISH-us) page 66 = favorable or promising. [From the Latin word for a "bird seer" describing those who watched the flight of birds to detect and interpret omens. Ancient Romans conferred sacred status on a special flock of chickens because they were used to determine strategy and predict the eventual outcomes of military undertakings.]

AWOL (A-woll) page 117 = the first letters of Absent-With-Out-Leave—a military term for abandoning one's post without actually deserting.

Bamboozling (bam-BOOZE-ling) page 131 = tricking, hoodwinking, deceiving. [Aside from its delightful sound, this word's possible origins include a Scottish verb for confusing or confounding, an Italian expression for reducing an adult to baby-like status, or, best of all, a French term for turning somebody you've duped into a baboon.]

Banshee (BAN-shee) page 63 = a spirit in Irish folklore whose wailing foretells bad news. [Although Ms. Bell's breed of Dumpies can be traced to the ancient Picts, they too were Celtic like the Irish, and lots of the Scots migrating to North America stopped over in Ireland for a while. So, given its settlement patterns, it's not all that surprising that a *banshee* is said to have haunted the banks of the Tar River in northeastern North Carolina ever since a patriot miller named Daniel Warner was murdered by British soldiers in 1781. It's possible that Ms. Bell had run across the tale while growing up in Chapel Hill.]

Bilingual (BUY-LING-wull) page 104 = speaking two languages.

Biped (BUY-ped) pages 13, 37, 179 = any creature with two feet. [Nature appears to favor balance and symmetry to such an extent that virtually all animals have an even number of legs—a single exception of sorts being the kangaroo which has adapted its tail to serve as its primary means of locomotion, resulting in a third leg for all practical purposes. Of course, you could make a similar claim for an old man with a cane as an ancient Greek riddle did.]

Blight (rhymes with "night") page 185 = a calamity or scourge that spoils or damages something. [In Britain, a person who's disliked is often dismissed as a "blighter," meaning that his mere presence is socially catastrophic.]

Bonanza (buh-NAN-zah) page 43 = suddenly acquiring something you greatly want. [This is actually a Spanish word variously meaning good weather at sea, good fortune in general, or the discovery of a rich lode in mining. It was the last of these meanings for which it was first adopted in English, implying a "lucky strike" which in turn became a cigarette brand that ravaged smokers' lungs—like a mining disaster, in effect.]

Bonbons (BAHN-bahns) page 83 = pieces of candy, especially those that are covered in chocolate. ["*Bon*" means good in French, so bonbons are goodies—or, if you prefer, goody-goodies. . . though that's how we refer to excessively smug or complacently virtuous people who aren't really all that sweet. As a matter of fact, chocolate itself is not very sweet for chickens as well as for dogs and cats for all of whom it can sometimes be quite *toxic*.]

•**Brouhaha** (BREW-ha-ha) page 128 = an uproar. [Note that this is one of those delightful words that imitate the sound of what it's describing—like "bow-wow" or "cock-a-doodle-do."]

Burbled (BURR-bulled) pages 87, 95, 98, 108, 179 = made a continuous murmuring noise, babbled, gurgled, or gushed. [This too is one of those very old words that sounds like what it means, first used to describe a flowing brook or stream.]

•**Capacious** (kuh-PAY-shuss) page 116 = roomy and ample, able to contain a lot.

Carnivore (CAR-nuh-vore) pages 31, 81, 200 = an animal that eats meat. [Despite individual exceptions, both humans and chickens are classified as omnivores, which means they'll eat almost anything that they can chew and swallow.]

Chivalric (shi-VAL-rick) page 87 = behaving like an ideal knight— with courage, honor, and courtesy. [Though admirable as an aspiration, such behavior is apparently as rare among humans of the male persuasion as it is among roosters. With the exception of Sir Galahad, that was even true of King Arthur's Round-Table knights.]

Coed (KOH-ed) page 99 = a noun or adjective referring to a place that's open to both men and women. [Originally, the term referred to a "coeducational" system open to students of both genders. In time it came to refer specifically to women at what had once been all-male institutions—although there was no comparable term for males intermingled with women. In a bit of reverse prejudice, however, roosters are slaughtered on large factory farms as soon as their gender is determined. For middle-sized operations that want some or all eggs to be hatched, the ratio preferred is one rooster to every 10 or 12 hens. Most poulterers believe their hens to be somewhat happier under such circumstances, but, in situations with no more than a dozen hens, most roosters refuse to tolerate any rivals, so there's likely to be a single rooster or none. As for urban chicken farms, municipalities tend to cite noise pollution as a reason for banning roosters altogether. In other words, the career path confronting male chicks is extremely challenging.]

Collaborationist (ko-LAB-oh-RAY-shunn-ist) page 198 = someone who willingly cooperates with the enemy.

•**Commiserated** (koh-MIZ-uh-rated) page 89 = showed sympathy for another's misfortune. [Chickens are among the animals known to show empathy for each other and even to feel one another's pain. This is especially clear among hens when their chicks are in distress.]

Condescension (kon-duh-SENN-shun) pages 12, 77, 121, 149 = as if looking down on someone.

Conform (kon-FORM) pages 126, 186 = to obey conventional customs, standards, or rules. [Conformity tends to be very important among chickens with every flock maintaining a rigid social arrangement or "pecking order" to determine the rank of each of its members. If there's no rooster in the flock, the biggest and most aggressive hen will literally "rule the roost," entitling her to first choice of everything from a perch inside the coop to the best place for a dust bath. But she's obliged by her position to be on constant lookout for any *predators* and for ushering others to safety when one appears. As a further sign of responsible leadership, although the top chicken has the privilege of eating first, he or she will generally stay on watch while others are taking their turns. Once the pecking order has been established, it's usually maintained harmoniously unless outsiders disrupt it—not so different from high school, in effect.]

●**Consternation** (kon-stir-NAY-shun) page 128 = dismay and/or concern.

●**Corpulent** (KOR-pyu-lent) page 139 = portly, overweight, fat.

Craw (kraw) pages 82, 107 = also called a "crop," a craw is a pouch in most birds as well as a few other species that's used for storing food prior to digestion. It's located near the throat and leads to the digestive system. Chickens will often swallow small pebbles and sand to act as grinding stones that make what they eat more digestible. [To say that something is "stuck in your craw" means to have something on your mind that's so puzzling or disagreeable that you can't stop fretting about it—another way of saying, "I just can't swallow that!"]

●**Debonair** (deb-uh-NAIR) pages 78, 106, 175 = charming, confident, and sophisticated.

Deciphered (duh-SYPH-uhhd) pages 28, 163 = made sense of a difficult text or of something written in code.

Deduce (duh-DOOSE) pages 55, 165 = understand as a logical conclusion from other things you've learned. [Strictly speaking, *deduction* moves from a theory to observation while induction reverses that process. Though both are highly logical, Ms. Bell is actually describing the latter.]

●**Delectable** (duh-LECT-able) pages 42, 83, 116 = extremely delicious. [Among the foods that most chickens find *delectable* are oatmeal (cooked or uncooked), cottage cheese, pasta, pumpkin, watermelon, and, yes, a little meat every now and then (see the endnote for page 19 about chickens, dragons, and dinosaurs). But their absolute favorite snack is mealworms, which can be found at bait and tackle shops.]

Derring-do (DARE-ing-doo) page 73 = bold and heroic action. [The late-medieval poet Geoffrey Chaucer used the phrase "dorryng don" meaning "daring to do." There were later misprints as "derrynge do" and "derring-doe," which Sir Walter Scott employed as "derring-do" in historical novels like *Ivanhoe*, making the term quite popular—especially in Hollywood when adventure films came along.]

Detaining (dee-TAYNE-ing) page 53 = preventing someone from proceeding or confining someone suspected of wrongdoing. [This word is often used as a *euphemism* or a sugarcoating of something that might otherwise seem too harsh or potentially embarrassing—as, for example, when students are punished by having to stay at their desks or in someone's office during recess or after school is over, it's referred to it as "detention" rather than as temporary imprisonment. Among the earliest uses of this *euphemism* was its application to Mary Queen of Scots while she was *"detained"* for 19 years in the Tower of London.]

•**Dispelled** (di-SPELLED) page 19 = made to disappear.

•**Dissolute** (DISS-uh-loot) page 202 = having loose and decadent morals.

Diverse (duh-VERSS), page 25 = showing or containing a lot of variety.

•**Dogmatic** (dog-MAT-ik) page 198 = asserting beliefs or opinions as if there can be no acceptable disagreement.

Dollop (DOLL-up) page 26 = a blob of something, especially food. [It can also be used more loosely as in "a *dollop* of adventurous intrigue." In English, it initially referred to a clump of grass or weeds in a field, though it may have been based on an older and more generalized Norwegian word for "lump." Many past inhabitants in the western isles and northernmost parts of Scotland first arrived there from Norway, and much of present-day England was occupied for centuries by Scandinavian invaders, so that might well account for the origins of this word.]

Domestic (duh-MESS-tic) pages 79, 87, 103, 120, 141, 142, 143, 171, 191 = related to a family, household, or locality—the opposite of wild. [This word has its root in the Latin "domus," meaning "house" and implying something civilized. So a *domestic* chicken, as opposed to a jungle fowl, is likely to have its room and board provided for it by humans.]

●**Donnybrook** (DON-ney-brook) page 44 = a brawl or free-for-all, a scene of wild disorder. [This term comes from the long-held Donnybrook Fair outside Dublin in Ireland and is therefore, in the eyes of many, a general comment on the public behavior of Celts. It should be pointed out, however, that Dublin itself was founded and named—as a city, at least—by Vikings who intermarried with the Gaels. So that supposed readiness of the Celts to fight (if indeed there is such a thing) might be attributed to the Norse, a condition they share with the Scots. Whatever the ultimate source, if you're a fan of football—meaning a game that's played primarily with one's feet— then you know all about the rival clubs of Celts and Rangers in Glasgow and the frequent *donnybrooks* at matches between the two.]

Ecology (ee-KOL-uh-jee) page 179 = the study of ways in which living things relate to their surroundings and to each other. [What the notion of "Mother Nature" implies is that everything that's alive belongs to the same big family that we should love and protect. (For a more sophisticated discussion of this idea, check out the Gaia Hypothesis on the internet.)]

●**Edifying** (ED-uh-fye-ing) pages 149, 150 = instructive, uplifting, enlightening.

Effervescent (effer-VES-sent) pages 104, 141 = bubbly, lively, vivacious. [This word can be used to describe anything that fizzes— like champagne and ginger ale or a room full of kids at Halloween.]

Egghead (EGG-head) pages 124, 202 = an insulting term for either a bald person or an overly intellectual person who lacks common sense. [Or, conceivably, for someone who's both at once, though that's better than being a blockhead!]

●**Egomaniac** (EE-go-MAIN-ee-ac) page 121 = someone who's so obsessed with himself that he can't really think of anything else.

•**Embellishment** (em-BELL-ish-ment) page 185 = an added detail that makes something more attractive.

Emphatically (em-FAT-uck-lee) page 20 = forcefully, without any doubt, with great emphasis.

Engrossed (en-GROST) pages 30, 149 = having all one's attention captured and held by something.

Epigraph (EP-uh-graff) page 178 = a short quotation at the beginning of a book suggesting what it's about. [There's an *epigraph* by William Blake at the head of this book's introduction.]

Errant (AIR-ent) page 59 = wandering off course or making a mistake. [Stories in the Middle Ages described "knights *errant*" who deliberately wandered off in search of adventure and a chance to accomplish noble deeds. Although Sunshine Bell might be called an "*errant* chicken," her adventures were hardly deliberate—and yet she was brave, resourceful, and generous to others. It may be that finding oneself must sometimes involve being lost.]

•**Esoteric** (ess-o-TAIR-ic) pages 150, 150, 177 = something that's obscure or hard to understand. [Originally, it referred to ideas or information designed to be known and shared by only a few.]

•**Euphemism** (YOO-fuh-mizzum) page 157 = a word or phrase used to prettify something that might otherwise seem too blunt, unpleasant, or depressing. [Often, it's simply a way of evading or refusing to acknowledge a hard but painful truth.]

Evaporated (ee-VAPP-uh-rated) pages 139, 204 = a liquid that's been turned into a vapor and therefore seemingly disappeared. [The word is sometimes used for things which weren't liquid to begin with or which haven't been fully vaporized. Thus so-called "evaporated milk" has really just been condensed with no more than 60% of its water removed.]

•**Expendable** (ek-SPEND-uh-bul) page 38 = unneeded and disposable—something that can be done without.

•**Facetious** (fah-SEE-shus) page 160 = joking, often in an ironic way that's deliberately inappropriate and not to be taken seriously.

Fascist (FA-shist) page 200 = a person or group with a strong political preference for ethnic or nationalistic uniformity emphasizing obedience to a single strong leader and a rabid distaste for outsiders or those who insist on thinking for themselves. [Sunshine Bell is unusual among chickens in her openness to other languages and species and her relative indifference to a rigidly established pecking order—an attitude that she attributes in large measure to her adoptive human family as well as her own innate inclination.]

•**Fastidious** (fa-STID-ee-us) pages 170, 187 = attentive to detail, but also picky, finicky, and even *persnickety*.

Fathom (FA-thum) pages 22, 134 = to discover the meaning of something. [The oldest definition of this word involved embracing something with one's outstretched arms, a measurement roughly equivalent to the distance from one fingertip to the other, eventually standardized at six feet or 1.8 meters. Then it was applied to taking soundings from a ship to determine the depth of the water and, more broadly, an effort to get to the bottom of anything including difficult problems of a more general sort. The American author Samuel L. Clemens (*Tom Sawyer, Huckleberry Finn*) once worked as a river pilot on the Mississippi, and the pen name he chose for himself— "Mark Twain"—meant the water depth was at the second mark on the line or two *fathoms* down which meant in turn that, in a constantly changing riverbed, it was safe for a steamboat to proceed. Twain became the most famous wit of his day, and, in 1866, he had this to say to a Salt Lake City reporter: "The man who lives next door to me on the right keeps chickens; and the man who lives next door to me on the left keeps chickens; and the fiend who lives across the alley in the rear keeps chickens. . . and the roosters crow the whole night long, and the hens lay an egg apiece at sunrise and then cackle about it the whole day long." He continued in his usual humorous manner to consign all chicken fanciers to perdition, but nevertheless, some four years later, he was notified that a complimentary membership had been conferred upon him by the Western New York Poultry Society. Finding this hard to *fathom*, he thanked them in a very *facetious* way and immediately went inactive. It seems fair to conclude that he preferred cigars to chickens.]

•**Fatuous** (FAA-chew-us) pages 121, 165 = silly, simple, or foolish. [See also *infatuation*.]

Feasible (FEE-zuh-ble) page 22 = possible or reasonable to expect [and often implying a combination of the two].

Foraging (FOUR-ad-jing) pages 83, 96, 102, 132 = hunting about for something to eat [though it also means to pillage or *plunder*].

Forlorn (fuhr-LORN) pages 66, 89 = miserable, sad, or dejected.

•**Fortuitous** (for-TOO-uh-tuss) page 194 = occurring by chance rather than by design, accidental or coincidental. [Note, however, that if something is fortuitous, it may or may not be fortunate.]

Fruition (froo-ISH-shun) page 40 = the point at which an undertaking becomes productive or, in effect, "bears fruit." [On the subject of fruit, chickens love eating apples, bananas, berries, melons, and tomatoes but aren't very keen on oranges. Some say they should avoid all citrus fruits in general, but, in fact, it seems the only things they really shouldn't eat other than certain seeds are avocado pits and skins, onions, rhubarb, coffee grounds, chocolate, and anything containing alcohol—which helps explain why you'll rarely see an inebriated chicken. They should also be discouraged from smoking, of course, which could easily become a very expensive habit.]

Furtive (FUR-tiv) pages 58, 113 = secretive, stealthy, or sneaky.

•**Garrulous** (GARR-uh-lus) page 92 = overly talkative. [As it happens, chickens are great conversationalists. They talk to themselves and to each other, and, in fact, a brooding mother hen begins talking to her chick even before it hatches. In the final stage of incubation, the unborn chick begins peeping back from inside its egg while its mother offers encouragement for it to peck its way into the world. Chicks in an artificial incubator like Sunshine Bell instinctively peep from inside their shells and, even if they hear nothing in return, proceed to hatch anyhow.]

Glossary (GLOSS-uh-ree) pages 151, 178, 179 = a vocabulary list, usually alphabetical and bearing on a specific subject or text.

Glower (rhymes with "flower") pages 57, 107 = to have an angry or resentful expression, to scowl or frown. [This is another word of Scandinavian origin that probably entered English via a Scots dialect.]

Gluttony (GLUTT-uh-nee) page 84 = overindulgence in eating. [Several of the ancients such as Socrates and Cicero are credited with some variation on "Eat to live, not live to eat." But no matter how much food is placed in front of them, chickens won't overeat—one respect in which they're superior to most of their human friends.]

●**Gobbledygook** (GOBB-uhl-dee-gook) pages 105, 199 = gibberish or meaningless talk. [This word was invented in 1944 by a U.S. Congressman from Texas whose name was Maury Maverick, a grandson of the man whose name had become a byword for an independent-minded person. Frustrated by the jargon and double-talk of bureaucrats in Washington, Congressman Maverick said they sounded like gobbling turkeys. On the other hand, like most of his colleagues, he probably used the phrase "talking turkey" to mean they were getting down to serious business. Consistency seems to elude many experienced politicians.]

Grandiose (GRAND-ee-ose) page 42 = very big and impressive, often in a pretentious way.

Guano (GWAA-no) pages 29, 30, 134 = the excrement of seabirds and bats. [Technically, this term is not used for all bird droppings because its definition includes the potential use of such manure as an organic fertilizer. Although it's true that, of all animal manures, what chickens produce is richest in nitrogen, phosphorus, and potassium, its drawbacks are its odor when over-applied on crops and, in the case of large industrial chicken farms, the danger of environmental pollution. Human waste, formerly known as nightsoil and more recently as "humanure," has served a similar purpose with similar problems—though, with appropriate treatment and composting, the practice continues in a number of places.]

Guillotine (GILL-uh-teen) pages 68, 176 = an apparatus for beheading people "humanely" that was used extensively during the French Revolution. [Its name is pronounced GHEE-uh-teen in France where, in 1981, its use was abolished along with capital punishment in general. However, in the United States and elsewhere, similar but more highly mechanized devices are still widely employed for slaughtering chickens as is capital punishment for humans.]

●**Gullible** (GULL-uh-bul) page 108 = easily persuaded.

Gyrating (JAI-rating) pages 63, 179 = spinning or turning, usually very rapidly. [For the related word "gyre," meaning a circular or spiral motion, see the endnote for page 12.]

Hackles (HACC-uhls) pages 45, 84, 86 = plumage or hair on the necks of some mammals and birds that rise up when anger or fear is felt. [In roosters, such feathers are often long and brightly colored and, when raised, can make them appear much larger and more ferocious to whatever annoys or threatens them. Hens, though less flamboyantly feathered, can raise their hackles too but tend to be less aggressive.]

Haven (HAY-ven) pages 79, 81 = a place of safety or refuge. [Derived from Old English, Old Norse, and an even older Germanic word for "harbor."]

Hieroglyphics (HIGH-row-GLIFF-ics) page 52 = a form of writing in which many different pictures and symbols represent words, syllables, letters, or sounds. [They're especially associated with ancient Egyptian inscriptions which took a very long time for modern scholars to *decipher*.]

Hokey-Pokey (rhymes with "okey-dokey") page 146 = a dance that involves a shaking about of the limbs often accompanied by a simple sort of nursery-rhyme song. [Some believe it originated in the 1940s, but in Britain, where it goes by the name of "hokey-cokey," its earliest recorded version dates from Robert Chambers' 1826 edition of *Popular Rhymes of Scotland* and goes as follows:

> Fal de ral la, fal de ral la:
> Hinkumbooby, round about;
> Right hands in, and left hands out,
> Hinkumbooby, round about;
> Fal de ral la, fal de ral la.

With appropriate anatomical changes, it sounds very much the same when sung in Chicken.]

Hunky-dory (HUNK-ee-DOOR-ee) page 123 = doing well, just great. [As with most slang, the origins of this popular term are *murky*, but it seems to have been used in children's street games in New York City during the 1860s. If so, it's probably based on a Dutch word *honk* meaning "home" or "home-base" in tag—so, with a silly rhyme tacked on, being safe at home was eventually called "*hunky-dory*."]

Illicit (ill-LIS-sit) page 52 = forbidden by law, rules, or custom.

Impelled (im-PELLED) pages 146, 147) = pushed forward or caused to happen.

Imperceptibly (im-per-SEPP-tuh-blee) page 103 = in a way that's so slight or subtle that it can't be perceived. [But what gets us in trouble most often is less what we're unable to see than what we refuse to see. It's easy to forget that perception itself can be both moral and creative.]

●**Imperious** (im-PEER-i-us) page 126 = bossy, arrogant, acting superior in a way that is often unjustified. [Derived from the same Latin root as "empire" and "imperial"—so, when applied to Rodney in Ms. Bell's story, it also implies "Napoleonic."]

●**Imposing** (im-POSE-ing) pages 24, 87, 186 = impressive in size or appearance. [As Ms. Bell has pointed out, this word isn't as big or obscure, but it's a good alternative for words like "awesome" or "terrific." For example, if someone should say, "He's very large for his age, don't you think?", you might reply with a thoughtful nod, "Yes, he's quite *imposing*."]

Impresario (im-pruh-SARR-i-o) page 44 = an organizer, manager, or producer of an event, especially concerts, plays, or operas. [An *impresario* is basically a showman, one of the most famous of whom was P.T. Barnum who, during the 19th Century, made a career of exhibiting curiosities, both human and otherwise, to equally curious humans including Queen Victoria. One of his exhibits, advertised as "A Man Eating Chicken," drew large crowds who, once inside, were merely shown a man who was calmly eating chicken wings—and, remarkably enough, most of his customers laughed at Barnum's joke. In 1854, he also staged a National Poultry Show at his museum in Manhattan and subsequently lent his name to the Barnum & Bailey Circus ("The Greatest Show on Earth"). Though he may not have actually said, "There's a sucker born every minute," he did write an autobiography that, according to him, sold more than a million copies—which, in the course of a year, works out to about one purchaser every two minutes, so its earnings weren't just chickenfeed.]

●**Impromptu** (im-PROMPT-too) page 83 = unplanned, spontaneous, and improvised. [Suitable for describing anything that's spur-of-the-moment or off-the-cuff.]

Inarticulate (in-ar-TIC-you-let) page 23 = unable to speak or express oneself clearly.

●**Incentive** (in-SENN-tive) pages 54, 74 = something that encourages or motivates.

●**Inconspicuous** (in-kon-SPIC-you-us) page 64 = not likely to draw attention.

Incurred (in-KURRed) page 147 = caused to happen, brought upon oneself.

Infatuation (in-FAT-chew-aa-shun) pages 72, 84, 160 = an extravagant passion. [Because it's derived from the Latin word *fatuus*, meaning "*fatuous*" or "foolish," *infatuation* suggests, in effect, what is often described as being "crazy in love," which some regard as merely a giddy prelude to a deeper and more stable relationship. In fact, there's considerable evidence that such powerful if irrational initial attractions among humans (as well as other species like prairie voles) tend to last long enough for wooing, marriage, and the birth of a first offspring—which is to say, for humans, a maximum of between 2 and 3 years, after which a more mature and responsible affection may or may not ensue. Incidentally, although some varieties of duck form lifelong mating pairs, chickens do not, whereas humans appear to be somewhere in between]

Infer (in-FURR) pages 79, 98 = to conclude or *deduce* on the basis of reasoning rather than simply guessing or being told. [There are some tricky shadings of meaning here. To *deduce* is to reach a conclusion based on a logical analysis of facts or premises that are assumed to be true. To *infer* is to riddle something out in a similar manner for oneself, though *inferring* may often involve a conclusion based on what is merely implied. To imply is to suggest something to someone else without specifically stating it. The one strict rule here is that you can't *infer* anything to somebody else, only to oneself.]

●**Insatiable** (in-SAY-shuh-bul) page 83 = incapable of being satisfied. [The most nearly *insatiable* bird—and, in fact, the hungriest creature of any sort other than insects—is the hummingbird, who must eat up to twice its weight in nectar every day. As a result of its fiercely energetic efforts to satisfy this need, the Aztecs of central Mexico regarded the hummingbird as the symbol of their war god, Huitzilopochtli, and assumed it must be immortal. In actual fact, though a hummingbird can starve to death in only 3 to 5 hours, its average lifespan is about 5 years and some have been known to live as long as 10 (assisted by the fact that, in the United States, it's illegal to trap or hold a hummingbird unless you have a permit).]

●**Interlopers** (IN-ter-LOPE-ers) page 115 = intruders.

Intuition (in-too-ISH-unn) pages 56, 72 = immediate insight or perception as opposed to conscious reasoning or analysis.

Iridescent (ir-uh-DESS-unt) page 87 = shining with colors that shimmer and seem to change hues when seen from different angles. [Some chicken feathers are *iridescent*, especially those that are blue and green, but as is often the case with other species, such flamboyance is most frequently confined to males—as are such descriptive terms as "popinjay" or "fop."]

Ironically (eye-RON-uck-lee) pages 151, 152, 159, 182, 183, 200 = unexpectedly, paradoxically, using wry or sarcastic humor to describe a coincidence.

Kith (rhymes with "with") page 55 = friends and other reminders of home. [This word is used today almost exclusively in the phrase "*kith* and kin," often defined as simply "friends and relatives." Both *kith* and kin are very old English words of Germanic origin, but though kin does indeed mean relatives or kinfolk, *kith* also refers to neighbors and friends and, even more generally, to one's homeland. It first appeared in literature in a 14th-century poem called *Piers the Ploughman* but largely disappeared from written usage until the so-called "ploughman poet" of Scotland, Robert Burns, took up the phrase again in the late 18th-century. Sunshine Bell has observed that Scots are often reluctant to throw anything away, confessing that she herself had wanted to keep the broken bits of her shell.]

Lexicon (LEX-i-kon) page 149 = a scholarly word for "dictionary."

Liquidate (LICK-kwi-date) page 202 = dissolve, eliminate, or kill. [Literally, to turn a solid into a liquid.]

●**Lilliputian** (lilly-PEW-shun) page 28 = very very small. [The word comes from the inhabitants of an imaginary island named Lilliput that's visited by a character named Lemuel Gulliver in a four-part satirical novel by the Irish author and clergyman Jonathan Swift. In that book, entitled *Gulliver's Travels*, the Lilliputians are reportedly only six-inches tall—almost exactly the same as Ms. Bell's height at the time of the incident she describes.]

●**Lollygagging** (LAH-lee-gag-ing) page 111 = dawdling, fooling around, spending time idly or without any purpose. [A word believed to have been introduced by Irish emigrants into American slang in the mid-19th Century, probably derived in turn from the Celtic language of Ireland. Even when idling, however, the Irish have prided themselves on excelling at what one of their poets and playwrights, Oliver Goldsmith, popularized as "blarney" or what others have called the "gift of the gab."]

Loutish (LAO-tish) page 198 = rude, uncouth, and aggressive.

Melee (MAY-lay) page 43 = a chaotic scuffle.

●**Mellifluous** (me-LIFF-lew-us) page 23 = flowing sweetly, especially of a voice or words. [From the Latin word for honey. Even roosters will frequently croon when wooing a hen, and hens often murmur contentedly when in the company of their chicks. Both sounds could be called *mellifluous*.]

Melodramatic (MEL-uh-dra-MAT-ic) pages 49, 98 = exaggerated or over-dramatized as in a blood-and-thunder stage play. [Such behavior often erupts when something upsets the established social order within a chicken flock, especially after a newcomer's been introduced. Considerable violence can occur before harmony is restored—as frequently happens with humans too when transfers of power don't go well.]

Mesmerized (MEZ-muh-rized) page 29 = spellbound, as if hypnotized. [The term is derived from the name of an 18th-century German physician named Franz Mesmer who developed a theory of "animal magnetism" which he proceeded to demonstrate by hypnotizing some of his patients—though it was a Scottish doctor named James Braid who coined the word "hypnosis." (See the endnote for page 25 about the source of Maud Gonne's name and how a famous Celtic poet tried to *mesmerize* chickens after he and his verse had little success with a human he admired.)]

•**Momentous** (mo-MEN-tuss) pages 29, 99 = of great importance or significance.

Monopede (MON-o-peed) page 149 = a creature with only one foot.

•**Morose** (muh-ROHSS) pages 51, 79 = gloomy, grouchy, or sullen.

•**Mortified** (MORD-uh-fyed) page 57 = acutely embarrassed. [Derived from the Latin word for death, as in "I could have died with embarrassment!"]

Mosey (MO-zee) page 39 = to walk or shuffle slowly with no apparent purpose.

Murk (MERK) pages 118, 163 = darkness and gloom. [From Old English, Old Norse, and an even older Germanic origin, it's sometimes spelled "mirk" in Scotland where the date of a total solar eclipse in 1652 was long recalled as "Mirk Monday."]

Myopic (my-OPP-ik) page 187 = short-sighted or narrow-minded. [The eyesight of chickens is extremely interesting. With eyes on opposite sides of its head, a chicken can simultaneously survey a field of approximately 300 degrees, nearly a complete circle and an important advantage in avoiding *predators*. By way of contrast, a normal human range is just short of 180 degrees. A chicken can also see a larger spectrum of colors and shades (it's especially drawn to the color red) and can use each eye independently on two separate tasks at once. Furthermore, apparently as a result of how it fits in its egg—having just one side of its head exposed to the light while incubating—one eye (its left) will be farsighted (useful for spotting *predators* in the distance) and other (its right) will be nearsighted. or in other words, *myopic* (handy for locating food nearby). But because its eyes have limited mobility in their sockets, a chicken must move its head instead in order to change what it's looking at (thus its characteristic nodding and bobbing). Another visual shortcoming is extremely poor night vision, a probable factor in its having developed an ability to sleep with one eye open and the other closed when roosting in risky situations. But—despite so many differences—like humans, chickens dream.]

Nincompoops (NIN-kom-poops) page 123 = dopes. [The great 18th-century scholar of language and literature, Samuel Johnson, who compiled the first English dictionary, believed this word was playfully derived from a legal phrase in Latin, *non compos mentis* meaning "not of sound mind."]

Nuptial (NUP-shul) page 83 = having to do with marriage or a wedding.

•**Oblivious** (uhb-LIV-ee-us) pages 103, 120 = heedless, unaware of or unconcerned about something that's taking place.

•**Ostracized** (OSS-tra-sized) pages 36, 170 = excluded from a group or clique. [Behavior as old as Ancient Greece and as recent as "mean girls" in school.]

•**Pacified** (PASS-ee-fyed) page 123 = soothed, rendered peaceable.

Paean (PEE-uhn) page 124 = a song or expression of praise. [Though rarely used as a verb, it was employed in that manner in 1968 by an American naval commander named Lloyd M. Bucher when, with his ship, the *USS Pueblo*, and all its crew, he was captured by North Korean adversaries. After having been subjected to torture and warned that his men would be executed unless he confessed to having done wrong by spying, he issued a written statement in which he declared, "We *paean* the North Korean state. We *paean* their leader Kim Il Sung." If that puzzles you as it did his captors, try reading it out loud.]

•**Palatial** (puh-LAY-shul) page 33 = like a palace, large and luxurious.

Palooka (puh-LOO-ka) pages 54, 151 = In boxing, a run-of-the-mill opponent who's probably easy to beat. In general, a clumsy or stupid person.

Pariah (pah-RYE-yah) page 127 = an outcast. [Outcast hens can be a real problem because, often with one or two exceptions in a flock, most of those already accustomed to an established pecking order will isolate and pick on a newly introduced hen or one that's from a peculiar breed or different in some physical way. (See the comment on *ostracized* above).]

Pâté (pah-TAY) pages 48, 200 = a paste or loaf made from the livers of various animals, especially geese, ducks, and chickens. [Many humans, especially in France, consider this food a delicacy but, because the animals in question have often been force-fed to produce a tastier liver, many others oppose both the process and the result. There are also counter-protestors who assert the right to eat whatever they want. No one has polled the donors to determine their position.]

•**Peccadillo** (peck-uh-DILL-oh) pages 145, 146, 149 = a trifling misdeed or minor offense. [In the Spanish language from which it was borrowed, it literally means "a little sin."]

•**Persnickety** (per-SNICK-uh-tee) pages 160, 187 = extremely *fastidious*, excessively fussy about details. [Ultimately derived from the Scots "pernicky" and later "pernicketie," possible variants of "particular".]

Pimentos (puh-MEN-toes) page 30 = small sweet peppers that are often mixed with cheese or stuffed inside green olives. [The word's derived from the Spanish language in which it's spelled "pimiento," the plural of which is "pimientos." In English, however, it's generally spelled "pimento" while its plural can be either "pimentos" or "pimentoes." To add to the confusion, pimientos come in various colors including red, green, and yellow, but in English-speaking countries the word is used almost exclusively for those that are red, most familiar because their contrast with the yellow-gold of cheese or the green of cocktail olives. Although few people seemingly knew or cared, the stuffing of those olives was done by hand until the 1960s.]

Pinochle (PEE-nuck-ul) page 30 = a card game for two to four players.

Pistachio (pis-STASH-ee-oh) pages 148, 149 = an edible nut related to cashews.

Plunder (PLUN-der) pages 125, 161 = stolen objects [especially in reference to theft or pillage in wartime].

Pomegranate (POM-uh-grann-et) page 30 = a reddish-colored fruit with lots of juicy seeds. [In Greek mythology, the *pomegranate* is associated with three different deities: Aphrodite, the goddess of love; Hera, the goddess of marriage and childbirth; and Persephone, the goddess of the spring, who was tricked into spending half of each year in the underworld with Hades because, while a captive there, she'd eaten a handful of *pomegranate* seeds. In a related belief, some say the forbidden fruit in the Garden of Eden was a *pomegranate* rather than an apple (while at least one pop anthropologist has suggested it was meat!) In any case, most chickens find *pomegranate* seeds irresistible too, but without any terrible consequences.]

Poult (POLT) page 97 and many following pages = a word that can be used for a young *domestic* chicken, pheasant, turkey or other fowl, but it's generally used specifically for turkeys—as *pullet* is for young chickens (see page 172).

Poulterer (POLL-tuh-ruh) pages 155, 179 = one who raises or studies poultry.

Precipice (PREH-si-piss) page 71 = a steep cliff.

Precocious (pruh-KO-shuss) pages 104, 150 = developing skills or capabilities at a very early age or sooner than expected.

Predators (PRED-uh-ters) pages 76, 89, 92, 106, 132, 156, 168 = humans or other animals that prey on others.

●**Predicament** (pre-DICK-uh-ment) page 71 = a difficult situation.

●**Preposterous** (pruh-POSS-tuh-russ) page 54 = ridiculous or absurd. [From the Latin *prae* meaning "before" and *posterus* meaning "coming after," so something that's reversed the normal order of things—like putting a cart before a horse.]

●**Prevarication** (pre-VAIR-uh-KAY-shun) page 195 = a way of deliberately misleading someone by evading or telling only part of the truth—in other words, to lie in an apparently innocent way.

Prodigy (PROD-i-jee) pages 149, 151 = a brilliant and gifted person, especially a child with unusual ability or achievement for one so young.

Prodigious (pruh-DII-juss) pages 12, 26, 137, 173 = anything extraordinary in size, skill, or accomplishment. [In other words, a highly gifted child is *prodigious*, but so is Mt. Everest. It gets even more complicated because the closely related word "prodigal" can mean either generous or wasteful, as in a "prodigal philanthropist" or the "Prodigal Son"—or, for that matter, "the prodigal hen" meaning an extravagant fowl who wanders and returns (as on page 137).]

●**Proliferate** (pro-LIFF-uh-rate) page 31 = to reproduce *prodigiously*. [Some breeds of chickens tend to be more *prolific* in laying eggs than others with the average for highly productive well-fed hens at 200 to 250 eggs per year. Many regard the Leghorn breed as especially good layers, but the world record of 364 eggs in 365 days was set by an Australorp (an Australian breed) in the early 20th Century. Hens everywhere are as a rule most *prolific* during their first 2 or 3 years and will typically continue laying with a declining output into their 6th or 7th years during a total life expectancy of 8 to 10 years. Assuming eggs have been fertilized and hens are permitted to sit, roughly 55% to 75% of the eggs will probably hatch, though the rate is often higher.]

Prolific (pro-LIFF-ik) pages 106, 172 = highly reproductive.

Pseudo (SOO-doh) page 124 = fake, bogus, or false.

Psychotic (sigh-KAH-dik) page 202 = crazy or demented, often in a dangerous way. [Strictly speaking, chickens aren't *psychotic*, but some breeds are fairly crazy looking—even, or especially one would suspect, to other chickens. For example, use the internet to look up photographs of the following: Onagadori (a Japanese imperial breed), Polish (though from the Netherlands rather than Poland), Silkie Bantams (from China), Modern Game Bantams (from England), or Saramas (from Malaysia).]

Pugs (rhymes with "bugs") page 30 = dogs belonging to a breed with a wrinkly flat nose and face.

Pullet (PULL-et) pages 42, 118, 171 = a young hen older than a chick but not yet fully grown—a teenager of sorts. [A young rooster is called a "cockerel."]

Putsch (rhymes with "butch") page 115 = a violent effort to overthrow a government as, for example, by assassination or revolution. [This word, borrowed from the German language, is equivalent to what the French would call a *coup d'état* (koo day-tah). It's particularly associated with Adolf Hitler's unsuccessful Munich beer hall *putsch* in 1923, not wholly unlike what occurred in Washington, D.C., on January 6th, 2021. Unhappily for the world, Hitler would later succeed in coming to power in 1933.]

Quadratic (kwa-DRA-dick) pages 37, 41 = related to a square. [From the Latin word for "four," this term is encountered most frequently in the phrase "*quadratic* equation" referring to a complex mathematical problem in which something has been squared.]

Quadrupeds (KWA-druh-peds) page 37 = creatures with four feet.

Rant (rhymes with "can't") pages 48, 86, 108 = a blustery tirade or harangue. [As in "cease and desist," both words in the phrase "*rant* and rave" mean roughly the same thing, but, like a lot of poetry, both phrases use repetition to emphasize what's meant in a very effective way.]

●**Ravenous** (RAVV-uh-nuss) page 83 = extremely hungry, often excessively so. [Ms. Bell wants us to know that this word is definitely not related to her distant and somewhat disaffected cousins the ravens who, though considered as smart as dolphins or chimpanzees, can nonetheless be very mischievous and even dangerous for unhatched eggs and chicks.]

Razzmatazz (RAZZ-muh-TAZZ) page 52 = another word for "razzle-dazzle." [It also imitates the sound of what it was used at first to describe—the vibrant brilliance of jazz.]

Rebus (REE-bus) page 52 = a puzzle using pictures and individual letters to represent words or parts of words.

Reconnoitering (RECK-uh-NOI-duh-ring or, sometimes in the U.S., REE-kon-NOI-duh-ring) pages 111, 113 = inspecting, surveying, or looking about very carefully—often used in a military sense of gaining strategic information.

●**Recuperating** (ruh-KOOP-uh-rate-ing) page 44 = recovering from illness or over-exertion.

Refugee (REFF-you-jee) pages 27, 200, 202 = someone forced to leave his or her country in order to escape persecution, war, or natural disaster and seeking safety somewhere else. [The Statue of Liberty, erected in New York harbor in 1886, contains an inscription by Emma Lazarus that reads in part, "Give me your tired, your poor, / Your huddled masses yearning to be free. . . Send these, the homeless, tempest-tost, to me. . ." ("Tost" is a poetic spelling of "tossed.") According to that poem, the statue is said to proclaim a "world-wide welcome."]

Relent (ruh-LENT) page 27 = give way or ease up.

•**Retaliate** (ree-TAL-ee-ate) page 36 = fight back, get even.

Rinky-dink (RINK-y-DINK) page 55 = shoddy, old-fashioned, amateurish.

Reveling (REV-uh-ling) page 57 = celebrating, making merry, or taking great pleasure in something.

Ruse (ROOZ) pages 63, 117 = a clever trick used to deceive, evade, or outmaneuver someone.

Sardonically (sar-DON-ik-li) page 91 = in a mocking, sarcastic, or cynical way.

Sashayed (sa-SHAYED) page 87 = strutted in the manner of a show-off.

Scree (SKREE) pages 148, 149 = heaps of rocks and pebbles on a slope or at the bottom of a hill or cliff. [From Scots and northern English dialect, derived from an older Old Norse word—all places where there's a high likelihood of encountering what the word represents. Obviously, flatlanders have little reason for borrowing or inventing such a term.]

Screed (SKREED) page 148 = a wordy long-winded text.

Scrofula (SKROFF-you-luh) page 59 = a disease related to pneumonia causing glandular swelling and scabbing on the neck and cheeks. [*Scrofula* was once known as "the king's evil" because it was superstitiously believed that the touch of a royal person could cure it.]

●**Sedate** (suh-DATE) page 22 = dignified, calm, unruffled.

Semaphore (SIM-uh-fore) pages 111, 207 = a way of signaling using flags, arms, or other usually visual forms of communication.

Sleekit (SLEEK-it) pages 81, 82, 195 = smooth-coated. [This is a word in Scots dialect which has also come to mean sneaky or crafty, which appears to be what Ms. Bell has in mind when she uses the word herself a few lines later.]

Smidgen (SMII-jin) page 147 = a very small amount of something. [Believed to have come from "smitch," a word in Scots dialect for a very small amount of something or an insignificant person.]

Spiel (SHPEEL) page 54 = a practiced, often glib speech generally designed to sell something or persuade somebody. [In some parts of Germany, this word is pronounced "speel," though in Yiddish it's "shpeel" while, in the United States, both pronunciations are used.]

Spree (rhymes with "free") page 101 = a period of time during which something, often irresponsible or fun, is done without restraint. [The word comes from Scots dialect, probably derived from Old Norse but possibly from the French or even from another Scots word for a cattle raid—regarded by some Scots in the past as a variety of fun.]

Spurned (rhymes with "burned") pages 25, 182 = rejected disdainfully.

●**Suave** (SWAV) pages 68, 112 = worldly, charming, *debonair*, and cool.

●**Subside** (sub-SIDE) page 70 = diminish or grow less intense, *abate*, recede, or die down.

●**Supposition** (sup-po-ZISH-un) page 151 = a guess, assumption, hunch, or *surmise*. [It's derived, of course, from "suppose" and medieval Latin but can be traced much further back to a Greek word meaning "hypothesis" or a theory.]

●**Surmised** (sir-MIZED) pages 115, 175 = guessed or suspected.

Swag (rhymes with "drag") page 181 = stolen goods.

•**Swashbuckler** (SWASH-buck-ler) page 72 = someone who engages in daring and romantic adventures with stylish abandon. [In Hollywood lingo, a *swashbuckler* is an action-adventure movie set in the distant past and starring a handsome rogue whose wit and skill with a sword easily win the heart of a damsel in distress. But the term meant something else in the past, as a "swash" was either a type of drum (producing a boisterous clamor) or the sound of a heavy blow (like banging a sword on something metallic) while a "buckler" was a very small shield designed to parry opponents' attacks but useful as a noisemaker too. So *"swashbuckler"* was coined as a word to describe a boastful and swaggering thug whose bluster was mostly an empty pose, and, Hollywood's leading men aside, most hard-pressed damsels, now as then, would do well to be advised.]

Tacit (TASS-it) page 48 = understood or implied without being spoken.

Testily (TESS-ti-lee) page 76 = irritably or impatiently or both.

Toxic (TOCK-sik) pages 154, 177 = poisonous. [Ultimately derived from a Greek word referring to the poison used on the tips of arrows. Thus, if someone's "intoxicated," it's as if he or she has been shot with a poisoned arrow.]

Traipsed (TRAYPSSD) pages 110 = walked about casually and idly. [This word also means trudged or plodded as if weary or out of sorts. What the two meanings have in common is that neither involves a brisk or jaunty gait.]

Tryst (TRIST) page 101 = a private romantic meeting or rendezvous. [Incidentally, though the word is derived from French, the phrase "a *trysting* place" has long been used in Scots dialect to mean a market or fair—so it's appropriate that Sunshine Bell's romance with Rodney began at a state fair.]

Tumbrel (TUMM-brul) page 68 = an open cart used to carry those condemned to the *guillotine* during the French Revolution.

•**Unanimity** (you-nuh-NIMM-i-ty) page 95 = total agreement.

Utopian (you-TOPE-ee-uhn) page 201 = pertaining to an imaginary place where everything is perfect. [The word "Utopia" was actually coined by Sir Thomas More in 1516 as an *esoteric* pun which, to those who'd studied Greek, meant either "no place" at all or "a place where all is good."]

•**Virulent** (VIRR-uh-lent) page 107 = poisonous, *toxic*, or malicious.

Wary (WHARE-ee) pages 36, 87, 96, 118 = cautious and on one's guard.

Woolgathering (WOOL-ga-thur-ing) page 192 = indulging in idle daydreaming or absentmindedness. [The pastime of gathering tufts of wool from brambles and hedges may have involved as much apparent wandering as the sheep themselves, though it wasn't without a purpose or even a meager profit. It would have been the equivalent of gathering bits of lint scattered about a textile mill, where workers were sometimes scorned as merely being "lintheads"—which leads us back to Ms. Bell's point about how we can best use our brains. The idea for Eli Whitney's cotton gin had only come to him after idly observing a cat attempting to tug a chicken through a fence while getting nothing but feathers. There are such connections everywhere, and though formal education is rarely based on this premise, we should learn to draw a distinction between mindless drudgery and the sources of creativity.]

•**Xenophobic** (zenn-uh-FOE-bic) page 69 = fearing or disliking strangers, especially those from somewhere else such as a foreign country. [As previously noted, chickens find the sudden introduction of outsiders to be very disruptive to the flock, but, when given time to work things out, most breeds of chickens adjust to living well together. Many humans are less *adept* in that regard.]

ENDNOTES
of
Quaint and Curious Lore

These brief elaborations on items in the text are designed to assist the reader in the same manner as the glossary by providing interesting bits of related information that, when used modestly and sparingly in conversation, will be seen as further evidence of a widely inquiring mind. Ms. Bell herself has added insightful comments throughout the notes.

Page 11: The *epigraph*—a quotation at the beginning of a book—is by **William Blake**, an English poet, painter, and visionary who lived at the beginning of the Romantic Movement in the late 18th and early 19th Centuries. Described by some as possessing a "child-like" wisdom, he had an intense appreciation of the natural world and was said to have on occasion conversed with angels. Although this is pure speculation, it seems possible that, as Ms. Bell has suggested, some of those conversations were actually with chickens. [See her own encounter with "angels" on page 133, though I recommend you wait until you've actually read that far.]

Page 11: **Frans de Waal** is a distinguished Dutch primatologist— someone who studies and compares a specific group of mammals including monkeys, apes, and humans. He's also a widely read author whose work on animal intelligence and emotions has done much to overcome human prejudice towards other species, even non-primates such as birds and fowls. Of particular note in this regard is his observation that, "It is hard to name a single discovery in animal behavior that has had a greater impact and enjoys wider name recognition than the 'pecking order' [research]. . . by a Norwegian boy [named] Thorleif Schjelderup-Ebbe, who fell in love with chickens at the tender age of six." Indeed, Schjelderup-Ebbe's later breakthroughs in his own field of research were largely based on journals he'd kept as a very young *poulterer*—an example which youthful readers of this book might want to take to heart.

Page 12: **Andy Sih** is an American scientist and professor who specializes in behavioral *ecology*—the ways in which living things relate to their environments. Many others might be cited in support of Professor Sih's comment about the likelihood of highly gifted individuals appearing in other species, including one expert who's declared regarding the capacities of poultry in general that "chickens make great pets, they talk to each other while still in the egg, they have a sense of time, recognize their friends and can run up to nine miles per hour. . . it's time to reconsider these unsung birds." [Both Ms. Bell and I agree, especially with that final observation.]

Page 12: **"I was born on a beautiful bug-filled day!"** Many readers will be familiar with the conversation of Alice and Humpty Dumpty in Lewis Carroll's *Through the Looking Glass*, during the course of which Humpty Dumpty quotes a poem that begins, "'Twas brillig and the slithy toves / Did gyre and gimble in the wabe. . ." He then proceeds to demonstrate his boast that "I can explain all the poems that were ever invented," turning first to the second word "brillig" which, according to him, "means four o'clock in the afternoon—the time when you begin broiling things for dinner." Ms. Bell has asked me to point out that in what would have been her own first sentence in Chicken—"*Kraak krak* **brrrlkk** ☼ *krūwwwk!*"—the third word meaning "bug-filled" is, in fact, properly pronounced as "BRILL-ikk," from which one can only conclude that, from his perch on a wall, Mr. Dumpty (or Professor Carroll, a.k.a. Dodgson, himself) had overheard a hen who was *burbling* to herself and totally misunderstood what was actually being said both by her and in the poem. . . that there were lots of bugs about on that particular day in the wabe. In other words, like many literary critics, Mr. Dumpty isn't as clever as he pretends.

Page 13: As noted in the glossary, a **biped** is an animal with two feet. [On one occasion, in response to the question "What is man?" the ancient Greek philosopher Plato is reported to have replied, "A *biped* without feathers"—whereupon an Athenian jokester plucked a chicken's feathers and declared, "Behold, Plato's man!" That was widely considered a very clever put-down until, more than two thousand years later, the American naturalist and author Henry David Thoreau repeated the anecdote to a French-Canadian woodcutter whom he'd encountered in the forests of Maine. When the woodcutter heard about that long-ago exchange, he shook his head. "*Mais non!*" he said, in effect, "a chicken's knees bend the other way, more like our elbows do." He was right, of course, as anyone should know who's ever bent over to peck at something in the dirt. Every species excels at what it's designed to do in order to survive.

Page 13: Regarding the "**genius label**," the author, having read over these notes, wishes to advise the reader that, "Though I admit to being a resourceful chicken—as you, no doubt are a clever reader—the truth of the matter is that, if you're initially underestimated, a display of even modest intelligence will often prompt astonishment. On the other hand, in urging me to subtitle this book 'The Autobiography of a Genius,' my editor has insisted that boldness and presumption are typical of what that claim implies. He cites the example of Napoleon, who insisted on crowning himself as the Emperor of France. But, having known at least one Napoleon-wannabe, I think it more likely that some have been so quick to call me a genius as a way of excusing their own mediocrity. That sounds harsh regarding my editor, but I happen to know him extremely well." [Speaking for myself, I accept both her modesty and her criticism, though I think the subtitle is a good one.]

Page 13: Largely because of his work in theoretical physics, **Albert Einstein** is widely considered the most brilliant scientist of the 20th Century. He is also known (somewhat dubiously) for having struggled with mathematics as a schoolboy as well as for loving music and playing the violin. He deserves special praise for having been an outspoken if somewhat absent-minded humanitarian and for having observed in answer to the age-old riddle about a chicken's reasons for crossing a road that, "The chicken did not cross the road. The road passed underneath the chicken." He truly said that.

Page 19: **Ali Baba** is the hero of "Ali Baba and the Forty Thieves," one of the stories in a collection called *A Thousand and One Nights* or simply *The Arabian Nights*. As a poor woodcutter in that tale, Ali Baba happens to overhear the magic phrase "Open Sesame" that unlocks the entrance of a treasure cave where a gang of forty thieves has hidden its fabulous *swag* ("*swag*" is a word for loot or stolen goods). He takes some of the treasure for himself but then must fend off the angry thieves from whom he's rescued by a clever servant girl named Morgiana who [as Sunshine Bell has pointed out to me] is yet another example of a reckless male bailed out by a prudent female. Ms. Bell wishes to add the following comment: "Strictly speaking with regard to my own experience, nothing that I happened upon in the room belonging to Jones and Zan Bell could be classified as *swag*, though many intriguing items that they'd been given or discovered had been stored on shelves or in drawers, including occasional edibles—so, to a naïve young hen like me at the time, it did indeed resemble an Ali Baba's cave." As a further gruesome footnote to the tale, the author reports that she once stumbled across a recipe for "Ali Baba Chicken," which recommends stuffing the main ingredient with forty cloves of garlic. It is to be hoped that knowing the right words (like "Open Sesame" as opposed to "Little pig, little pig, let me come in") and meeting the right people (like Morgiana) can prevent those like Ms. Bell from becoming such gourmet *swag* themselves. We ourselves should never forget that a frantically squawking chicken might be trying to tell us something.

Page 19: It's worth pointing out that the **dragons** of myths and fairy tales have generally been depicted as huge ferocious lizards and that the largest lizard alive today is called the Komodo Dragon. In reality, however, although dinosaurs—the biggest lizards ever—had become extinct long before human beings appeared, we now know they were closely related to the earliest species of birds. To underscore this point, contemporary scientists maintain that chickens are, in fact, the closest living relative of both the Tyrannosaurus Rex and the fearsome Velociraptor. Ms. Bell suggests we should all bear that in mind before dismissing anyone as "chicken-hearted."

Page 23: "**The poetry of earth** is ceasing never" is a line in a sonnet by the English Romantic poet **John Keats**. The poem is entitled "On the Grasshopper and the Cricket," both of which, according to the author, are quite delicious. [While living in northern Thailand, I myself have eaten deep-fried versions of both and found them fairly tasty.]

Page 24: As with any language, **the best way to learn to speak Chicken** is by listening and observing, but to help you get started, there are many useful websites on the internet—as, for example, *www.tillysnest.com/2018/04/listen-chicken-vocalizations*, or, to hear Chicken spoken with an English accent, there's the equally delightful *www.youtube.com/watch?v=8zrmI6zOLH4*. You'll find a wide range of examples with which to practice your listening skills at *www.youtube.com/watch?v=V5-q90QaV5Q* and a bit of comic relief (if somewhat shaky camerawork) from a region through which Ms. Bell has traveled at *www.youtube.com/watch?v=TrSftKiD-Oo*. [It's very ironic, Ms. Bell has said, that we're now studying Chicken by using the same technology that helped her learn to write in English.]

Page 25: **The poet's name** was **William Butler Yeats** who, for many years, was hopelessly in love with an Irish actress, revolutionary, and women's rights activist named Maud Gonne—though in the end each of them married someone else. Perhaps with the memory of having been *spurned* in mind, when Yeats was later appointed as chairman of a committee to choose designs for the Irish republic's coinage, the selections he reported included no portraits of women. But that didn't exclude all females because, for one side of a penny, a depiction would appear of a mother hen with her chicks. Oddly enough, it's reported that Yeats himself was in the habit of trying to hypnotize hens which, if he'd only known the secret, would have proved a good deal easier than his similar efforts with Maud Gonne. [To learn how easy it is, look up "Chicken Hypnotism" on the internet, though Ms. Bell points out that chickens have a remarkable ability to nap throughout the day for intervals as short as 15 seconds which, according to her, is probably what's going on rather than true hypnosis. In any case, it seems quite clear that, since chickens typically sleep from dusk to dawn while the average household cat sneaks in as much as 16 hours a day, their so-called "cat naps" aren't all that brief, and we ought to be striving for "chicken naps," which she thinks we can learn to do.]

Page 26: **The Grateful Dead** was Boykin Bell's favorite rock-'n'-roll band—though that must have been despite a 1962 recording by its leader, Jerry Garcia, of a song entitled *Crow Black Chicken* containing the unfortunate line, "I love chicken pie."

Page 28: The earliest known version of the story of **Chicken Little** (called "Henny Penny" in Scotland) is a Buddhist folk tale from some twenty-five centuries ago—though, in that account, the role now assigned to a chicken was played instead by a hare (as it would be yet again in one of the Br'er Rabbit stories). It's a disturbing *irony* that, however slight the evidence might have been in the past, climate scientists today have confirmed that the sky is indeed, in a manner of speaking, about to fall and the joke will be on those who fail to listen.

Page 30: **This famous alarm** was supposedly delivered in mid-gallop by **Paul Revere**, a silversmith and engraver in Massachusetts who was really just one of as many as forty largely forgotten men who, on that evening of April 18th, 1775, warned the rebellious colonists that British troops were advancing towards Lexington and Concord. His "midnight ride" was later made famous by the American poet Henry Wadsworth Longfellow, who chose to ignore the fact that numerous British patrols that night had made whispered warnings far more likely than shouts. But it's certainly true that, once alerted, the colonists would repel the British in skirmishes that began with what another American author, Ralph Waldo Emerson, described as "the shot heard round the world"—though no one knows for sure by which side that shot was fired. [Ms. Bell has asked me to remind you that, despite the absence of such poetic commemorations, Scots Dumpies were used to sound similar alarms long before America had even been "discovered." (For other comments on that subject, see page 143 and one of the endnotes for page 46.)]

Page 30: [I myself might have mentioned this anecdote to Sunshine Bell as we were putting this book together. It was in an article I'd read in one of the Sunday papers when I was a student at Oxford in the late 1950s and early '60s, though I've never been able to track it down. As I vaguely recall, **the old woman** lived in Apulia or possibly in Calabria and, in any case, close to the sea—which underscores Ms. Bell's basic point that, like most humans until fairly recently, the vast majority of chickens will rarely have traveled more than a very short distance from where they were born. Although books, computers, and television now offer convenient ways of learning about the rest of the world, the essential challenge still lies in retaining a sense of wonder and surprise—as that old Italian woman had clearly done.]

Page 33: Built of white marble in Agra, India, as a memorial for his former queen, the **Taj Mahal** was erected by Shah Jahan in the 17th Century and is, in the opinion of many, the most beautiful building ever built. [Taj Mahal is also the name of a legendary blues singer who happens to be a personal friend of mine. Both the building and the singer are very *imposing*, and, though cracks have appeared in one and wrinkles on the other, neither should be described as anything less than majestic.]

Page 35: **The names of Sunshine's coop-mates** were drawn from various sources. Thor—the name that Zan proposed—is the hammer-wielding god in Norse mythology who's associated with thunder, lightning, and the protection of humankind. Thorazine—the name that was chosen instead—is a medication administered to mental patients instead of previous treatments that resembled being hit by the hammer of Thor. Jo, Meg, Beth, and Amy are the sisterly heroines of Louisa May Alcott's ever-popular novel *Little Women*—which Boykin Bell had presumably read and from which she may even have remembered a passage in which Amy, having traveled to Britain from Massachusetts, reports that in England, "The very cattle looked more tranquil than ours, as they stood knee-deep in clover, and the hens had a contented cluck, as if they never got nervous like Yankee biddies." What a pity that Amy didn't travel farther north where she might have met some of Sunshine's even less nervous and more contented kin!

Page 37: Actually, **some hens do crow** very much like a rooster, though they're generally not as loud. As a rule, this occurs in the absence of a rooster when the hen that's top of the pecking order assumes the same sort of authority and asserts it as a rooster would do by crowing repeatedly. Not all top hens feel a need to crow, however, unless there's previously been a rooster in the flock. But even when there is a rooster, there are two other somewhat rarer reasons that a hen might begin to crow. One is an apparent desire to irritate him because of his boastful and bullying manner, and the other involves certain physical changes in which the hen stops laying eggs and, in every possible way, simply becomes a rooster. Whatever the reason, many male humans have traditionally resented strong and clever women, so they've often repeated a proverb that warns "a whistling woman and a crowing hen will always come to some bad end."

Page 37: **The Rolling Stones**, an English rock band formed in 1962, took their name from the familiar saying that "a rolling stone gathers no moss." The question raised by that particular proverb—along with complaints in several of the band's most successful songs that "you don't always get what you want" and "I can't get no satisfaction"—is whether gathering moss should be regarded as an *embellishment* or a *blight*. It may be inevitable in some climates if the stones in question are stationary, but it's highly unlikely if they've been set in motion by earthquakes or volcanoes. Presumably the Rolling Stones prefer the latter sorts of disturbance, especially since, even late in their careers, neither Mick Jagger nor Keith Richards appears to have gathered much moss. On the other hand, The Doors lead singer Jim Morrison, whose biography is entitled *No One Here Gets Out Alive*, died too early to tell when he was just 27 while the oldest chicken on record only lived to the moss-less age of 16.

Page 38: **The Hottentots** (which isn't the name they used for themselves) are properly called Khoikhoi ("people people" or "real people") and had lived in Southwestern Africa for a thousand years before they got in the way of some newly arrived European colonists. Today only a few true Khoikhoi survive, and their culture has been almost totally destroyed. They're like the quagga—a variety of zebra that, until the late 19th Century roamed the South African plain in great numbers but is now completely extinct. South African chickens appear at first glance to have fared somewhat better than either the Khoikhoi or the quagga—though, in fact, the so-called "native" species of poultry in South Africa are believed to be immigrants from India, China, and Southeast Asia. [In any case, I urge you to read Maya Angelou's very short and informative book *My Painted House, My Friendly Chicken, and Me* which is set in South Africa.]

Page 40: **Wofford College** is a small but highly regarded liberal arts institution in upstate South Carolina where, when Bevin Bell was a student there, a retired psychology professor named John Pilley made international headlines by proving that the language-learning ability of his **border collie, Chaser**, was far greater than anyone had ever supposed to be possible. The same result has been achieved with many of Wofford's students.

Page 40: **Sequoyah** was an illiterate Native American silversmith and blacksmith who, in 1821, without knowing the alphabet of any other language, developed a way of writing in Cherokee—a feat rarely equaled by any other individual in human history. Unlike our letters, his system of 86 characters (later 85) represented different syllables. For example, the word for chicken, *tsitaga* (pronounced chee-TAH-gah), is written as ᏥᏔᎦ in Cherokee.

Page 40: During the late 1950s, so-called **beatniks** (or "beats") conformed to a mode of non-conformity that included growing beards, dressing in black, and playing bongo drums. They differed from subsequent "hippies" in that they were generally encountered in ones and twos as opposed to crowds or tribes and tended towards existential sulking as opposed to hallucinogenic ecstasy. It wasn't clear whether they took their name from the heavy beat of the jazz to which they listened or from the fact that their listless "cool" made them appear exhausted. They later claimed they'd merely been beatific, possibly because of foreign substances.

Page 40: "**Little Annie Rooney**" was a popular comic strip about an orphaned girl and her dog named Zero that ran in American newspapers from 1927 to 1966. The name was taken from a well-known 19th-century English music-hall song that begins by describing a young woman with "a winning way, a pleasant smile, / dress'd so neat but quite in style." However, there's also a Scottish saying that "she's having an Annie Rooney" meaning that, whoever she is, she's in a furious snit. In this case, the song better suited the actual person.

Page 40: **Marcel Proust** was a 20th-century French author whose extremely long masterpiece *In Search of Lost Time* (also translated as *Remembrance of Things Past*) is talked about by many and read in its entirety by few. It is, however, one of the greatest novels ever written—and, if you consider the life expectancy of a chicken, you'll understand what a commitment of time it represents for the author to have read it. . . either that or what a fast reader she is.

Page 41: **The colonel** in question here was a so-called "Kentucky Colonel" named Harland David Sanders, who was awarded that strictly honorary title by the governor of his state in 1935 and had it reaffirmed in 1950. The service for which he was so honored consisted of killing large numbers of chickens and frying them for consumption by the citizens of Kentucky and, later in his career, throughout the United States and the world. After selling its franchise, he continued to serve as the mascot for Kentucky Fried Chicken, also known as KFC. His image was carefully managed to convey a feeling of southern charm, but to "meet the Colonel" remains a grisly prospect for any chicken or chicken-like substance.

Page 42: The seven-spotted **ladybug** found throughout the United States is also the most common variety in Europe, where it is better known as the "ladybird"—a term appropriated as a nickname for the wife of Lyndon B. Johnson, the 36th President of the United States. Lady Bird Johnson, whose rarely used birth name was Claudia Alta Taylor, was renamed in childhood by a nurse who declared that she was "purty as a ladybird." Although there is some uncertainty about whether Mrs. Johnson's nurse had a bird or a beetle in mind, the ladybug is so widely admired for its looks and its assistance in pest control that it serves as the official state insect of Delaware, Massachusetts, New Hampshire, Ohio, Pennsylvania, and Tennessee. However, as every *fastidious* chicken knows, its flavor leaves much to be desired. (*Fastidious* just means "picky," but it'll be a showstopper if, when anyone insists on telling you what to eat, you answer them by saying, "Thanks very much for your concern, but I'm extremely *fastidious* when it comes to food!") [By the way, two states, Rhode Island and Delaware, have designated a chicken as their state bird and, as Ms. Bell has pointed out, the latter has also been "admirably *persnickety*" in specifying that what they've chosen is a hen.]

Page 43: **The "counsel"** (or advice) is that of **Thomas Babington Macaulay**, a 19th-century poet, historian, and statesman whose belief that Britain and a few other western nations had achieved a uniquely high level of civilization is paralleled by the equally *myopic* notion that human beings are uniquely capable of reason (myopic means short-sighted or narrow-minded). In his defense, it should be noted that, in addition to his later achievement as a very fine storyteller, he was a Scottish Highlander's son who, as a bright lad of about four, had replied to a visitor who apologized for having spilled hot coffee on his leg, "Thank you, madam, the agony is *abated.*" *Abated* means it decreased, but, needless to say, for having used words in such a way, he was instantly seen as a genius. Nevertheless, he appears to have remained more sensitive to the pain of spilled hot coffee than to that of colonization.

Page 44: **The Festival for the Eno** is an annual musical gathering held over the July 4th weekend in Durham, North Carolina, to benefit the Eno River Association. The Chicken Wire Gang, a popular bluegrass group from nearby Chapel Hill, has frequently performed at the festival. Greg Bell is its leader.

Page 45: "**Croker sack**" was until very recently a term confined to a narrow geographical band stretching across South Carolina (where Boykin Bell grew up) through Georgia, Alabama, and Mississippi. The singer Willie Nelson and author Franklin Burroughs have made the usage more common. No one knows how the term came about, though some have speculated that the sacks were originally designed to carry gigged frogs or "croakers" while others maintain they were used for gathering crocus bulbs for saffron. [Whether called croker or burlap, the loosely woven sacks have also been fashioned into clothes during hard times like the Great Depression—though, needless to say, feathers are on the whole a more attractive mode of attire even when worn on a bonnet.]

Page 46: In Scotland, the fearsome battle cry in Gaelic of the West Highland Clan Cameron was *"Chlanna nan con thigibh a' so 's gheibh sibh feòil"*—"You sons of the hounds, come here and get some flesh!" Members of that clan made up half of the original Black Watch regiments who, during World War II, were the last British battalions to go into battle wearing kilts, maintaining their reputation for courage under fire and earning themselves a nickname as "The Ladies from Hell." [Because Scots Dumpies had served those very same clans so long and well as ambush alarms, it seems only right that Ms. Bell should compare herself to "**a chicken from hell**." As she once observed to me, "Never underestimate a Scot—whether in feathers or in kilts!"]

Page 46: We might suppose such intense **emotion over the loss of a single hen** was something only another chicken could feel. But a woman named Nancy Luce—who was born on the island of Martha's Vineyard in 1820 and, without ever visiting the mainland, lived there alone for 70 years with her chickens and a cow—wrote and published a long *eulogy* for several hens who were dear to her. The poem is entitled "Poor Little Hearts" and begins with these heartfelt if somewhat ungrammatical lines:

> Poor little Ada Queetie has departed this life,
> Never to be here no more,
> No more to love, no more to speak,
> No more to be my friend,
> O how I long to see her with me, live and well,
> Her heart and mine was united,
> Love and feelings deeply rooted for each other,
> She and I could never part,
> I am left broken hearted.

She also wrote a prose work entitled "Hens—Their Diseases and Cure" in which she observed, "It is as distressing to dumb creatures to undergo sickness and death, as it is for human, and as distressing to be crueled. . ." [Visitors to the island thought she was merely an amusing simpleton, though I'm of the opinion that, had he lived long enough to read her 32-page *Complete Edition of the Works of Nancy Luce, of West Tisbury, Dukes County, Mass.*, the English poet William Blake, who completed his own masterpiece *Jerusalem* in the year that she was born, might well have thought her to be as wise as he in a childlike way.]

Page 47: The only benchmark I could find for **ransoming chickens** involved a trucker in Montana named Christopher Hall who, in 2014, decided to withhold more than 35,000 pounds of frozen chicken valued at roughly $80,000 until he was paid an undisclosed amount by his company, Dixie River Freight of Nampa, Idaho. The company refused, so he abanoned his trailer at the Town Pump Flying J truck stop west of Missoula, making off in the cab and leaving the carcasses to rot. Assuming he asked for the full value of his load, that would have amounted to slightly less than 44¢ per pound which, given an average weight of 5 lbs. per chicken would have worked out to 7,000 chickens at about $2.00 each or, in today's prices at a North Carolina supermarket, a sum equivalent to the cost of 16 eggs. A live egg-laying chicken currently sells for about £15 in the UK and between $20 and $50 in the U.S. depending on the breed, with Scots Dumpies going for as much as $150 or more. As a local celebrity, Sunshine Bell might well have fetched a fairly tidy sum.

Page 47: It's not clear whether **Pennzoil the duck** got his name from a popular motor oil or from the company that manufactures it. Any further connection is obscure except for the fact that an oil gland at the base of a duck's tail helps keep its feathers soft and pliable which, as a result, not only keeps them waterproof but prevents them from breaking and improves its ability to fly. Ducks use their bills to spread this oil by their constant preening.

Page 48: **Calliope the rabbit** is named for the ancient Greek muse of epic verse (*kallos* means beauty, *ops* means voice, combining to indicate a "beautiful voice" like that of a classical muse). But, as noted later in the text, a calliope is also a musical organ on wheels with pipes and whistles grinding out tunes—which hardly suggests the mute character in this story, and, though the ancient poet Homer begins his epics by asking the muse to sing through him, there wouldn't be much point in directing that plea to a rabbit. . . unless, of course, she and others of her species are simply holding their tongues to avoid being overheard. In actual fact, without being as talkative as the cartoon character Bugs Bunny ("Ehhh, what's up, doc?"), rabbits do have a fairly elaborate language of grunts, thumps, clicks, honks, ear wiggles and body positions—not exactly musical to our ears, but maybe even poetic to them.

Page 48: **The bantam rooster Runnymede**'s name apparently derives from the water-meadow in the Thames Valley of England where, in 1215, King John signed and sealed Magna Carta (the Great Charter), agreeing to limitations on his power and taking a major step towards establishing the authority of Parliament. The nobles on that occasion were reported to be as feisty as their namesake in this story.

Page 50: Knowing world history well, Sunshine Bell is thinking of **the Colosseum in Ancient Rome** as opposed to the Omni Coliseum in Atlanta, which closed its doors in 1997. Runnymede was showing his years by referring to it, but so was the Omni after lasting merely 25 years because of poor design and construction. The Colosseum, still largely intact after several thousand years, was an oval stadium built out of rocks, stone, and concrete towards the end of the first century in the Common Era. It held between 50,000 and 80,000 people, with the average number of spectators being roughly 65,000. Most of the "entertainments" were very violent, ranging from gladiators who fought against each other to people who were literally fed to the lions—which is why Runnymede's comment sounded so ominous to Ms. Bell. There is no known instance of any species other than humans having organized the suffering of others as a form of mass amusement.

Page 51: **Tic-tac-toe**, also called wick-wack-woe in Asia and noughts-and-crosses throughout the British Commonwealth, dates back some two thousand years to the early days of the Roman Empire and, possibly before that, to ancient Egypt.

Page 52: Just as dogs and cats often get ticks and fleas, so domestic chickens can find themselves irritable, stressed, and even sick because of **fleas, lice, and mites** lodged beneath their feathers or emerging at night from crevices in their coops. It's one of the reasons chickens indulge in a dust baths, but humans can help them a lot without resorting to pesticides, especially by adding some garlic to their drinking water. In that regard, it's intriguing to note that humans themselves have long believed that, without resorting to bullets or stakes, garlic could keep them safe from such purely imaginary bloodsuckers as vampires. That may be because of several blood diseases formerly known as porphyria that could cause disfigurement of the lips and gums as well as a painful sensitivity to light and an intense intolerance of foods containing high sulfur content such as garlic.

Page 56: On the subject of **using all parts of your brain**, studies of great inventiveness and creativity have repeatedly found that geniuses of every sort have developed a problem-solving habit of feeding all relevant information into their conscious minds before putting their subconscious minds into play by setting out on a walk or taking a shower or simply going to sleep—after which, as if by magic, a brilliant new "solution" surfaces in their conscious minds. It's apparently no coincidence that the ancient Greek thinker Archimedes had his legendary "Eureka!" moment while reportedly taking a long hot bath, and many have found a similar approach to be just as effective in preparing for quizzes at school. . . though this method, derided as mere "*woolgathering*" by its skeptics, should generally be employed either outside class or away from the workplace and is not recommended for use while operating a chainsaw.

Page 61: It was the late-medieval Italian, Dante Alighieri, who so memorably described the pain of **recalling a joyful time in the midst of wretchedness**: "There is no greater sorrow," one his characters says, quoting a martyred philosopher named Boethius, "than thinking back upon a happy time in misery." Dante's poetic masterpiece, *The Divine Comedy* (or *La Divina Commedia*) is one of the very greatest works in world literature.

Page 62: Sunshine Bell is paraphrasing a fellow author and Celt, James Joyce, who once described his own strategy in life by having a fictional character declare that, "I will tell you what I will do and what I will not do. I will not serve that in which I no longer believe. . . and I will try to express myself in some mode of life or art as freely as I can, using for my defense the only arms I allow myself to use— **silence, exile, and cunning**." Ms. Bell's allusion to this passage is further evidence of how widely she has read.

Page 67: No one knows for sure, but historians believe North Carolinians were first called "**tar heels**" because, during much of the 18th and 19th Centuries, their state was the world's major source of tar and other naval supplies. Tar was a by-product of burning pine tree logs which was, on the whole, as messy a job as one could find. As a consequence, the nickname was initially regarded as an insult, but, after troops from North Carolina stubbornly stood their ground in several Civil War battles, they began to boast that they'd stayed in place as if they'd been stuck in tar. Perhaps inevitably, the University of North Carolina calls its athletes "Tar Heels"—even though immobility is not a desirable trait for most competitive sports.

Page 67: The mascot for the University of South Carolina in Columbia is **a gamecock** while his counterpart at the University of North Carolina at Chapel Hill is a ram—specifically, a Horned Dorset Sheep named Rameses who's most conspicuous at football games for which butting heads is more appropriate than in sports such as basketball. Both institutions refer to themselves as "Carolina," which only intensifies their rivalry despite there being no known instance in the natural world in which chickens and sheep have quarreled with one another. In traditional Chinese astrology, however, a pairing of the two is said to be less than harmonious, which may suggest that—as mascots, at least—the gamecock and the ram will never be on friendly terms.

Page 67: **Harry Houdini** was a famous Hungarian-born escape artist who died in Detroit, Michigan, in 1926. Though he was a professional magician whose stunts were often amazing, he never claimed to possess any supernatural powers and sought to expose as frauds all those who did. To "pull off a Houdini" is to free oneself from a very threatening situation.

Page 71: In 1990, the pop musician Prince (who'd previously dispensed with his middle and last names, Rogers and Nelson) announced that he would use the unpronounceable symbol ♀ instead and thereafter should be referred to as "**the artist formerly known as Prince**." In 1993, however, he reverted to his previous first name. In a similar manner, Sunshine Bell has largely abandoned a brief attempt to be known as Yrkkkk-☼-Krak.

Page 71: **The so-called "Auld Alliance" (Old Alliance) of Scotland and France**, formed to resist invasions by England, dates from 1295 and, with Scotland's overwhelming opposition to leaving the European Union in 2016 still persists in many minds today. Not only did soldiers from Scotland go to the aid of Joan of Arc, but Mary Queen of Scots, who'd spent most of her childhood in France, was briefly married to its future king. In the midst of World War II, General Charles de Gaulle declared in a speech in Edinburgh that, throughout his country's history whenever it was in danger, "there were always men of Scotland to fight side by side with men of France, and what Frenchmen feel is that no people has ever been more generous than yours with its friendship." [Nevertheless, Ms. Bell's implied link between that historic past and amorous attraction seems purely *fortuitous*—which means it's merely a matter of chance or, as the French would say *pas une question de destin*, not a matter of destiny.]

Page 72: **Wattles** that dangle from the throats of healthy chickens tend to be bright red like the combs atop their heads and serve ornamentally as signs of their vitality. Both wattles and combs are smaller on hens, but for hens and roosters alike they're a very practical means of dealing with heat, like radiators in automobiles. Only a few species sweat, mostly primates and horses, while others rely on different means to regulate body temperatures. Dogs pant, for example, while sweating just a little from their paws while chickens with far less effort rely on their wattles and combs. Jackrabbits and elephants use their ears. Humans wear hats when it's cold and nudists wear nothing at all for reasons that seem obscure.

Page 75: Rodney is shouting the name of a famous Native American leader, warrior, and medicine man named **Geronimo**, spelled Géronimo in France where it's pronounced as Rodney pronounces it. From the age of 21 until he was 57, Geronimo led his fellow Apache tribesmen in battles against the armies of Mexico and the United States across much of what is now the American Southwest. A great deal of his motivation derived from the murder of his family by Mexican soldiers, but eventually he surrendered and remained a U.S. prisoner of war until his death in 1909 at the age of 79. He had been fierce and often brutal in combat with such a remarkable ability to evade and outmaneuver his opponents that many supposed him to have supernatural powers. Inspired by a 1939 Hollywood movie, U.S. Army paratroopers began a tradition of shouting Geronimo's name as a way of showing no fear when they leapt from a plane. That must have been in Rodney's mind as he jumped with Sunshine Bell from the truck.

Page 75: *Paul et Virginie* (or *Paul and Virginia*) by Jacques-Henri Bernardin de Saint-Pierre is an 18th-century novel familiar to nearly all French readers. It describes two young lovers on the island of Mauritius where they live initially in happy harmony with the world around them—as was once the case with the most famous native of that island, Ms. Bell's tragic cousin the Dodo. [Coincidentally, in 1983, before either Jones or Zan had been born, their future grandfather Pa Ben wrote and starred in a National Public Radio children's series called *Radio Free Dodo*, which included a song that began, "On the island of Mauritius / Where dodos were delicious. . ." For animals other than humans, nothing's more fearful than hearing the word "delicious" applied to themselves.]

Page 77: It's true that **"a chicken in every pot"** was a slogan used by the Republican Party to help elect Herbert Hoover as President in 1928. But Hoover himself apparently never uttered the phrase, which had first been used by King Henry IV in 17th-century France. Furthermore, so far from being an easterner as Rodney seems to imply, Hoover was actually born in Iowa, spent parts of his childhood in Oklahoma and Oregon, and went to college in California. In other words, Rodney seems to have been guilty of inventing "fake history" or, at least, of *prevarication*. But no matter who said it first, it was a terrible idea from a chicken's point of view.

Page 81: **Sleekit** is the second word in the opening line of a poem by Robert Burns entitled "To a Mouse," which is supposedly addressed to a field mouse whose nest has been overturned by a plow. Burns, who's widely regarded as the national poet of Scotland, died in 1796 at the age of 37. In a recent Scottish poll, he was named the greatest of all Scots, narrowly beating out the warrior William Wallace, who died in 1305 at the age of 35. Most humans live longer, but few achieve as much as either of them in their short lives. (For a more recent reflection on the plight of dispossessed mice, see Art Spiegelman's graphic novel *Maus*.)

Page 84: **Spurs** are short, sharp, horn-like growths on the back of a chicken's legs, sheathed in a substance called keratin that's also found in rhinoceros horns. Spurs are roughly the size and length of a claw and are used for fighting or self-defense, stabbing or slicing at very close range more or less like the gladius or two-foot-long sword employed by the armies of Ancient Rome. Although they're most commonly found on roosters, all chickens have a bud that sometimes develops on hens as well. If the spurs aren't trimmed, humans can often be injured and even, in rare cases, killed by an overly protective rooster looking out for his flock or simply acting territorial. It's quite common for owners as well as intruders to be chased about a chicken yard by an aggressive rooster.

Page 85: **The notion that not seeing something may be evidence that it's really there** may sound altogether nutty. But, according to many scientists, that's exactly what tiny particles do, and, if you should find yourself in conversation with a pretentious non-scientist using words like "physics" or "theoretical" or both of them together, that may offer you a high-risk opportunity to sound like a very thoughtful genius. In that situation, you should wait until a pause occurs and say, "Yes, of course. . . the Heisenberg Principle." You may have to practice a bit to pronounce it in a casual way (it's HIGH-zen-burg), but there'll probably be an almost magical reaction, assuming the person you're talking to doesn't know any more than you yourself will know after reading this note. If he tries to call your bluff (and it's almost certain to be a man) by asking what exactly you have in mind, you should patiently explain that "Watching really does change what you're looking at, you know." He'll nod and say, "Of course. . . but I'm very surprised you've even heard of Heisenberg." To which you should answer, "I see," and let it go at that. For any true understanding of Heisenberg's ideas or of quantum mechanics, the notion of changing something simply by the act of observing it is, to be sure, only a very small part of what the theory is all about. But because so few know anything more than that, you should, in the unlikely event of being challenged any further, simply frown and say, "You know. . . the Uncertainty Principle." Your challenger will almost certainly back off, and, if he or she does not, the chances are good that he or she has already won a Nobel Prize for Physics. In that case, you might as well confess that you'd be grateful for a little further instruction on the matter.

Page 86: To find out what happened to **Bambi**'s mother, I urge you to read a translation of Felix Salter's book, *Bambi, A Life in the Woods*, or see the 1942 Walt Disney animated film. The fate of Bambi's mother is only one of the disturbing aspects of the story, another being the total absence of any chickens. [To Disney's credit however, one of his Silly Symphony cartoons, *The Wise Little Hen*, released in 1934, retells the story of *The Little Red Hen* in Technicolor

—though it's best known today for having introduced a new male character named Donald Duck. (This beautifully preserved film is actually quite delightful, and you can watch it on the internet at *www.youtube.com/watch?v=A5dowCyaP7I* in its full nearly eight-minute length.)]

Page 88: Only one Christian Gospel, that of St. Matthew, mentions the visit of an unspecified number of **Magi** (MAY-jai) or Wise Men from the east bearing gifts of gold, frankincense, and myrrh for the infant Jesus at an unidentified time and place. Tradition has it that the number of wise men must have matched the number of gifts, that they were kings named Melchior, Caspar, and Balthazar, and that their arrival coincided with that of a group of local shepherds on Christmas night at a stable in Bethlehem. Frankincense and myrrh are gum resins from trees used for incense, medicine, or perfume, and, like gold, they were in high demand at the time. What became of their precious gifts remains unclear.

Page 89: **"They flee from me that sometimes did me seek"** is the first line of a poem by the Elizabethan poet Sir Thomas Wyatt—probably referring to various court ladies by comparing them to deer which, though formerly tame, have now become skittish. Some speculate that he was thinking specifically of Anne Boleyn, who later caught the eye of King Henry VIII with tragic consequences for her. [Although the rumor that Anne had six fingers on one of her hands is almost certainly untrue, she apparently had an extra fingernail on her right hand while Henry VIII, like Bluebeard, had six successive wives, of whom Anne was the second. In an interesting parallel, the Silky or Silkie breed of chickens, with which Scots Dumpies have occasionally been confused, has produced a number of six-toed chickens, though most of that breed have only five while it's an indisputable fact that roosters of virtually every breed expect at least as many wives as Bluebeard and Henry VIII combined.]

Page 90: A very close equivalent of this Scots Dumpy proverb was recorded by the 16th-century Dutch humanist Desiderius Erasmus who advised, **"Don't crow until you're out of the wood."** And, of course, everyone is familiar with a related saying—"Don't count your chickens before they hatch"—to which Rodney will later allude.

Page 94: *"Travail, Famille, Patrie"* (**Work, Family, Fatherland**) was the motto of the *collaborationist* Vichy government in France during the Nazi occupation from 1940 to 1944, temporarily replacing the traditional national motto of "Liberty, Equality, Fraternity." Although he had been called "the Lion of Verdun" during World War I, the Vichy leader, Marshal Pétain, was accused of having become a chicken in the worse sense of the word during the next world war—though it's "rat" that comes first to mind. After the war, he was tried and convicted of treason.

Page 95: *E pluribus unum* is a Latin phrase meaning "out of many, one." It has served as the traditional motto of the United States since 1782, though "In God We Trust" was adopted by Congress as the country's official motto in 1956. It's important to note that the concept of one out of many originally referred to a unified nation made up of 13 different colonies and many different nationalities. It did not imply that there should be a single *dogmatic* way of thinking or the rule of a powerful and despotic leader, king, or president like that against which the colonies had rebelled.

Page 98: The turkey hens' description of **Rodney yelling Sunshine's name** causes her to recall a scene from the movie of a famous play called *A Streetcar Named Desire* which is set in New Orleans. There's a violent and *loutish* character named Stanley Kowalski (played by Marlon Brando) who at one point stands in the middle of the street after quarreling with his wife whose name is Stella, shouting that name out at the top of his lungs. [Coincidentally, as a young acting student in a class taught by a different Stella—Stella Adler—Brando and his fellow students were told to act like chickens in the midst of an atomic bomb attack. While the other would-be actors flailed about in a Chicken Little sort of panic, Brando sat unruffled, pretending to lay an egg. When asked to explain his reaction, he explained, "I'm a chicken—what do I know about bombs?"]

Page 99: **Haggis** is a traditional Scottish dish made from sheep's innards mixed with oatmeal, onion, and other ingredients. It is for many an acquired taste at best, and, in fact, it's illegal to import haggis from Britain to the United States. But in a poem entitled "Address to a Haggis," Robert Burns called it the "great chieftain o' the puddin'-race," and even the French *Larousse Gastronomique* (an encyclopedia of gourmet cuisine) has declared that "Although its description is not immediately appealing, haggis has an excellent nutty texture and delicious savory flavor." [Some heretics believe that, like the forebears of many Scots, the original recipe came from Scandinavia.]

Page 104: According to tradition, **Balthasar** was the second of the Magi (or Wise Men) in the Christmas story who, as his gift, is supposed to have offered frankincense. Although turkeys, like the Magi, were long thought by many to have come from the east (which helps explain why the bird and the Middle Eastern country share the same name), in reality they're a native American species.

Page 105: It may be worth pointing that, in riffing on **"In the beginning was the egg,"** Sunshine Bell quite knowingly and Rodney Junior unwittingly were echoing both religious and scientific accounts of how, at the beginning of time, order emerged from chaos. But Rodney Junior not only mixes his two languages up, but changes "gobble" to "gobbledygook—meaning, in effect, utter confusion or, if you will, that "the earth was without form, and void; and darkness was upon the face of the earth." In short, he accidentally makes a case not just for wisdom flowing forth "out of the mouths of babes" but out of the beaks of chicks as well.

Page 106: **The Marquis de Lafayette** was a French aristocrat who served as a general on the rebellious colonists' side during the Revolutionary War and was later made an honorary citizen of the newly formed United States. Like every nationality, the French have had their military ups and downs, but, even when wounded, the courageous Lafayette was known to have fought on without considering surrender, and Fort Bragg, the largest such facility in the world, is in Fayetteville, North Carolina, which was named in Lafayette's honor. [No one is perfect, however, and Sunshine Bell has asked me to point out that, though Lafayette, as an *ardent* advocate of democracy would have disagreed with Rodney on every political matter, he had one quite disturbing shortcoming. When he visited Mount Vernon, his friend and host George Washington would always try to serve what he knew to be his old comrade's favorite meal—a casserole of chicken and rice prepared with pepper and nutmeg. One wishes it had been something else, but, as Ms. Bell observes, "Though a Frenchman's heart and head may be aligned, his stomach often is not." [See related comments about *pâté* (page 170) and *carnivore* (page 154).]

Page 108: Rodney's words—***"Die Puter sint unser Unglück"***—are an adaptation of an anti-Semitic slogan used in Nazi Germany during the 1930s and early 1940s. With similarly hateful intent, Rodney substitutes *Puter* ("turkeys") for *Juden* ("Jews"), and, though it's not clear where or how he'd picked this slogan up, anti-Semites had held prominent positions in the Vichy regime in France during the German occupation. The French philosopher Jean-Paul Sartre wrote a story ironically entitled "The Childhood of a Leader" (*"L'enfance d'un chef"*) which outlines the career of one of Rodney's ambitious human counterparts.

Page 109: **Benito Mussolini** was a *fascist* dictator in Italy from 1925 to 1945. Like his German counterpart Adolf Hitler, he became a rabid anti-Semite, which means he was highly prejudiced against Jews. In the end, he found his people were rabidly anti-Mussolini.

Page 111: **Club Med** or *Club Méditerranée* is a string of French holiday villages around the world founded in 1950 by a Belgian water polo star and currently owned by Chinese investors. Conceived as an "all-included" vacation option, it established a reputation for low-cost pleasure-seeking.

Page 114: Beginning with his wife's small flock of chickens in 1920, **Frank Perdue** became one of the country's most prosperous chicken farmers. Experimenting on his chickens, he developed a special marigold-blossom feed that produced a golden-yellow skin. Then, experimenting on his customers, he launched a nationwide advertising campaign that featured the jaunty slogan, "It takes a tough man to make a tender chicken." When his workers sought to unionize, he experimented on them as well by reportedly hiring a mafia boss to help discourage that undertaking. [In 1999, when I encountered Mr. Perdue and his wife at a birthday party for a young Cuban *refugee* named Elian Gonzalez, Mr. Perdue, as the result of a recent accident, was wearing a medical device called a halo, which caused him to move his head like a very large chicken, though without a golden-yellow hue.]

Page 114: **Shangri-la** is the name of an imaginary earthly paradise in a secret valley in Tibet. It was invented by the best-selling author James Hilton for his 1933 novel *Lost Horizon* which has been adapted several times for the movie screen. The name has become such a by-word for a *utopian* society that, in 2001, a Chinese county bordering on Tibet officially changed its name to Shangri-la as a means of attracting tourists. [I'm sorry to report that there's also a product sold in the UK as Shangri-la Chicken Flavour Noodles, sometimes advertised as "Paradise in a Bowl."]

Page 117: The term "**Napoleonic**" refers, of course, to the French emperor Napoleon who, though he was a military and administrative genius, became a tyrant whose long string of victories ended in a decisive defeat at the battle of Waterloo, after which he was exiled to a remote island in the South Atlantic Ocean. Although the term is often used to imply that someone is short in stature and as a consequence excessively ambitious, Napoleon was actually of medium height for that era, approximately 5 feet 7 inches tall. It is therefore more accurate to say that, though he was of medium height, he was ambitious in a way that resulted in the loss of huge numbers of human lives. [Though he apparently had an indifferent appetite, he had chickens always roasting on spits at the Tuileries Palace in Paris, and, according to legend, so enjoyed a dish called "Chicken Marengo" after a battle at that location that he ordered it prepared for him after every subsequent battle. That story might be a hoax, however, because his victory over the Austrians at Marengo in Italy was fought on June 14th, 1800, a time of year when tomatoes—a necessary ingredient for that dish—were out of season.]

Page 118: **Lady Macbeth** is best known as a complicit character in William Shakespeare's tragedy *Macbeth*, in the course of which her husband, who kills and replaces a king, is compared to a "kite" or bird of prey and the wife and children of one of his enemies are referred to as a hen and chicks whom Macbeth has caused to be murdered. [Though Ms. Bell isn't truly like Lady Macbeth, Rodney may strike many readers as a cross between a feathered Macbeth and Geoffrey Chaucer's Chanticleer, a rooster driven by vanity.]

Page 122: **Coq au Vin** ("Rooster with Wine") is a French recipe for which, despite its name, the principal ingredient is a hen.

Page 122: National Public Radio, also known as **NPR**, is a wide-ranging source of important information and amusing entertainment. [See the end note for *Paul et Virginie* on page 194.]

Page 123: During the Nazi era in Germany and other parts of Central Europe, **kapos** were prisoners in concentration camps who received special privileges in exchange for helping to "maintain order," often with great brutality. It's not clear how Henriette learned this term, though she might have heard it on television during her time in the owner's house.

Page 124: What Anna undoubtedly meant in calling the other hens **"eggheads"** was that they were as thoughtless and naïve as unhatched chicks. But the word, which initially meant a person who was bald, came to be used for people—especially politicians—who were said to be overly intellectual and therefore lacking in common sense. One such politician, an unsuccessful presidential candidate named Adlai Stevenson, once ruefully observed in Latin that *"Via ovicapitum dura est"* ("The way of the egghead is hard"), proving that he was indeed an intellectual and a witty one at that. Neither could be said of Anna and Henriette's fellow hens.

Page 124: **Nero** was an emperor of ancient Rome who, in addition to being a *dissolute* and *psychotic* killer, believed he had a beautiful singing voice. He tended to *liquidate* his critics, and, when Petronius Arbiter, one of the best satirical writers of his time, chose suicide over execution, his last words were said to have included a statement that, "Nero is the worst singer in Rome." Nero himself, who'd begun his reign while not yet seventeen, would die at the age of 30 in the midst of a rebellion.

Page 124: **Elvis** Presley lived somewhat longer than Nero and was a better singer.

Page 132: Mardi Gras or Fat Tuesday is a carnival celebration just before the beginning of Lent, a period of fasting and sacrifice that lasts until Easter in the Christian calendar. In the Cajun country of southern Louisiana (largely settled by French-speaking refugees expelled from Canada after the end of the French and Indian War in 1763), there's a tradition called the *Courir de Mardi Gras* (or Fat Tuesday Run) that's said to have originated in the medieval French countryside. Included among the festivities is a so-called "chicken chase" in which people in colorful costumes pursue the crucial ingredients for a community-wide feast of gumbo at which there's music and dancing for all except the unfortunate chickens. In most places today, the meal's prepared well ahead of time, so those particular *poulets en fuite* ("chickens on the run") may be spared to crow another day—but vegetarian gumbo has yet to catch on.

Page 132: It may stretch a point to suggest that the reference to "**fowls of the air**" in Psalm 104 should include chickens, but, despite the fact that chickens were imported from the east as early as the 6th Century B.C.E., they weren't widespread until later and there are very few specific references in the Bible—several to roosters strutting and crowing, another in Psalm 91 to finding refuge under the wing of what may or may not be a chicken, and one in the gospels of both Matthew and Luke describing a mother hen that gathers and protects her chicks. [Ms. Bell has admitted to me that, in the midst of great uncertainty, she was seeking reassurance and found it in the language of that passage.]

Page 134: The **moose** species—known as elk in Europe and Asia—is currently found in Canada, Alaska, and parts of New England as well as in Scandinavia, the Baltic States, Poland, and Russia. Because its name in English comes directly from the Native American Algonquin and Narragansett languages rather than from European origins, its plural is formed according to different rules. So instead of plurals like "geese" (or, for that matter, "feet" and "teeth"), more than one moose should still be referred to as "moose" although more than one noose (derived from Old French and Latin) should be "nooses." Languages teem like bugs on a log and are often not very tidy.

Page 135: When Pa Ben and Annie Rooney were young, it seemed that everyone who knew the color of Rudolph the reindeer's nose could also quote a four-lined poem that went

> I never saw a Purple Cow,
> I never hope to see one;
> But I can tell you anyhow,
> I'd rather see than be one.

It was written in 1895 by a man named Gelett Burgess and, almost immediately, became so popular that, in 1907, the students of Williams College in Massachusetts voted to make a purple cow its mascot. [When Zan Bell quoted the poem to me, his Uncle Ben, who'd gone to a rival college called Amherst, nodded his head and said, "You can say that again!" However, the Amherst College mascot is now a mammoth, from a species best known for its extinction.]

Page 139: [Sunshine Bell has pointed out that, during the Yukon Gold Rush at the end of the 19th Century, a miner in Dawson City was called "The **Evaporated** Kid," a nickname that suits her fancy as well. "So, really," she's written, "I wouldn't mind at all if somebody someday spoke about me as 'The Evaporated Hen'—except," she adds, "and it's a big exception, I want my true story told so people and animals everywhere might be a little more inclined to live with mutual respect." She thought for a moment and added, "not just people and animals, though—all living things and even the planet itself."]

Page 140: **That Prince** is named Hamlet, the main character of another famous play by Shakespeare entitled, as you might expect, *Hamlet*—or, more elaborately, *The Tragical History of Hamlet, Prince of Demark*. Although there's some dispute about who really wrote the plays of Shakespeare—just as there's been about the authorship of this book—there's no doubt whatsoever regarding Shakespeare's abiding interest in chickens. For example, one of his sonnets begins by comparing the less than responsive woman he loves to "a careful housewife" who'd rather chase after a chicken than attend to her adoring child, and it concludes by suggesting that, after she catches the chicken (a rival suitor, no doubt), she might kiss and be kind to him (that is, to the lovesick poet) as if he were "her neglected child." Scholars have pointed out that, because of their short legs, Scots Dumpies would have been easier for such a housewife to catch, increasing the likelihood that Shakespeare might have had that particular breed in mind because the chase would have ended sooner. [It's noteworthy too that poultry-centric lines also appear in Act I, Scene 1 of the very play in question: "The cock, that is the trumpet of the morn, / Doth with his lofty and shrill-sounding throat / Awake the god of day." However, despite Alan Coren's admirably provocative essay, "Awaking the God of Day: Was Shakespeare's Muse a Chicken?" (*Poultry Journal of Islip and Noke*, XIII, May-June, 1961, 28-39), most literary experts have rejected Coren's thesis.]

Page 140: In Chapter 6 of Lewis Carroll's *Through the Looking Glass* (as noted in an endnote on page 179), Alice has a lengthy conversation with Humpty Dumpty in which he talks very haughtily about the meaning of words and whether they can mean whatever you want them to mean. At one point, he observes somewhat pettishly that, "It's very provoking to be called an egg—*very!*" Shortly afterwards, he says to her abruptly, "I suppose you don't mean to stop here all the rest of your life." Then he adds with great finality, **"That's all. Good-bye."** [Among other things worthy of note in both *Alice in Wonderland* and *Through the Looking Glass* is that, although dozens of different creatures appear, no chickens are mentioned anywhere except for a passing reference to "a very large gnat" estimated by Alice to be "about the size of a chicken." For all his remarkable wit, Charles Dodgson (aka Lewis Carroll) was himself a very odd duck, and scholars have yet to explain this disappointing omission.]

Sunshine Bell at the time of her interview with Zan Bell for *The Ephesus School News* in 2009, when she was preparing to become a contestant on the television quiz show *Jeopardy*—only to learn that chickens were excluded.

Ben Dunlap's acquaintance with chickens dates from the fall of 1950 when, as a Boy Scout with little interest in knots or semaphoring, he earned a Poultry Keeping merit badge after unexpectedly winning 450 baby chicks from a Reddy Kilowatt exhibit at the South Carolina State Fair. Decades later, as an adult at the same State Fair, he ignored several of Scouting's precepts when he lost a game of tic-tac-toe to a nameless hen who, as he now recognizes, deserved but did not receive a merit badge of her own. Though the title character of this book is, in fact, a real-life chicken, Ben Dunlap's contribution is in part a belated effort to address that incident from the past. Wherever that unknown hen might be, he wishes to apologize for insisting she must have cheated.

THE DIVERS COLLECTION

Made in the USA
Coppell, TX
28 June 2021

58256994R10121